THE LEGEND
OF CAPTAIN SPACE

THE LEGEND
OF
CAPTAIN SPACE

John Harvey

COLLINS
8 Grafton Street, London W1
1990

William Collins Sons & Co. Ltd
London · Glasgow · Sydney · Auckland
Toronto · Johannesburg

BRITISH LIBRARY CATALOGUING IN PUBLICATION DATA

Harvey, John, *1942*–
The legend of Captain Space.
I. Title
823'.914   [F]

ISBN 0 00 223556 0

First published 1990
Copyright © John Harvey 1990

Photoset in Linotron Trump Medieval by
Rowland Phototypesetting Ltd
Bury St Edmunds, Suffolk
Printed and bound in Great Britain by
William Collins Sons & Co. Ltd, Glasgow

FOR EKATERINI

ONE

The Lotus came to rest in a lush damp meadow, with several yards of barbed wire round its front wheels. The two men fell out of it into the grass.

'Are you in one piece, Barney?'

'No.'

'That's all right, then.' Nick got up precariously. 'It's the drink that saved us – kept us relaxed.'

There was a sign nearby, stuck up on a post.

'What's it say, Nick? Slow on the curve?'

'No, mate. It says Beware of the Bull.'

The bull was a low black hump in the distance.

'OK.' Nick uprooted the signpost.

'Where you heading, man?' Barney sat up bloat-faced in deep grass, but Nick was already tramping towards the bull. 'Bull!' he shouted at the top of his voice.

Barney got up and felt himself. He was large-built and fat, there was a lot of him to bruise. Nick was a thin black shape against the green.

'Christ! Come back, will you?'

He came up with Nick, as Nick came up with the bull. Two yellow eyes in the blackness watched them.

'Er Nick, do you know this bull?'

But Nick was absorbed, confronting it. His overhanging forehead came forward like a shelf, he looked as if he might butt the bull.

He banged on the board. 'Get up and fight!'

Barney goggled. 'Slow down, man.'

Barney's legs melted, a cloud hid his sight, as the bull stirred bulkily and lurched to its feet. When he saw clear, still the bull stood staring at Nick, and Nick, dead white, stared at the bull. He kept giving quick blinks, the muscles of his neck stood out like ropes, he had the look he had when racing-driving. He held the sign upside-down, so it was more like a cricket bat than a cape.

The bull lowered its head, its heavy wattle hung down in a curtain.

'Nick, let's shove.'

But Nick was struck rigid.

Barney nudged his arm, the bull stayed where it was. Eventually they began to walk away. Nick looked at the ground, his face drawn to a point.

There were only seconds in which they heard the thudding pads. They swerved and turned, saw the bull growing big at them, black, smoking, like a container lorry on top of them.

It had gone between them. Now like slow-motion it braked, turned round, and pawed the ground as it saw where they were. But Nick was ready, he stood forward at the bull waving the sign.

Barney's heart banged as the bull ran again. He could hear it through the ground. He saw Nick jump as the bull went by, but immediately it turned and came again. Again Nick jumped and this time, as it passed, he gave the bull a great thwack on its rump with the sign.

Barney gazed. The bull seemed surprised: and Nick too, for the sign had split, and as they looked at it the bottom half hung down and dropped off.

They looked at the bull, the bull looked at them. It slowly butted its head, appraising them.

'Come on, you bugger!' Nick shouted.

'Here, man, enough is enough.'

The bull moved. In a lumbering run it moved past Nick

8

and trotted some distance up the field, where it turned its
head and scanned them.

'Right, Nick, that's it, time, all out.'

They backed away. When they were at a good distance,
the bull sat down again.

They got out more beers from the car, and lay in the
sweet grass, drinking. Afterwards they jacked up the car,
took off the front wheels, and unwound the wire. They
reversed out of the field the way they had come. Then
their rear wheels spat, they were quickly back to eighty.

At dusk they paused on a hilltop, with the shadowy
Midlands below them. There was a huge moon, like a
bronze wheel on the edge of the world.

'I don't have to go through with this.'

Barney was miles away. 'What's that, Nick?'

'I could take off. We've got the car, we could clear off
in the other direction.'

Barney eyed him sideways, Nick looked again in his
dangerous mood.

'You can't get out of it now, Nick.'

Nick stared ahead. He seemed to see something Barney
didn't see, a black wall on the hills.

Wobbling his head, comical, Barney warbled, 'A man's
gotta do what a man's gotta do.'

Abruptly Nick turned to him. 'We'll shake it up tonight.
We'll take the place apart.'

He flashed his famous grin, in which his mouth smiled,
wide and tight, showing his teeth while his eyes were
sharp. He raised his head, and bayed at the rusty moon.
Barney joined him, in a high long canine howl which
descended in a series of yelps. Presently a sheepdog in the
valley below gave a surly, growling bark. They barked
back, the sheepdog snarled, then some little whippet
further off began a furious yapping. Another dog came in.

Nick and Barney stopped, and sat back getting breath while further and further away dogs and more dogs joined in, and a ripple of dogs barking passed outwards, expanding through the lowlands of England.

Nick slapped Barney hard on the shoulder, so his head wobbled again. 'Let's hit the road, man!'

The car-engine revved, they slid down the hill.

There was commotion inside the house, women's voices laughed.

'You'll see her tomorrow, Nick, you're not to see her now.'

Sandy's friend Pearl stared at them a moment, her round potato face flushed and bright-eyed, then she ran upstairs. All the women must be up there, trying on clothes.

Nick shouted after her, 'We'll be down the Wagon. Send Vince down the Wagon if he turns up!' Someone laughed him away.

They drove to the pub. 'We'll live it up tonight. Woo-hoo!'

The Wagon was solid, everyone bawling. Barney sat back with his drinking look, eyebrows up, eyes shut, mouth pursed small, his belly slack in front. He looked virtuous, like a soft monk. Nick crouched forward, scowling at his glass.

'I could go up Vanessa's.'

Barney made big blinks. 'Up Vanessa's? That's a dead letter, man.'

'What you mean? I could go to Vanessa now. I'd say, "Come with me, darling" and she would.'

'Are you serious? You and Vanessa – that was death. You're well out of that, Nick.'

'There's Karen, she'd come running.'

'You're sure of that, are you? It hurts, doesn't it, Nick. But still, it's happening. I never thought I'd see you get

married. Because Nick, if truth is told, you're bad. I mean,
frankly Nick, admit it, and I only say this as your friend
– you're a bastard.'

'Right.' Nick laughed, looking depressed.

'No, but she's a nice girl, Sandy. I mean, she's really
nice. And besides, you *can't* go, can you?'

'What you mean?'

'Well, you know . . . bun in the oven.'

Nick eyed him slowly, then he stood up.

'Drink?'

He took the glasses to the bar. There were two women
behind the counter. One was behindhand hurrying
through the orders, banging down glasses so the beer
jumped out of them, chucking change on the counter,
catch it that would have it. The other did nothing but
wash and dry glasses – she paused and puffed fluff off a
glass – while her eyes were far away.

'Come on, darling,' Nick shouted at her. She ignored
him.

He took the beer to the table and drank it fast. Barney
had got maudlin, he'd decided he was in love with Sandy's
friend Pearl.

'And it's true her face is a bit round, Nick –'

'Round? It's like the rising sun.'

'But what lips, eh?'

Nick shrugged at large, and eyed the pub ceiling.

Barney put his lips forward, and kissed the smoky air.
'Mmmm!' he said.

'By Christ!' Nick kicked his legs out. 'Ah, you wait till
I'm a racing-driver. I won't stay around then.'

'Forget it, man. You're a wage-earner now. You won't
be a racing-driver.'

'Thanks a million. Bastard. You're a good friend, aren't
you, Barney?'

'I'm a man in love.'

11

When Vince arrived with Sandy's father Barney was sitting back with closed eyes, babbling about his dream-girl. Nick they could not find at all.

'He went to get some air,' Barney said at last.

They looked round the car-park. They found Nick hanging out of his car unconscious.

'Nick.' They shook him. 'Here, Nick.'

A bloodshot businessman came by with his wife. 'What's wrong with him?'

'He's getting married tomorrow.'

'Good for him!' The businessman burst into laughter, and moved on laughing.

They got Nick and Barney into cars, and drove them back to the house. They supported Nick up the stairs, lolling and mumbling, 'Don't let Sandy see me.' At the top of the stairs they met Pearl and Sandy supporting Sandy's mother full of sherry to the bedroom.

'Don't let Nick see me,' she murmured. 'Oh, I'll be so ashamed in the morning. Sandy, you must help me unzip.'

In the living-room Pearl sat by herself on the sofa: she livened when Vince and Barney came in. Barney was already half undressed, he paraded in the room white-bodied, fat-bellied, with a towel round his waist. Pearl moaned, 'I'm left on the shelf!' Barney drew up beside her, and reached round her a fat white arm.

As he tried to sleep, Nick repeated, 'Vanessa.' While his bed tipped over, and his stomach and head rolled like cement in a mixer, he knew that in the morning he'd bolt.

He woke in the early hours, alone in bed and thinking of Sandy. Warm-coloured, freckled all over, she'd huddle in bed with the sheet to her nose. But marriage? There were other couples that didn't get married.

He got up, and slouched round the kitchen. He stuck

his head out of the door, but it was fresh and bright like any good morning, the birds still on the go. He'd nothing to do but sit over his Nescaf, and listen for the noises as the others got up.

'Hey up, Nick! Can't you wait, then?'

'It's not that, mate. I couldn't sleep.'

They came and went, brittle people nursing their heads. Later they had a stand-up breakfast, then they started to change while Nick sat on in his old sweater and jeans, smoking with Barney.

Pearl came in and saw him. 'Nick isn't getting ready,' she shouted up the house.

Nick shrugged. 'I'll go as I am.'

His mother arrived, brought by cousin Harry. She stepped briskly into the kitchen.

'Wotcher mate!' Nick cried. 'How are you?'

'Nick, aren't you dressed?' She sat down at the kitchen table.

Harry said, 'Nicholas, you really ought to be ready.'

'I'm dressed, aren't I?'

His mother only twinkled at him. They chatted about small things.

Harry told him, 'Your mother fell off her bike the day before yesterday.'

Nick looked his mother over. 'You know your trouble, mate? You drive too fast!'

Harry was shocked. 'Your mother hurt her heel!'

'Good gracious, Harry!' the mother cried. 'That's all right!'

Harry shook his head seriously while she smiled at Nick. Then she got up. 'Nicholas, go and get dressed.'

He did. All the house was cheerful, smartening up for the wedding, crowding the mirrors and shaving and lipsticking and curling eyelashes together. The men in singlets shone with aftershave. Barney was active with an

13

aerosol of shaving cream, till Pearl had moustaches and the upstairs looked like the arctic.

Spruce and excited they collected in the kitchen. Even Nick made an entrance: pale, clean-shaven, fragrant, his hair combed down like a Hollywood Roman, tall and good-looking in his pencil-slender suit. He had a modesty on him and moved softly in the room, while everyone looked at him. His mother said quietly to Sandy's mother, 'He *is* a good-looking man!'

'He's marrying a good-looking girl!'

'Well, it's getting on, you know,' Harry started saying, waving his watch. No one had seen Sandy yet, it wasn't clear if she was ready or not.

In the end they were all there, bar Sandy. Sandy's father, a quiet man, had appeared in immaculate morning dress. Even Barney came out dapper, in his best salesman's suit, of a silvery stuff without a fold or pucker anywhere. For he was best man, he had a complacency, a dignity. Nick's mother, notwithstanding, said loudly to Sandy's mother, 'He's no good, that Barney. He was very bad for Nick. Oh, I'm glad Nick's getting married.'

Barney took Nick off in the Lotus.

Pearl came back into the kitchen. 'Can someone come? I don't know what's the matter with Sandy.'

'She was ready before any of you,' her mother said, surprised.

'Yeah, but she's stuck.'

Her mother and father looked unhappily at each other.

'I'll go and see her,' her mother said.

Sandy, in a white trouser suit, sat head-drooped on the bed.

'Sandy love, what is it?'

Sandy's head came up. Her big freckles looked like sprinkled trouble.

'There there, love, everyone's nervous.'

14

Her mother sat by her, not touching.

'I feel I'm jumping off a cliff.'

'Well, but Sandy. Nick is a difficult person. But I don't think he'll hurt you. Let's hope he changes, let's hope he settles down.'

'It isn't Nick.'

'Whatever is it? Tell me, love.'

Sandy clenched her eyes.

'I mean, Sandy, Dad and I, we thought you were impatient, you know, to have your own home. We thought – oh, I don't know, stupid things, but we thought that, being adopted like, perhaps you never felt you really belonged to us, perhaps that was why you wanted, you know, to make your own home as soon as you could. We thought that's why –' She stopped.

'That's why what?'

'You know.'

'Do you mean, why I got pregnant?'

'No, love, no. Well, not really.' Her mother stroked her back. It was the wrong time, her hand sprang away.

'It's the baby as well.'

'What do you mean?'

'I feel wrong about it.'

'I don't understand.'

'I'm frightened of it, Mum.'

'Everyone is, it's ever so difficult, having a baby.'

'It's not that –'

'What then, love?'

Sandy hunched lower.

'I feel it's something bad.'

She looked at her mother, but her mother avoided her. Eventually she said, 'You could still – you know, stop it. Why ever didn't you . . .'

Sandy looked away.

'Well, I don't know. What a terrible thing! What are we

15

to do?' Her mother's hands fluttered useless in her lap.

Sandy stood up. 'Mum, if it comes to a bad end – will you take me back?'

'Oh Sandy. Sandy. Oh.' Her mother hugged her, patting her.

'Here comes the bride.'

Sandy stood in the kitchen door. She was round-shouldered with shyness, showing off her white suit. Her thick auburn hair was light and feathery. She was blushing, she looked warm.

'Oh,' the two mothers said, in falling voices. 'Oh. You do look nice.' Her father nodded, still tense.

She smiled quickly, while her big-lidded eyes glanced nervously.

The Registry Office was a new building in light brick with little gardens round it. The vestibule was crowded, with other weddings standing in groups, and washed children being good.

They were led down a corridor, to a blue-painted room with rows of chairs. A fair-haired secretary sat at a desk. 'The Registrar won't be long,' she told them.

The Registrar was a short, upstanding man in a light grey suit and a sapphire tie. He had a white, taut, hygienic face, and a glitter in the eyes as if he wept or drank. He shot through the ceremony – but with an unction in his voice, so it was quite like church without the religion. When Nick had to speak he was quiet and shy like a good boy at school. Sandy was inaudible. Her father was dignified. Barney stood tall, looking deeply solemn as if at a funeral. The two mothers sat rapt, with raised heads.

It was quickly over. They signed on a page headed 17 June 1972. The mothers peered closely at the dates of birth.

Outside, the mood changed. Nick elbowed Barney. 'Hey

man, did you see that tie? All I could think about was that tie.'

Sandy's father took photos, and every photo, when developed, showed Barney above, behind or underneath Nick, gaping, goggling, gawping. They found a little sign saying 'No confetti', and stood round it in a group while Barney and Vince made a blizzard.

Vince asked Barney, 'Get your oats last night?'

'Yeah, the big girl.' Barney nodded towards Pearl.

They went back to the house, where Sandy and her mother brought out from secret places a buffet of canapés, chicken-limbs, trifles. Barney shook up the champagne bottles so they fountained. Vince went to work at the table. Harry talked insurance with Sandy's father.

Nick came in. He was slender and dashing, the centre of attention, taking it for granted he was talking to them all.

'Where you heading, Nick? The Côte d'Azur?'

'Nah, 'fraid not. I went round the travel agents Wednesday afternoon, but it was early closing.'

Sandy joined him. She had changed into a different suit: Lincoln green, it went with her hair. She stood close to Nick as if he were a shelter. Her cheerful eyes looked round cautiously as if only half of her wanted to be seen.

'Might take a room down the Wagon,' Nick said hopefully.

Sandy's hands went to her hips. She stepped back and, publicly, stared at Nick hard.

Nick watched her be cheerful with her friends. She had a lovely laugh, her head came up as the quiet laugh came, as if she were quietly bubbling over.

A little later they slipped away, and the party only realized afterwards that they had gone.

The others sat smoking and chatting. Pearl sat by

17

Barney, who was affectionate in a drooping, hangdog way, and started to look at his watch.

People drifted from the house. Harry took Nick's mother home. At the door she said, 'That's no way to get married.' Sandy's mother sighed.

Barney gave Pearl a lift. Vince put on his leathers and left in a roar. Sandy's parents had the house to themselves.

'Sandy,' her mother said, sitting forward in her chair, raising her head. Her husband looked down, blinking.

TWO

For cheapness' sake, they settled in a farm-labourer's cottage in the country. There were three small houses in a terrace, surrounded by fields of rape, sharp yellow. The walls were painted the colour of peas, but the old cottage furniture was nice, it was all knobs and spindles, with the bars of the chairs twisted like candy-sticks. Upstairs was a brass bedstead, that creaked but was grand. They made love in every room, and in the garden also, and far out, one night, in the moonlit field of rape.

Sandy had never believed Nick would settle in marriage: he was a wild man, thrilling as a knife. He'd always be on long hauls, or off in fast cars, or boozing with Barney. But he surprised her, he suddenly loved home. At night he'd lie back, watching her rest his clean underwear on the polished rail of the bed.

'That's great, Sandy.' He was amazed at someone doing this for him. He did no housework, but he was at home all the time he could be. He used his car only for going to work. He even took up gardening. He dug their patch, later she saw him stooped down with a trowel. He was planting some sweet peas he'd brought home. In the evenings all he wanted was to sit at home watching the telly with her. Perhaps he was strung too tight before. He took things easy, he was happy.

She made the house nice. She loved working on the floors and furniture while the young sun shone into the small rooms. There was crusted old lino on the floor, but she scrubbed it with wire-cloth till it shone.

She had shocks. She looked up once just as a mouse scurried in from the next room. As soon as it saw her, it tried to retreat, but its scamper was too fast. It slid on the wet lino, spinning, till it bumped her, got purchase, and shot away again. It had gone before she could shriek. When she'd caught her breath, she was amused: the mouse had been more scared than she was.

Slowly she got the house to rights. She cleared the furniture from the living-room, they would paint it together. The bare box of space was filled with sun. She stood in the centre in a calm trance. 'It's my home,' she repeated. She had only ever had corners in other people's places.

She looked at the curtainless window and the brilliant even stretch of rape. Hours could pass and nothing would change, no one would come. She was glad Nick was out.

She wondered, do I miss the office? It had been hectic there with Pearl and the others, while all day she answered telephone enquiries. Such different people rang, there were brisk men and slow men and old men and young men, there were men who were old women and women who were bossy men, and women who purred and women who husked and men who were lost and men with oily caressing voices that crept from the phone and brushed her ear.

Now she had silence, and no phone for a mile: it was a holiday of peace. Perhaps I'll miss them. Coming here was like waking up better from a fever.

She sat outside, listening to the birds and looking at her garden. Nick had tidied the groundsel, his sweet peas stood in a line with their sticks. A pale-yellow butterfly zig-zagged towards the chicken-wire fence, and moved back and forth and then flew through it. She stretched back in the deck-chair, and closed her eyes and raised her head to the sun.

'Heaven.'

Among the unstoppable birdsong she made out the noise of the brook beyond the hedge. It dropped over stones, making a sound like someone filling a bath in the distance.

She looked down at her belly. With two fingers she nervously pressed it.

The neighbours kept to themselves. On one side was Mr Boyce, a retired labourer with a gammy leg stiff as a rod and a blind eye. His face was thin and weathered and scorched-looking. Whenever he spoke to her, Sandy couldn't look away from the pale whitey-blue eye that couldn't see her. He came and went at odd times, he walked by himself in the woods. Sometimes she heard him shouting in his cottage.

'You won't get the best of me!' the thick voice called. 'No. Never. Don't think it.'

On the other side was Mrs Wilmot, an enormously old lady. Her skin was like screwed-up paper, her jaw trembled all the time. Sandy would see her over the fence on a sunny day, in her brown cardigan buttoned tight, making her way down her yard with a pan of ashes. And when Sandy looked again, ten minutes later, she was still on the same journey, she moved so slowly: her face determined, with nothing frail or helpless in it. Always one of her stockings was down round her ankle.

When she wanted to talk she did, and Sandy had to listen. Her family had been labourers here for years, she described the area as it used to be. There had been several farms then, with smaller fields, and sheep and cattle and lots of trees, and people too that had all gone.

Under her spell, Sandy imagined it – harvests, wagons.

21

She described it all to Nick when he came home. 'Isn't that sad, though?'

'Yeah, all we've got now is rape for miles.' He laughed.

'Oh, I think rape's lovely, it makes you think the sun's shining when it isn't.'

'No, that's what you do, lover.'

'Nick, what a lovely thing to say.'

'And the way you've done this house – you know, it's something, Sandy. I was mental, I thought marriage was the end of the world.'

'Nick.'

One evening they walked down the lane that led on from their cottage. Rooks called, rabbits scampered, tiny flies dodged in the air. It was so warm and peaceful they kept stopping, and looking round them and loving. Out in a field a hare stood up on its haunches.

'It's like a film, Nick. I'm very happy.'

She looked at him beside her: he was handsome, with his large square temples, straight sharp nose, nice mouth with loving lips. His eyelids were calm, he looked strong and wise, she'd never known him like this in the old days. She thought, where has all his danger gone? His days were spent in long-haul driving, but still he was content. With zest she snuggled closer, she felt safe from all the world.

On a fine day her mother came to see her. Red poppies ran round the edge of the rape-field, and grew in pockets beside the door of the house.

'Sandy, you *have* made it nice!'

It was a pleasure she had never imagined, showing off her own home. She took her mother into every corner, her mother cooed and liked it.

'Will Nick be home to tea?'

'I told you, he's on a long run.'

22

Her mother shook her head, and asked what it was like, living married to Nick.

'Well, it's not what I expected. He's turned out domestic.'

Her mother looked sceptical, but drank her tea.

She said, 'I saw Pearl the other day.' She passed on gossip from the office. Sandy laughed cheerfully.

Her mother was thoughtful. 'Don't you get lonely, love?'

'Oh no, I love it here, I don't want other people. I like it when Nick's here and I like it when he isn't.'

Her mother seemed to want to find some sort of snag. She asked gravely, 'How are you really, love? I mean the baby. Do you feel better, dear?'

Seeing her face, her mother said gently, 'It doesn't show at all. Have you felt it yet?'

'No.'

'Still, dear, you must make a start. I mean, there's a lot of shopping to do, you know. You'll have to get a playpen and a cot and a highchair and the Babygros, and a lot of them you can get in the small ads, they're always coming up, and all you've got to do is give them a good scrub with a bit of boiling water, and it all comes off you know, and anyway you can paint them all bright colours so they're ever so nice.'

Sandy nodded, but her head felt as if it was filled with lead.

'Have you won any competitions, Mum?' Her mother had a system, and got one free holiday a year.

'Not yet, dear, no, it's a little worrying. We'd been counting on it, rather. We're spoiled, you know, what with the Bahamas last year and Trinidad the year before.'

They both laughed, and got back into the bright mood. They went into the garden. 'Oh, you could do a lot with this, Sandy.'

'Nick's made a start.'

'Nick! I don't see Nick out here with a spade.'

'He put those flowers in. He looks after them, too.'

Her mother prepared to leave.

'Sandy, it's very nice here,' she said, as if she couldn't believe it.

'I love it.'

But there was a drag on her happiness as she came back in the house. She looked at herself in the mirror that evening. Was she plump? But she couldn't see a difference. Perhaps there is no baby, she thought, but this thought cried like a ghost baby inside her.

Later it was clear, her tummy was bigger. The baby jumped. Nick curled round her and pressed his ear in, chuckling sharply. She lay back with her eyes half-closed and rolled her head as she felt the stirring.

It grew fast, till it looked as though its feet hung in her pelvis, while bottom and body leaned out in front. Alone in the house, she'd waddle bare in front of the mirror thinking, I'm just a big ball, with a leg either side, like a toad. Her eyes looked back at her, terrified. The farmer had harvested and it seemed wrong, some days, being all alone out here in the wilds, with such emptiness stretching away, and this creature inside her swelling. She gazed for hours at the bare field, and at a bush in the garden where a nest with one egg left tossed in the wind.

There were classes she should go to but it was difficult getting into town. She panted at each step and had to hold on to things. Nick wouldn't walk slow enough if they tried to go out. All he did was smile. He'd feel her belly to know where the baby was, and think he was finding its head or its heels. He was so gentle when he touched her then, it was quite different from his normal touch. He was loving the baby through her, she was simply a skin

24

with a baby inside. And she thought, I'm too small, how will it get out? It's eating me. I'll be split open.

He was struck gormless, while she sobbed. 'I can't face it, Nick, I can't. I'm not ready for it. I don't want a baby. I've told you and you don't believe me. But I'm young, I want to be young, I don't want a child.'

'Sandy. Love.' As she sobbed and he caressed her, he saw her hair spread out and thought what lovely hair.

Her tears didn't stop. He gazed over her, helpless.

'I'd lose it if I could, Nick. I just want to be free of it.'

'It's a bit late for that.' His voice sounded like earth in his mouth.

When she was tired he got a bottle. 'Let's cheer up.'

'Oh no, Nick, I mustn't. I mustn't these days.'

'It's all right, little bugger, give him something to wet his whistle.'

They drank the whisky till they were cheerful, sexy, confused. Drunk they went to bed, but in the night she woke him.

'Nick, he's not moving.'

Nick shifted. He was in a heavy slumber, leaden, he didn't want to wake.

'Nick, wake up. He's all still.'

Now Nick woke, he knelt beside her and rested his ear on her belly. She'd put the bedside lamp on, she watched his eyes rolling as they strained to listen.

'Oh no.'

'He'll be all right, won't he, Nick?'

He'd begun to caress and massage her belly.

'Oh Nick, what should we do?'

He listened again. 'He must move.' But there was no movement.

'What if he's dead?'

'He isn't dead! Gerraway!' But his face was yellow, it looked old.

25

They lay side by side, sick. Nothing moved, they were all three still as the furniture. He was horrified when he saw her face: she looked dead herself, she took all the blame.

'He'll be all right, Sandy. He must be.'

In the morning it was so. The baby stirred and shifted.

'Can you feel him, Nick?' Her eyes had their saucy look, her quiet laugh bubbled. She was happy, happy to have the baby, happy as she had not been since she became pregnant.

'You know what it was? Little bugger was pissed. He's full of booze.' He said to the belly, 'You're sloshed, mate, canned.' They both laughed, happy together.

Night shift in the baby factory. All round her beds stretched in avenues, laden with women who panted and groaned as they heaved in the half-light. It would go on all night, it was a train accident hospital with no anaesthetic. The woman beside her gave quick little squeals, like a baby herself. Sandy clenched, her own pain pulled her belly inside out. She opened her mouth wide but no sound came.

Later she called, 'Please, nurse, I want the toilet.'

'Oh Christ!' the nurse muttered, and came over with the bedpan and roughly helped her on to it. Perhaps out of grievance she had just sterilized it, it was burning to the touch. Her grey head, tight-lipped, stooped in Sandy's sight, as Sandy worked to achieve release. Then the nurse went but the pain returned. Sandy lay panting as everything tightened and the globe of pain expanded. Again she gave her dry non-shriek, her head turned on its cog from side to side. This was the slaughterhouse. Around her the carcasses bellowed or whimpered, it made no odds, no one could help them. Nothing alive could come out of here.

It was day and Nick was beside her. He was pale, he looked handsome with his brow all knit, but what use was that? Never mind, Nick, you're safe outside. You can't help. She'd been terrified of having a baby, and yet she hadn't a glimmering of how it was. She'd seen mums with prams and never known they'd gone through death.

They gave her a baby, blood still on it. They held it up over her. Were they trying to scare her? She could only stare. All she wanted was to swoon back dead, and this baby hung over her, it had a huge open mouth like a sucker. Take it away. They touched it to her. She shuddered, she wanted to cry and couldn't.

They'd taken it off. She vaguely knew she'd done something criminal, their round faces looked at her. But she was tired, she let herself sink.

Nick thought she was asleep but, as he approached, her heavy-lidded eyes opened slowly.

'Hello, Nick. Oh, they're nice.'

He had a big bunch of carnations. She clasped the stems loosely.

'Feeling better, lover?'

She nodded drowsily. He bent and kissed her, smelling the flowers and her warmth together.

'You look good.' She was tired still, but her skin was flushed as if she'd been sunbathing. Her auburn hair shone, spread round her like a sun over the pillows and bolsters.

Beside her was a little bed. He could see a bundle of white cloth with a pink bulge on top, with brown hair. He stroked the fine hair gently and fingered nervously the soft place in the middle.

'I can feel his brain! Poor bugger!' He couldn't bear to touch the head now, but he touched the large cheeks, then put his finger to the baby's mouth. At once the tiny jaw clamped, the small mouth sucked.

He laughed quietly. 'Just like a milking machine.'

And presently a nurse arrived briskly. 'It's time for his feed.' She had picked up the small bundle, and passed it to Sandy and gone. Sandy held the baby like an awkward package, and puckered as if she'd cry. She gave the baby a freckled breast. The baby sucked angrily and Sandy winced, she was hurting. Then both relaxed, the baby sucked steadily like a lapping cat.

'Gor, I envy him!'

'Nick!' She nodded towards the other beds. He looked round at them without interest. She rested back drowsily, the child sucking. Her eyes began to smile, a little as they used to if she were caught flirting. She had a fat luxury Nick couldn't share. He blinked, pleased. She'd been so down about this baby.

'When'll you come home?'

She murmured inaudibly, lying back warm. She was almost asleep, the babe in her arms sucked in its sleep.

'Bye,' he said quietly and stole from the ward. He wasn't needed. She was together with her child and he was outside what they had.

THREE

Sandy came home. She was frightened of being alone with the baby, out in the middle of nowhere; but Nick had done wonders with the cottage. He had tidied and cleaned everything, even the lino, and had ironed the baby things and arranged them neatly. Everything was welcoming, he had even bought an electric fire with artificial coals. He had shopped as well, the pantry was full of food and baby food. Sandy was amazed.

'Nick, you're so domestic!'

He had taken a day off to see her settled in, then he had to go back.

'Oh Nick, don't go to work today.'

'I've got to, lover. I've got a long haul.'

'When will you be back?'

'I don't know.' He was awkward. 'Can't your mum come?'

But Sandy's mother couldn't come, she was in Tenerife on a holiday she'd won. Sandy didn't want Nick's mum, she would take the place over.

Nick drove off. She found she was cosy, snuggled with her baby by the electric coals. They were the one warm spot in the empty wilds. The baby cried desperately, but she held him and fed him till he stopped.

'Davey, Davey,' she crooned.

In the orange light the baby lay back, drunk with milk, its plump arms limp, its eyes nearly closed, its mouth bubbling milk. Utter abandon, happy sleep. She curled on the rug beside it.

Nick was there most evenings, they'd wash and change the baby together. If the baby cried at night, Nick would comfort him. He would pace the bedroom, holding the baby and patting its shoulders.

'There, there, lover,' he said to it, using the words he used to her.

He was better at quieting the baby than she was. Her nerves were torn by it, it had a rhythm of crying. In the daytime, when she was by herself, it would cry and cry till she cried. It cried with fury.

'Are you hungry, Davey?' She didn't know what he wanted. He was crying at her. When Nick came home in the evenings, he was annoyed she couldn't make the baby quiet.

'Do something, Sandy, for Christ's sake. I've got to sleep tonight, I'm up at five.'

There were days when she felt at the bottom of the world, as if the space inside her from which the baby had been taken was still there, and still growing, and now the baby had left it, she had fallen into it. She stood by the cot. This was not her baby, her baby had died and this was another creature. She was a husk, an old incubator, life had used her and chucked her out.

Spring was arriving, and the baby only cried more.

She was alone in the house and the baby cried.

She cooed, and rocked the cot steadily, but the baby cried.

She picked up the baby and held it close, cuddling it and rocking it. The baby paused, coughed and cried.

She walked back and forth in the room, and from room to room, holding the baby so it looked over her shoulder while she patted it. The baby snuffled, then cried steadily.

She smacked it. The baby stopped. Its eyes, its mouth, goggled wide, then it howled.

She put it back in its cot, and shook the cot quietly. It cried. She shook the cot vigorously, then violently. The baby roared.

She left it and went elsewhere in the house. The walls were thin, wherever she went she heard the baby.

She went upstairs, but in the bedroom the baby's noise made a dull big echo. She came down again, and the noise grew louder as she approached the living-room. It split her head, she could take the baby and shake it, bash it.

She went outside, but from the garden she heard the baby crying.

She walked out into the field of rape, but still she heard it. She walked further, trampling through the acid blossom. She tramped on in a daze, it was like swimming through a sea stained fluorescent with yellow chemical.

She stopped in the middle of the field. All round her like a prairie the bright chrome yellow stretched. The row of cottages was tiny, like a chocolate bar marked out by kids to be cut in three pieces. The world was flat, the sky was huge – and silent, there was no traffic noise, nothing. Thank God. She wanted to cry. She looked at their cottage: and she heard, tiny, a baby's cry. Now she heard it, she heard it louder. She realized she had come the wrong way, the wind was blowing the sound to her.

She walked on through the field but the cry continued. She couldn't tell whether she really heard it or whether the crying was in her head.

She entered the copse beyond the field, her head banging with the baby's cry. She stumbled through brambles, whips in her face. The broken sky streamed behind the branches, she heard her own crying, her own tears ran.

There was a noise in the wood. An animal, something wild? She stopped. Sticks cracked. It roared, it shambled.

It was a man. It was their neighbour, Mr Boyce, flinging his stiff leg forward, reeling, shouting at the top of his voice, his head back, his white eye flaring.

'You don't put me out to grass!'

He came through a thicket and saw her: and stopped dead, staring, his mouth wide like the baby's. She ran.

At the other end of the copse she faced whiteness, a huge white sky and the ground gently fell in a field of grass. She crouched down, a ball, she couldn't go out in all that white. She hugged herself, and listened hard. She heard the wind, it made a noise like water as it shoved through the wood. Perhaps she heard Mr Boyce, crashing through undergrowth in the distance, but nothing else, no cry. She listened, and listened keener. Silence. Oh praise God. She sat back and breathed great breaths. She could rest here safe.

The silence continued. She got up, and began walking home. Sticks cracked loudly. The wood was full of sounds and wind-noise, but she heard no cry.

She walked faster, hurrying till she saw sharp yellow, like a sunrise of Heaven behind the trees. When she broke clear, the yellow sea reached in all directions. Her eyes darted to the tiny row of houses, knowing that the moment she saw them the crying would break on her.

Silence. Even the wind made no noise now. Well, the baby was asleep. It was dead. Cot death, it had choked itself.

She waded back through the yellow, she ran. The wind pushed her face, she had to walk, she was exhausted. She stopped in the middle. No sound. She thought, why run, the baby's dead. She flooded with relief. It was dead, she could walk. Then she gasped, oh how could I? She was the monster. She ran.

She got home and looked in the cot. The baby lay on its back, plump, contented, snoring like a grandma.

She looked at it, not believing. There was silence in the house, no noise at all except for the quiet snoring of the baby like a purring cat.

She went into the kitchen for a drink of water, but before she reached the tap she sank on to a kitchen chair.

In the evenings, with Nick home, the baby was fun. He lay on his back in the small plastic bath, and splashed and wriggled and chortled. Nick made legs of his fingers and walked them on the baby's belly, then suddenly tickled and the baby went wild, bouncing in the water, kicking with his feet so he slid up and down, laughing while water went everywhere.

Afterwards he lay on his back for his new nappy, his bottom and little prick and balls in the air, displayed to everyone as he held a foot in each hand. He looked up at them and laughed, full of delight, and they laughed.

'Dirty bugger! Dirty old man!'

'Oh Nick, you shouldn't!'

Nick put his head to the baby's, and a smile on both faces steadily grew so she couldn't tell who was the mirror. They were nose to nose, the baby's eyes goggled, its mouth opened wide in a lopsided grin as it paddled its arms.

'It's so unfair! I'm with him all day, and he only ever smiles when you come home.'

'He's a pig,' Nick said, and leered at the baby. 'Arncher, mate, look at those beer muscles!' He poked him in the ribs and the baby squirmed, wobbling its belly, with the bulging fleshy knot of navel.

'Nick, stop it! Poor Davey!'

Nick snatched him up and cuddled him. He was rough, his cuddles hurt, but Davey looked towards Sandy out of Nick's arms, and his small round eyes had a funny look, as if she were another child who wanted cuddles, but he had the cuddles and she didn't.

33

'You're spoiling him, Nick. Don't. It makes him worse.'

'Spoiling him? Who's spoiling him?' He started throwing Davey up in the air. He threw him up high, so he looked as though he'd bang his head on the ceiling.

'Here goes Captain Space! Up in the sky! Flying away!'

Davey laughed in mid-air as though Nick's hands were round him even then.

'Nick, don't, you mustn't!' Sandy screamed laughing.

But up went the barebum baby, over their heads like a chuckling moon.

On one of his long hauls Nick visited Barney.

'How's the married man, then?'

'Oh, it's great, Barney, you don't know. Sandy keeps the place all nice. I'm really happy when I'm driving home. And it's great having a kiddy. It's different from what I imagined. You don't get any idea looking at other people's kids.' He sprawled back with his glass, contented. 'I was up the pole the way I was before.'

Barney nodded into his glass. He was serious and lugubrious, Nick was surprised.

'What's up, Barney? You're not the man you were.'

Barney sighed. 'I'll tell you what it is, Nick. I'm in love.'

'In love, Barney? Get away! Who is it, then? Pearl?'

'Oh no, Nick, that wasn't real.'

'And this is the real thing?'

'Nicholas it is. Don't ask me how come. Maybe it's seeing you and Sandy.'

'Yeah, mate, I reckon that's right.'

Later, Nick met the girl. She was round-faced and shiny with apple cheeks, a bright, big, country-looking girl, and cheerful all the time.

'I've heard about you,' she said to Nick, and laughed and for some time couldn't stop laughing. Whenever she looked at Nick, she laughed.

34

'Nice to meet you, love,' he said.

But with Barney she didn't laugh, for Barney's life-style was utterly changed. All he did that afternoon and evening was sit around the flat with his girl, his brows raised in surprise, while they listened to classical records he put on, or sat together looking at art-books.

Nick soon had enough. 'See you, Barney. I must hit the road.'

'Bye, Nick, bye, Nick.' They stood in the door like man and wife.

Nick shook his head as he drove away. Barney too: domesticity had caught them all.

FOUR

The downpour pelted, but thicker than the rain was the oily muck off the road. As the wipers shovelled the brown stuff aside, new brown covered the glass. He sat cramped to the misting windscreen, his shoulders aching as his feet ached in the lead-heavy boots. The sky was black, the air was so sodden with mud and oil he couldn't see the other lorries in the many-laned road, all ploughing as he was through churning steam. Their red lights showed where they were. It wasn't a road, they were ships in a gale.

Orange lights flashed and the container in front of him, big like a stretch of Stonehenge, slid from the fast lane into his path. It walled in his view, the spray from its wheels sluiced his glass. It moved left again, and swung away like a warehouse leaving the road. Small cars came in, vans like woodlice, he almost couldn't see them.

'Oh Christ alive!' He pumped the brake pedals as the little saloon, which had just dodged in front of him, stalled. It was below his sightline, he would roll it out flat.

As his brakes bit he slithered, the whole lorry snaked and slipped in the road. He held it steady.

He relaxed. He was still behind the car and at a safe distance, but he'd lost his speed. It was the snails' Derby now, God knew when he'd check in. He was hours behind schedule.

'Gee up, grandma, for God's sake, please!'

Behind her he stayed, while the old dear took her time deciding which lane she felt most at home in. Her wheels left black tracks. He felt stationary and trapped, while on either side, end to end, the other lorries passed. They disappeared ahead of him, riding swirling smokes of spray. The rain drummed on his lid like shingle.

He dropped back further – then, release, the lane beside him was clear. He pressed the accelerator to the floor and waited while, imperceptibly, his speed increased. His engine juddered, he was beginning to eat road. He was coming on like an avalanche over the saloon. He set his lights flashing and slowly moved sideways. The car dropped behind him. He was at high speed, as the other lorries were, their wheels invisible in skirts of spray, the road invisible in oil and water, the rain pelting headlong like shot on his glass. He was on the fast track heading to the depot.

The lorry swerved wildly, he spun the wheel, frantic. A puncture? He straddled the road, skidding broadside. Brake-lines severed? He steered into the skid, pumping the brake in quick jerks. The controls were jelly, but the lorry came straight. But a heavy swinging and drag to the side. His load coming off? He wobbled and veered crazily, side to side of the road. An axle gone? He had to lose speed, how could he lose speed? He was hurtling breakneck for all his braking, he'd almost crashed times into other cars and lorries. How funny, to have this burden on his trailer he might shed at any moment, and this burden of speed he could not shed.

Minutes sliding: the lorry driving sideways, back to front, he knew it would jack-knife but he swung it round. In a crazy way he was riding the slide. He was elated, exhilarated, this was the sharp edge.

He was travelling slower, at the side of the road. Control went finally, but he was up on the crash-barrier and in a grating slide like a slow collapse, skewed over, twisted, he came to a stop.

Strength ran from him, he sat back eyes shut and lungs empty. He shook his head quickly, kicked the door and jumped down. The lorry might burn, cars crash into it. The rain soaked him instantly, he could drink the rain, swim in it – the pouring cold sweetness of the rain. He had survived. He had steered straight against the odds, he had managed to stop without a smash. He'd driven on his reflexes and he'd driven like a miracle. He still felt the happiness of steering on the brink.

'Nice one! Ace!'

A fat man came towards him, with a large pudgy head, in blue dungarees pushed forward by his belly. Beyond him, up the road, a tanker had parked.

'Oh I thought you'd get me,' he was saying. 'I thought you couldn't miss. And if you'd hit me, well by Christ, that would be World War Three in a hurry.' He roared with laughter. 'You all right?'

'Yeah, I'm just shook up.'

'Oh, you're all right. But look at that! By Christ, your gaffer won't be pleased.'

Arms akimbo they stood in the downpour, looking at the shining lorry, half off the road, its different sections set at odd angles. The load of crates, with engines inside, was hanging half off. The net of ropes just held them but some of the crates were split. Raffia hung out like innards.

One of the lorry's wheels was a jagged club of iron, like an uprooted tree-end, with rags of rubber sprouting. The rest of the tyre would be in pieces among the skid-marks back down the road.

The tanker-driver laughed and whistled. 'Co! Look at that! You've got a beauty there. I'll say this, boy. If you can drive with that, you can drive.'

38

The wheel-end was such a mess the tanker-driver had to kick it.

'Give me the number, I'll phone as I go.'

The tanker drove off. Nick got back in the cab, and waited.

Eventually they came: the police, a breakdown lorry. The rain had become drizzle. Later the boss came in his Audi. He got out, banging the door.

'Oh Christ! Jesus wept!' Nick couldn't tell whether he'd explode or cry.

He walked round the lorry, sighing great breaths and saying, 'Christ!'

At the end he said to Nick, his eyes shrivelled up, 'You sodding cowboy!'

'What do you mean? It wasn't my fault! The bloody tyre blew!'

'The tyre blew! You must have been losing rubber for miles. You wouldn't have been all over the road like that if you'd been driving right.'

'All right, I wasn't hanging about. I was late, and you know why. Anyway, I reckon I was within the limit.'

But the boss wasn't listening, he could only stare at his lorry.

'Look at that. It breaks my heart. You bloody maniacs.'

'I was driving all right. If you want to know, ask the bloke who rung in. He saw it all. He was right behind me, in a tanker.'

'Ask another driver? You must think I'm bloody mad. I know you buggers, you stick together. I'll tell you now, I don't believe a word. And I know you, Grant, you speed.'

'I haven't since I married.' Nick's sense of things collected. 'I'm not having this, about my driving. I saved that lorry. If it wasn't for me it would be upside-down, and cars underneath it and kiddies killed and God knows what.'

39

'Saved it? You call this saving it. I know you lot. Ace drivers. Champions. In for the Grand Prix.'

'I could have bailed out, and let the whole lot smash.'

'Bailed out?'

'I'd have stood a better chance.'

'Christ!'

Nick closed his eyes. His head filled with blood. His fingers closed and opened and closed.

He turned and started to walk away.

'You come back here, Grant, or you'll never drive again.'

'Keep your fleet, Nelson.'

'You'll be out of a job.'

They looked at each other down a length of kerb. The rain had stopped. Nick saw the boss hesitate. He hated his drivers, but he hated finding new ones. He had to curse, seeing his lorry in ruins, but he hadn't given Nick the sack. Nick saw he had come to a limit: that was where he liked to be.

'Keep your job.'

The boss gave a shrug, and turned back to the works.

The sun at that moment came out, low under the heavy lid of cloud. It lit the wet road, and the yellow crane stooping to the buckled red hulk, and the ruddy faces and shining clothes of the workmen and policemen standing round: from all of which Nick tramped away up the motorway. There were cornfields beside the road. He was free, a free man, he felt good.

FIVE

Nick opened the door. 'Had a good day, lover?' He clumped in and sat.

'Nick, you're so late.'

'Yeah, well, I won't be tomorrow. I'm out of work.'

'What do you mean?'

'I jacked it in. I'd had enough.'

'What are you saying, Nick? You've lost your job?'

He didn't hear sympathy, so he described the crash.

'You could have been killed.'

'Yeah.'

'Oh Nick.' She crouched by him. 'Nick, you should have said.'

'I'm right as rain now.' He shook himself. He was light-headed from the crash, the world was bright and papery.

'Nick.'

They both woke in the night, shaking from the crash as if it had just happened. They held each other close.

Next day they considered.

'Still it's a pity about the job, Nick. How will we manage?'

'We'll manage.'

'But Nick, if you didn't need to lose it. Oh, I don't know . . .'

'I know,' he said, annoyed. He'd thought she'd back him taking a stand. Instead she was critical, though she wouldn't come out in the open.

'I'll find work in no time, don't you worry.'

*   *   *

It wasn't so easy. He put his name down and waited, but no one called. He went round the transport yards but they were laying off, not taking on.

He couldn't look for work all day, often he sat round the house. His mood was sour, with Davey he was irritable.

'Let's shake it up, let's rave,' he'd say in the evening, but they had no money to go out. All they could do was sit watching the telly, for as long as they could afford the telly.

He slept late, and when he got up sat slummocked round the house in his socks, his vest, an old shirt not fresh. He moped while she prepared the meals, and lost his temper when she was impatient. He wanted respect.

She stood up from the kitchen table and faced him.

'Nick, I think you should go and ask for your old job back.'

'I've got my pride.'

'What are you proud of, Nick? You were a good driver, that was worth being proud of. Go on, go and ask.'

He felt his head would explode.

'I'm not staying to hear this.'

He banged the door, she heard car-wheels tear the dirt of the lane.

Later she asked, 'How can we go on running that car?'

'We're not selling the car.'

'But Nick, how will we manage? How can we possibly keep a sports car?'

'The car stays.'

He sat back, his lips pressed tight. The car was part of him, it could not go.

Next day he took them out in the car. He drove up the trunk road, overtaking in lay-bys. He zipped round corners in a dusty cloud, in whirling handbrake turns. She squealed, Davey cried: but she was thrilled, it was like

42

the old days. She watched the hair blow back from Nick's pale, pointed, straight-line face.

Later he sold the car. She hadn't had to insist, for they needed the money. He joked about it when he got back, describing how the bus-driver demon-drove home. Sandy's chest hurt, hearing him and seeing him. He was like a man who'd lost a leg, he sat around the house with a dazzled expression, vaguely shaking his head.

The money from the car disappeared quickly. They were three unhappy people on top of each other in a tiny hole at the back of beyond. They had a scene one evening about the housework, after which Nick helped: he would wash up and clean a bit. In return he complained about the way she was with Davey.

'Why can't you be normal with him? What are you afraid of? He's your kid too, you know.'

She bit her lip. 'He doesn't like me.'

'Doesn't like you? Make him like you. He's your own kiddy.'

She started crying. 'Nick, you're mean to say that. I do all I can.'

He didn't comfort her. She stopped crying and said, 'I'll tell you something, Nick. You've got very small since you lost your job. There's nothing you do for me, you're no good at all.'

He was sorry for himself. 'It's true, I haven't done much. I haven't been feeling great, you know.'

'Not feeling great? You've gone to bits. Hit me, then. The big man. The tearaway. You know something, Nick, I've lost my job too. And I miss it a lot, especially now. We don't ever talk about that.'

They quarrelled often, she was afraid he would hit her.

She put on the green suit she wore for their honeymoon. He watched her do her hair.

'Going somewhere?'

43

'I'm going to get a job.'

He filled the room. He said weakly, 'I support us.'

'But you don't, Nick, do you?'

He stared at her. He was surprised, he was hurt.

'I'm sorry, Nick. But what can I say? We need money.'

He was breathing through his mouth.

'Well, I'm off now. Look after Davey.'

He followed her to the door, she was relieved to get outside.

She walked to the bus stop and went into town. She tried for the kinds of work she knew, and had no better luck than Nick. Finally she took a job part-time, waitressing in a tea-shop.

'The pay's peanuts, Nick, but I should pick up on tips.'

'Yeah?'

She washed and ironed the blue dress and the white hair-band the boss had given her. She tried them on.

For once Nick smiled. 'That's really pretty.'

Each day she went in, and left Nick to look after Davey and the house.

'Garoo goo!' Davey gurgled from his play-pen, wanting to play.

'Can it, mate. I'm not in the mood.'

He sat slumped, staring at the switched-off coals.

The tea-shop was hectic and the tips were bad, and her arms and back soon ached. But she liked the kitchen, she felt a girl again joking with the other girls. When they were hungry, they put a chocolate cake in the microwave till it melted; then smothered it snow-white from the cream-dispenser. They threw food or dropped it, by the end of the day they were skating on the floor.

'Hey, Sandy, that's not all. Come on.'

They fought over tips, they all kept back some of what they got.

After work each evening she had a long trip home. When she arrived, she was exhausted.

'Christ, Nick, you've done nothing! I work all day and then I come here and cook. A great life!'

He sagged on the sofa, letting her slang him.

'You've got to pick yourself up, Nick.'

He nodded. 'You're right.' He looked up at her with frank eyes. 'I need to be moving, Sandy. I can't just sit here still.'

She sighed, he was more depressed than before. What was it with him, why was moving so important? Why was sitting in a car better than sitting in a chair in the garden? There was something odd in the middle of him.

The following days she was too tired for his dumps.

'Get off your arse, Nick, and clean the bloody sink! Coming back to this place is like coming back to two kids.'

She'd become like the bad-tempered mother of both of them.

He'd no answer, he wasn't even violent. He looked up, helpless. He had been a big good-looking man, he had become a sack of human stuff.

She wanted to howl, and he couldn't help her.

It was the world's relief when he got a job. This time it was tip-up trucks. He came home in the big, battered square lorry, which filled the lane with its throaty broken cough, and pushed the hedges back. To impress Davey he made the truck stand on end.

He felt good being back on four wheels, he'd drive as if the lorry were a formula one car. He held it to the line for corners and straights. He raced the country roads, with Davey strapped in beside him. Sandy was amused, it amused her to ring her mum and say, 'Guess what Nick's bringing me in! You'll never guess, it's a tip-up truck.'

She was glad to leave the tea-shop. The boss had become difficult, asking at bad times for extra time.

Nick bought a car: a saloon from the small ads, but it must serve. Life was better now they were in tip-up trucks.

SIX

Nick bounced down the road in the lorry. What a heap, it banged like a load of dustbins.

He threw the lorry round a corner, loving the clatter, and turned the radio deafening. He lolled as he careered, an arm out of the window, feeling the air blow through the cab.

She stood on the verge like something impossible. It was a country road, she was in deep grass. She seemed to be wearing men's shirts in layers, but it was clear she had nice breasts, a good waist. Was she hitching? She eyed the truck, then raised her eyes to the sky. Well, if she wanted a Jag, let her wait. Her fair hair was almost white, her eyes pale blue. As her eyes passed his, he saw her notice him.

Promptly he stopped. A rain of sand pattered on the bonnet, as the load in the truck lifted. He laughed to see the road turn yellow, already he was reversing in a straight even line, till he was beside her. From his high cab he smiled. The lorry-engine throbbed, the metal sides of the cab vibrated. She frowned back, her white face puckering so her small teeth showed.

'Are you going to Newport?' Her voice had a rough edge.

'A bit of the way.' He tipped his head to the door the other side. She frowned more, then came round and clambered in. She had legs that seemed more than half her body.

'OK, darling?'

47

Nick got in gear suavely, and trod the pedals lightly so the lorry moved off like a limousine. Soon he was at top speed, but smooth not banging, straightening the road. He could tell she was tickled, being taken in a lorry. And he was awake, having a passenger like this. He'd been in prison, stuck at home these weeks. He'd almost stopped being a man.

'What's on in Newport?'

''sa gig.'

'Who's playing?'

She said, but the name meant nothing to him. He thought, I'm right out of touch.

'If the pigs don't close it down,' she went on. Her voice had a funny catch that he liked, she was educated, but talking rough. He drove at speed round a long left bend, so a pressure like a gentle hand, and not him at all, moved her towards him.

They talked about groups, then about driving. She'd been to Brands and Snetterton.

'Do you do rally driving?' She sat towards him, her lip lifted.

'Nah. What I want is a single seater.'

'You've been racing?'

'Well, I been to racing school. What I haven't got is money.'

'What, to get a car?'

'Right. So I'm nowhere.'

He swallowed drily.

'Will your boss sponsor you?'

'Yeah, of course. He's just waiting for me to ask.' He laughed.

'You'd better get a different boss.'

He looked at her. The blue of her eyes was pale and transparent. Her small straight nose was soft as a baby's. He could see her nipples through her white man's shirt.

48

'What you do?'

'I'm doing retakes.'

As she explained about exams, the roughness left her voice. There was something delicate in her face. He liked her more and more.

He was off his route now, and driving further from it, but here was a chance he couldn't let go. His excitement grew keener, he became nervous, with each moment she was more important. Maybe they'd stop at a transport caf, he'd get her a meal, get to know her better, then they'd drive on –

'Stop – would you stop, please.'

'Here?' They were in the middle of a small town.

'Yeah. Thanks. I'll get out here. Ta very much. Bye.'

'See ya.'

But he wouldn't. She was already gone, and he had to drive forward, leaving her behind. He punched his head. She was an old hand, she knew how to hitch. All the time it was her taking him for a ride.

He sighed, declutched, advanced. He was exhilarated, none the less. He'd got something back which he'd lost. It was funny to think that all this time he'd been faithful to Sandy. He hadn't expected to, but in the event it was what he'd wanted. Now he'd come through a door, he was back in the world.

SEVEN

Sandy was again alone with Davey. He had started crawling, and she was happy when she crawled with him. He
would smile at her, wicked eyes, till she pounced. He
chuckled and rolled over, then he was off, on hands and
knees. She crawled after him, a racing-crawl, clumping.
When she caught up they went round in circles, till they
collapsed together tickling each other and laughing.

Other times he was fractious, as if he blamed her because Nick was away. He knew how to work on her
nerves. He would look at her wickedly, and do the naughty
thing. He would watch her put out food then send the
bowl flying.

'Oh Davey, don't do that.' She mopped the sopping
highchair tray.

'Do eat, Davey, there's a good boy.'

She stood by nervously.

'Please, Davey.'

He let her wait. His bright eyes sparkled at her, his red
cheeks shone over his plastic bib. He bulged out of the
highchair all importance, like a funny fat vicar in a too-
tight pulpit.

She lost patience and shrieked. 'Eat it, dammit, or I'll
wring your bloody neck!'

Davey gawped, but she was scared too. He stared at her,
testing, then down came his fat arms in the bowl itself,
the food shot all over him but he only laughed, and
brandished and banged his dripping arms so the food

splashed everywhere. There was nothing in the room but this fat demon up on its throne, flinging havoc. She got up to clout him, but slipped in the mess. She sat on the floor and cried, she bawled. He stopped and looked at her – dismayed, a bit lost, but not with kind eyes.

'Oh Davey, why can't you be nice? I am your bloody mum.'

The next day he played with his food but ignored her, while she stood at the door scared of him, not wanting to come in, her arms clasped up in front of her in a kind of imploring.

'Davey, what is it you want?'

She was trapped in the cottage. Nick was out all day, but she didn't drive, she had no bike, she was at the mercy of the bus service, which didn't run often. She looked out of the window at continuous cloud flowing low overhead. There were few trees round them, and nothing to break the wind that poured over the big fields. When the farmer fertilized his land, a grey dust blew up that settled on everything. She hurried to Davey out in the garden. He was crying and the dust, with its chemical smell, was falling on him like rain. She snatched him up and bathed him desperately, trying to wash off each grey speck.

While Davey played in his pen she moped. She had nothing to do. No one came to see her, why should they? She missed the tea-shop: it was hectic and steamy and the work was low-paid, but at least there she saw other people. The girls laughed in gales while for lunch they made themselves gigantic sandwiches, with layers of prawns like a double-decker bus. The boss was all temper, then sudden sweetness when she wanted extra time. It had been a break, she couldn't come back to being cooped up at home.

A telephone would talk to her, if they had one. In daydreams she was back in her old office, answering the calls that came sometimes from foreigners: they made

51

mistakes but they had style, when she heard them she shivered and imagined such kisses. The air of the office was people talking. Yes, she had wanted to be with Nick. But still it was odd to live alone, with all that talk switched off and dead.

Since he'd gone back to work Nick was impatient. He'd come home tired, and chuck off his boots and sit in his socks, waiting for food. He would fall asleep in front of the telly like a middle-aged man. She wondered what he did when he was away from her. They didn't make love much. He'd got into the rut of the fed-up husband, home was where he came to complain, while he sat in his underwear and his belly sagged.

'I've got problems too, Nick.'

'Garn, you're at home all day.' His humour with her was rougher.

'I work as hard as you.'

'You've got it made.'

'Nick, I've got to get out of here. I can't take it any more. I've got to get away.' Nick stared. She was shouting.

'OK, lover,' he said.

She talked about moving into town. Nick nodded, but his face was sullen. She saw he was simply keeping her quiet.

She knew she must move. Whenever she could she took the bus into town, and lugged Davey round in a pushchair. She ran out of back-streets. She became like a gypsy, pushing her child on an endless journey.

She stopped on the kerb. The lights changed, and changed again. Why cross the road, nothing waited on the other side? Why stay this side, there was nothing here. The lights changed prettily and people passed. She crossed and later crossed back again.

She began to notice men again. She hadn't looked at them while Davey was little, but now she was emerging from the box she'd been in. She wondered, will they notice me? She tightened her waist. She washed her hair often, to keep it fluffy. The world was full of other people having fun, she saw groups of them gossiping and laughing. She had forgotten them but they were there all the time. She looked at them wistfully as she shoved the pushchair, while Davey sagged fatly so his little limbs, in their too-big plastic tubes, stuck out all ways. He'd collapsed in his seat as if he needed punching into shape like a cushion.

'Oh do sit up, Davey.' He was a drag in town.

One day she met Pearl.

'Sandy, what's happened to you? You look so old!' She didn't mince words, Pearl. And she didn't listen when Sandy talked, she wanted only to give her own news. 'I'm in London now, it's so exciting you don't know, I work in this new hairdresser's and the people who come there, oh I wouldn't go back to living here, not ever.'

Pearl lived in a flat in Queen's Park. The house was run down but that didn't matter, she was out every night. She had so many men, she played them all off against each other. One was a black man. She got new clothes every week, there was so much to choose. She'd seen Prince Philip in the street, trousers she'd never seen such creases, with a detective on either side.

Afterwards Sandy thought of Pearl, taken out to restaurants and casinos and jazz clubs. That was where life was. On clear days, when the sky was big, she thought of London.

She sat in the living-room, looking out on the fields. Nick was at work, Davey had been naughty. She saw the white light behind the trees, and heard the scraping sound of the rooks. She said aloud, 'I'm young. I haven't had my life.' Her eyes filled with tears.

She looked up startled. Davey was in the doorway, on all fours. She stared at him and felt nothing.

53

His head bobbed higher, his eyes widened, his mouth opened ready to grin: he was on the verge of crawling pell-mell at her. She prayed, oh don't come now. He was growing so fast, his head was huge and square like a box, before she knew it he'd be walking.

He didn't come. His mouth was still open but his eyes had stopped shining, they only stared. A string of saliva looped from his mouth.

She thought, now he'll cry. She didn't want to hold him. She hunched tiny.

But he only gazed, bewildered, as if he had made a mistake. In Tesco's she'd seen a child run excited to a woman, then the woman turned and the child saw it wasn't his mother and stopped. But he didn't cry because this was not his mother and crying would do no good. So it was with Davey, he stared at her as if he'd only just realized she wasn't his mother.

They eyed each other. He was crouched across the room like a funny animal with a big head. She thought, where has he come from? He'd come out of her, but he was nothing to do with her, he was an alien from a film, he had come from somewhere else and crept inside her.

She murmured he's my Davey, I must go to him.

She didn't go to him, she went to the window and gazed, gazed through its whiteness, as if it looked out on a different planet.

She was on a cliff over a plain, the sky was black. The distant object on the horizon was the shape and colour of a humming top. It came nearer quickly till she couldn't see anything else except the giant spinning vessel. It was painted bright colours and was full of windows, and there were people in the windows, and the windows were shop-fronts. There were whole arcades on the wheel of its rim, and buildings and derricks and domes on top of it, and escalators.

As it approached its spinning slowed and the thick wheel of its rim was on a level with the cliff. She saw it was crowded, people strolled comfortably, it was their talk that made the hum. It came in like a ship reaching a quay. The people were all busy laughing with other people. They were smartly dressed and had their hair all styles, they'd got everything.

The edge was close, only yards away and turning slowly. The individuals on it were able to see her, they waved a bit.

'Can I get on?' she shouted.

The man there nodded, he looked kindly.

She didn't move, it was difficult. She asked again, 'Can I get on?'

They nodded, she hesitated. Then she crouched to jump, she would step across. Had she left it too late? The vessel was leaving, she fell on to a mattress, blinking at dead blackness.

She lay in the dark: she had seen London.

EIGHT

'Oh, Nick.'

The boss's wife only slightly raised her voice, but it was clear to Nick across the yard.

'Mrs Saunders.'

'You're going through town, I think. Drop me off, will you?' She didn't wait, but climbed in the cab.

She lit a cigarette, and called through the window, 'Be an angel and bring those bags.'

'Mrs Saunders.'

He wobbled his eyes at a mate, and carried the plastic bags to the lorry. She was absorbed in her handbag. He started.

She ignored him now, as though he were a chauffeur. But he was glad to be driving her. He was always excited by her smoker's voice, and her white, slightly puffy, indoor skin. He knew she fancied him, she had called him Nick from the first time she saw him.

She sat turned away, absently watching the hedge. He was aware without looking of her cigarette moving slowly to her mouth, to pause barely touching and then move away again. When he glanced at her, he felt she could see him with her back, with her shoulder blades, she was so still. He was nervous, he fixed his eyes dead ahead. When he looked again she had changed her position, she was looking straight at him, staring. His eyes darted between her and the road. His mouth was dry as though he had fluff in it. He looked ahead, he looked at her.

The seat-spring stirred. She moved her legs, her skirt moved high. He trembled as he drove, his heart walloped.

At a break in the hedge he slowed and turned, and drove up a track towards some trees. He was thinking, 'You're asking for it, darling.'

He pulled the brake on. She curled her body and raised her face. She kissed him passionately. He was surprised, frightened, his excitement paused.

They got out and walked under the trees. He thought nervously, if the boss could see this –

They kissed again and looked at each other. Her face had become young like a teenage face and shining.

She stood quiet and like a girl, while he took her clothes off, kissing her. She lay down naked on the grass, completely still and waiting.

After they fucked she was lazily cheerful. They smoked and laughed. She chatted easily about the boss.

He dropped her in town, then took the long route to his destination. He had a large load to handle, he was ages in a traffic jam.

He came home late and tired, the boss's wife was long ago.

'What is it, Nick?'

'I'm whacked, that's all.'

She frowned at the stove. Something wasn't right.

The next night he took Sandy out in the truck. Mrs Wilmot had said she would have Davey for once.

Nick drove nervously. He watched Sandy sniff. Was there scent in the cab?

She was holding a cigarette-butt, red at the end.

'Stop here, Nick.'

He didn't.

She opened the door, she had half stepped out. Beneath her the road blurred past.

He rammed on the anchors, the lorry swerved to a stop.

Sandy got down. From the road she called back, her face chalky, her eyes black balls.

'I'll get even with you, Nick.'

'Sandy!'

But she'd gone, tramping back to the cottage. By the time he'd turned round, he could see no trace of her. Now he was stuck – but why, did she own him? He drove to the pub, drank in a foul mood, and came home early. But she said no more that night.

NINE

They headed for the party, two smartened-up people in a shuddering truck. The mates would be there, Barney had come south. Davey was safe asleep at Nick's mother's. They were both excited, they'd hardly seen friends since they married.

'We'll have a good time, Nick.'

'We'll live it up, lover!'

'Nick, let's!'

They needed a party, things had been sour between them for weeks.

'Do I look good?'

'Mmmm!' He blew kisses at her with both hands, working the steering-wheel with his knees.

'Nick!'

He slewed the lorry round a corner and drove into an estate. They stopped by a house with all its windows lit. They could hear the party.

Vince opened the door. He looked an unhappy host.

'Sandy, Nick – great to see you! Liven things up if you can.'

They could see it was a party that needed something. There was music like a road-drill but no one was dancing. People hung in knots, and drank not talked. Barney stretched on the floor, pretending to be dead. His hands were folded on his hill of belly, his bumptious shut-eyed face was pious.

Nick stood over him. 'What, has Barney kicked the bucket? My good old mate.'

People looked up. 'Hello, Nick!'

Nick stepped across Barney, 'Excuse me, Madam!' He changed the record on the hi-fi, and grabbed Barney's hand. 'May I have the pleasure!' He heaved Barney to his feet. They started to dance, Nick doing the Fred Astaire and Barney sticking out parts of himself. They sang to each other, 'Why were you born so beautiful? Why were you born at all?'

Others started dancing, the party woke. Girls came round Sandy, who described the tip-up truck. They had arrived like stars.

'Where have you been, Sandy? We haven't seen you for months. Do you like being a mum?'

'Oh it's great, I wouldn't change it.' She felt good, she wanted everything to be good.

She saw herself in a mirror. It was a girl of freckles with auburn hair, happy in a happy group. She had forgotten she was like that.

Others chatted, the girl in the mirror raised her head laughing. She heard her own strong laugh, it's a long time since I heard it. She started dancing, it was a long time since she had danced. Her arms made happy small movements.

'It's great that you could make it, Sandy!'

Vince danced past her, with a weeping-willow blonde so much taller than him that she stooped to rest her chin on his head. She smiled to other people, while Vince made sedate fat movements, never raising his eyes above dead level.

She saw Nick across the room looking taller than usual. He and Barney were dancing solo. People chatted to him and about him.

'Hello, Nick, I heard you come. Engine sounds a bit rough. Shock absorbers gone, are they?'

'That's Nick, he does the ton over a hump-backed bridge.'

Nick grinned sharply but didn't waste words. She watched him. He was dancing with his head down, with a slow good swivel of his hips. He was pale and a bit haggard but so good-looking, with his big brow and black eyes and sharp nose and nice mouth. She thought, he's beautiful, he's a lovely man. She danced more slowly.

Barney's girl got in her laughing mood, all the time she burst out in peels and chimes. She laughed so much she had everyone laughing. Barney was lifting his arms and knees, he seemed to be climbing a rope as he danced.

'Doing a hornpipe, Barney?'

But he said it was a fling, and it was. He puffed out his cheeks and sucked them in, and rolled his eyes like casters. He reeled and pitched and tossed and lurched, he danced like two fat men in one suit of clothes. He danced on his toes, he danced on his arse; he danced with his girl, he danced with Nick, he danced with a cushion, with a bottle, with a cabbage; he did jumps and hops and springs on the spot, and a dance like a kangaroo doing a tango. His girl was in fits, she shouted laughter, but still kept dancing so she was many odd shapes, hopping wildly doubled up.

Other people had partnered. Vince danced with his wife, a short hook-nosed girl who looked round in worry as the party livened. The tall blonde was with a tall man, evidently they belonged together, they bowled round the room like two trees dancing. Sandy looked for Nick, it was time he came for her, but he was on the far side with someone else. It was someone she didn't know, and someone he didn't know, she could tell: he was putting on a show, swinging his pelvis. She could see he was interested, his eyes as well as his smile were sharp. That was Nick, any new woman at a party was his. This one

61

was a cow, with tits like shopping bags. It was one like this he'd had in his lorry. All her thoughts came back, of what he did away from her.

He saw her looking, at the next dance he came. 'How about it then?'

Sandy looked at the floor. 'I don't care.'

He stood over her, glowing and smiling. 'Come on, lover, let's boogie!'

She made him wait. After an interval she stood and danced. But still he was doing his number. What a show-off, he didn't really want a partner at all. He was doing a Zorba. He had his eyes shut, his arms outstretched, while he stamped and shuffled his feet. The temperature in the room had gone up, he took off his shirt and danced in his T-shirt, swooning as he danced and displaying his body.

Sandy said, 'I'm going to sit down.'

He came and sat too but had nothing to say. He sat on the chair-arm, gazing at the party with his big brow knit, as if he'd paused between words and the pause went on. She said nothing. The party he had brought to life still crashed on but they were outside it, on the shore watching, two people at odds like little hard nuts apart on the floor. She thought, anyone can see the sort of marriage we've got. Across the room she saw Vince's wife, sitting by herself huddled small in a chair, looking round suffering as beer splashed the carpet, and a cigarette, which had got lost in the upholstery, was found by its smell. Sandy looked at Nick, he was watching intently the other girls dancing.

'Good for you, Nick.' She got up and walked away.

'Please yourself.'

He sat a few moments indifferent, then jumped up. Someone had put on a blues record. He shouted, 'Here, here, too much soul!'

Barney joined him, 'Too much soul!'

Nick changed the record.

'May I?' he said to Barney's girl. She nodded, and stopped laughing for serious dancing. Still her smiles bloomed, it was a great thing dancing with Nick.

Across the room was a fair-haired man in a shirt and tie. He was a draughtsman somewhere, his name was Brian. He was everything Nick wasn't. Sandy went up to him.

'Shall we dance?' She hadn't done this in ages. She felt a risky smile come, she knew her eyes were smoky and bright.

His face, as he stood, was like someone woken suddenly.

'I'd like that.'

His dancing was quiet. He was slender and nervous and like a handsome boy: she thought, he's nice, and all this time I'm stuck with Nick! She sparkled like a new glass of champagne. It was a happy dance she gave, my life could be different from what it is. Nick would be watching her, dancing with Brian.

Nick's eyes were tight and shiny like marbles. He turned the music as loud as it would go, and danced with the woman he was with before. The house vibrated, people held their ears. Sandy danced faster. The room was reeling, the floorboards throbbed. Any second the glasses and windows would shatter, the bricks in the walls would turn to powder, they would all be vaporized by the music.

Spinning she glimpsed Nick, gone wild. He was shivering his hips towards the woman. Next to him Barney was being an aeroplane, he had his arms out like wings and swooped on couples blowing raspberries like farts.

There was a crash. Someone took the record off. Vince's wife cried while Barney stooped down, his trouser-seat stretched, collecting bits of vase. He hollered in a squeaky voice, 'Don't worry, don't worry, just get me the Superglue!' People round said, 'Christ, Barney!' Vince was down with him, nursing fragments.

'Come on,' Sandy said. She and Brian slipped upstairs. In the bedroom she made big frightened eyes, as if he'd brought her there, up to no good. She gave him her mouth.

'Brian, what are you doing?' She coiled, helping him loosen her clothes. She thought, this is terrible, Nick would go mad. Brian was beautiful. His chest was shallow and his arms were thin, but he had a lovely white body, it looked new-made of milk. She couldn't find anyone more different from Nick. As she curled within his arms she gave a quiet wicked excited laugh.

It was not bim bam, he caressed her nicely. It was different from Nick and not thrilling like Nick, but sweet and she lay quite quiet as he held her.

'Sandy!'

The light was on, Nick was shouting, they turned startled and there was Nick in the doorway enormous, but he was on top of her and the floor came at her. She had her hand up, Nick's fist was over her, his voice in her ears.

He didn't hit her. Barney came from nowhere, she saw his fat legs, his fat back. He was shouting, 'You hit her, Nick, and I'll put one on you.' Nick stared, drop-jawed. Barney gave him a great push in the chest so he lost his balance and reeled back.

'You do that again, Barney, I'll murder you.' Barney did it again, and again as well, he shoved Nick out of the door, Sandy saw Nick's astonished face.

There was a racket outside. Brian, white-faced, was getting dressed. Vince had come in, he was saying very seriously, like an undertaker, 'Are you all right, Sandy? Are you all right?'

'Pig!' Sandy muttered but she felt shaky. She huddled the bed-clothes round her.

64

TEN

Nick said nothing after the party, though he eyed Sandy heavily as she moved round the house. She ignored his looks and didn't try to make up, but she did her job: his dinner was ready, his clothes were clean. Her voice when she spoke was more like a man's. It all made him furious, his chest was an oven: and she sat across the table with a hard-faced look, as if, for two pence, she'd spit in his eye.

On the road he wondered what else she did. He was away long hours, anyone with half a moped could visit her. Or she could bus into town, leave Davey with a friend, see who she wanted. But she wouldn't, it wasn't like her. But he couldn't stop seeing her in bed with the man. He felt as if his blood made a burning sediment. He'd hear himself swearing. He would crowd other vehicles or make a noise hooting.

Out on the motorway he was overtaken by a racer. It was up on a trailer and all bright colours, yellow and green with red flashes and darts, and ads all round it, brilliant in the sun. He revved to keep up with it but he couldn't, it was flying. It was facing the way it wanted to go, it was his old dream, his hope, leaving him behind. The road ran straight across the valley and the racer was little in the distance like a model. It had gone over the crest, and he was still tied to his steam-roller lorry.

He pulled off at the next Services feeling sick. I was right at the start, I shouldn't have married. If I hadn't, I'd have got into racing somehow. As it is, I'm up to here in shit.

In the next town he came to he was stuck behind a cyclist. The busy road twisted, she wouldn't make way for him. He sounded his horn.

'Move it, darling.'

But she simply swung to the middle of the road. She cycled slower, making a pantomime of each push of her legs.

'Oh baby, just wait!' He was down into bottom gear, crawling.

She started to zigzag, wagging her bottom as she stood on the pedals.

'OK then, lover, take your time.' He began to be delighted. They made a slow progress through the crowded town: the swinging cyclist, and the reverberating juggernaut.

When the road widened he overtook her full-throttle, but a little way past her he stopped. He smoothed his hair in the mirror, then he climbed from the cab. He stood in the road watching her come. She eyed him uneasily and glanced to each side. Should she cut up a side-street? She wobbled towards him snail's pace, with comic-guilty rollings of her eyes.

She stopped, and stood astride her bike. She scanned him, and he stood tall.

He called, 'Can I give you a lift, darling? You're not making too good time.'

She gave a snorting laugh. 'I know what you're after.'

'What's that, then?'

They eyed each other.

He motioned with his head to the bike and to his cab.

'You can have a lift if you want one.'

He waited.

She shrugged and sniffed.

Lightly he lifted her bike into the lorry. Like a fancy gent he handed her up into the cab.

'Where to, then?'

'You can drop me at the underpass.'

As he drove he looked at her sidelong. She had a rude sexy face, with a big wide mouth, a fleshy nose, and bulging dark rolling eyes. He wanted to fondle her and suck her large breasts. He wanted to fuck her now, he hadn't been so impatient. I'll find a way, this'll pay Sandy.

'You've made me late, love.'

She tapped the tin fascia. 'Why d'you bring this through the middle of town?'

'Yeah, right. But it takes an age to go round.'

She gave a wide smile. 'Well, today it took you an age to come through.'

'That's all right, love. I had a nice view in front of me.'

She laughed. She started talking about her boyfriend, and finding fault with him then saying she liked him. OK, he thought, you want a new one. That way he could do what he wanted.

But what did he want? The road, the girl disappeared: he saw Sandy, looking up at him scared from Brian's arms. Oh it's coming to you, Sandy.

The girl was saying something, he shook his head.

'Say it again, love.'

She said it again, again he didn't hear. What about Sandy then, what's she doing right now? She'll be at it.

He looked at the girl: his mood had changed. His anger with Sandy had come into the cab. Be your boyfriend? I can't be bothered to go through that caper. What I want's a legover, hello and goodbye.

They'd come to the underpass, and stopped. The cab was hot. They both sat. Should he make his move? He thought, if I start here, that's my marriage down the toilet.

67

His mood had gone sour, he didn't want to do anything. Sandy's screwing had cut off his balls. The girl was sexy and it made him angry.

'Here we are then.'

He got her bike down.

'Thanks.' She frowned.

'Goodbye, then.'

'Cheers, love.'

He didn't look back. He was fed up with her, with Sandy, with himself.

He drove on in fury: what's wrong with me, why didn't I?

At times he'd repeat, well it was right not to – I'd better think of my sodding marriage.

When he got home, Sandy was impatient.

'Did you get the bread, Nick?' She could see he hadn't.

'No, I didn't. I was at it all day.'

'But we need it, Nick. How can we live without bread?'

'Bloody Christ! Couldn't you get the fucking bread?'

'How could I get bread? I'm shut up here.'

'Well, it's not my job to do the shopping. I work hard enough, don't I? Christ! Bloody sod!'

She went on getting the dinner, but her face looked so set it would damage the cooker. Every part of her said, 'You're in the wrong, Nick. You said you'd get it and you didn't get it.'

He thought, what I could have tried, and I didn't try today.

He went outdoors with Davey.

'Let's go down the lane.'

'Lane!' said Davey. 'Lane!' He was already in the pushchair.

'That's the ticket. Here, mate, don't forget the seat-belt!' He strapped up the harness.

68

In the lane he pushed the chair slowly, while Davey bounced and started to complain.

He sprinted. He pumped his long legs, the pushchair was juddering and shaking all over. He had the front wheels up for better balance, Davey lay back gasping. They were at top speed.

'Lean into the turn, mate.' He slowed and swung the pushchair round, turning it on one wheel tipped right over. Davey screamed with delight. They stopped.

'You're the racing-driver. You'll tear them up at Brands.'

Davey chuckled. Nick stood back, looking round. They'd come a long way from the cottage. He stood in a study while his gaze continued, over the hills and far away.

'Rrrrm rrrm.' Davey strained in his harness, bouncing in his seat as though he were revving to fly out of it.

''Fraid not, mate. We gotta get sodding home.' Not racing, Nick pushed the pushchair back.

ELEVEN

Davey was getting more of a handful. Sandy knew he didn't like her. And every day he was bigger, he kept wanting new clothes.

'Oh go on, do.'

She flexed the small rubber welly, and tried to force it on his foot.

'It's no good. I don't understand it, Nick. His feet can't have grown that much.'

'Big foot!' Nick called to him. 'You flatfoot, you'll be a copper.'

Davey, up on the cupboard, chortled. He couldn't swing his foot because Sandy was pushing at the welly. He looked at Nick full of bad fun. Nick shrugged and smiled over Sandy's head. The hard time she gives us!

'Nick, I can't buy him new shoes again.'

'It's OK, we'll get him bovver boots.'

'It's easy to say, Nick. I can't get anything on the money you give me.'

'I give you what I get, and I bloody work for it and all.'

'Yes, Nick, right, you give me what you've got when you get back from the pub. Oh, sod it!'

She gave up, and stood. She caught Nick and Davey exchanging looks.

'Nick, are you encouraging him?'

'What you mean?'

'I'm not having it, Nick. You encourage him against me. You've got like a bloody kid.'

70

'What?'

'He gets at me and you get at me, you do it together. It happens every day. I've had a bloody 'nough of it, Nick, I'm telling you now.'

'Just get his shoe on, will you?'

His face swelled and reddened, she winced away from him. He itched to hammer her, ever since the party.

She looked him over. 'Clint!' He'd have hit her, but she'd bent down to force the boot on. Davey looked at Nick, sparkle-eyed, bewildered, not sure what trick to play.

'That's what he's doing.' She understood: he was clenching his foot inside the boot, in a little fist so it wouldn't come on.

She shouted in Davey's face, 'Get your bleeding foot straight!'

She forced again and this time she succeeded, the boot slid on. Davey was excited, he banged his feet. The boot flew up and caught her, he had kicked her on the nose.

'You little sod!' She stood up, her nose red, her eyes weeping. Her hands went to her face, Davey goggled. Then her hand came down, with the anger of months she clouted his head.

His mouth dropped, his eyes yawned. He took breath then roared.

'Shut it!' She caught him a swipe that sent him flying off the cupboard. They heard him bang on the cooker. She gasped as he fell, his head slit open, he was on the floor but already Nick had punched her, such a blow, an iron punch, she was reeling back her hand over her eye, her eyeball had burst, she didn't know if she hurt yet.

He was bending over Davey, who was shrieking.

'How is he?' she asked.

'Christ!' he was saying. He got up and swarmed all fury towards her.

71

She picked up the breadknife. 'Get away, Nick! Get off!' She held the breadknife in front of her, it waved in her hand.

'Try it!' His face was bloodless. He made a feint to one side, jerkily she stabbed.

He was called off by Davey's shrieks. She approached, but as Davey saw her he howled louder. Nick turned on her, 'Clear out!'

She ran out and up the lane. She stopped in a copse, by the little stream. She put some water on her face. It was freezing. Her eye had closed completely, but by forcing it open she found she could still see with it.

She waited crouched down saying, I'll never go back. Ages later a voice called her name. It was Nick, she huddled smaller in the ditch. He came nearer till she could see him through the branches, looking round and hollering. Someone answered him, it was Mr Boyce.

Nick shouted, 'Have you seen Sandy?' He sounded worried not angry. She knew, with a feeling like a lid closing, she would go back.

'Ain't seen her,' Mr Boyce called.

'Funny.' Nick looked round some more then went away. She stayed where she was. Later she came up from near the stream and crouched at the edge of the copse. She could see their row of cottages end on. Dusk was falling, some lights were lit.

Nick went out in their car. She hid as it passed, lights blinding. Nick was either looking for her, or taking Davey to the doctor. She stayed where she was.

Nick came back, she saw him carry Davey in. Evidently he was all right. It was getting very cold.

It was dark, and damp. An owl made its noise. She thought, they must think I'm far away. Isn't it funny, when all the time I'm so near. She was so cold she didn't want to move. She felt she was getting smaller. She huddled and shoved, trying to make a nest in the under-growth. There was a drift of leaves, she burrowed among them till she was covered. She found she could breathe there.

It got darker and colder. Did she doze? She was a creature curled up in the chill, a little clod, a log.

She woke frozen. Stiffly she got up, she moved like a robot. She came out into the lane. She thought, I don't need to go back, they think I've gone. I'll walk off now, I'll never go back. She went to the cottage, and upstairs to bed, and fell asleep.

TWELVE

She stood and looked. It wasn't a mirror, because in it she saw not Sandy but the monster. It was a scarecrow of the farmer, come at her out of the field of rape. Its hair stuck all ways, it had a swollen turnip face, with one eye cut wrong, in a bulge that was red and black. Whenever she looked, there it was, it stalked her with its dead stare. Even her mouth couldn't open straight, the swelling was falling down her face.

Nick would come up to her saying, 'Sandy' in a voice that sagged. She shook him off, she didn't want that from him, or anything. Still he was careful and went on tiptoe, and looked at her anxiously and said shush to Davey, as if she were a corpse going round the house. Davey was frightened. If she went into a room and the two of them were there, they'd look up like two worried kids. She didn't care.

Old Nick was at a loss. He started saying, 'Come on, Sandy' or 'I've said I'm sorry' or 'I don't know what else I can do.' When those fell flat he'd stand with his arse against the rim of the sink, sniffing loudly, getting red in the face.

'What more do you want?' He had his hurt look.

She didn't want anything.

She watched the telly a lot. Often she saw people in London, they lived a real life.

She and Davey were wary of each other. She could still hear the sound, as he hit the cooker. The cut didn't show

74

but she still saw blood. But he had kicked her in the face. He was Nick's son.

At first he was frightened by her new ugly face, then he got used to it. He would creep up on her quietly.

She looked round from the mirror: Davey was in the doorway. He'd stopped at the threshold, rubbing crookedly on the doorframe.

She shut her eyes tight. When she opened them, he was moving backwards. He kept on till he was behind the doorframe, then he charged away down the passage. Later she heard him talking to himself. At least, nowadays, he'd play for hours by himself. She let him be, she'd given up on him. If he didn't like her, he didn't have to.

The days passed and her face came back, even the puffiness was absorbed. Nick started to put out his charms.

'Let's be mates.'

She looked at his face, the high brow, the not big but straight nose, the hurt-dog eyes. It was all like looking at a creature on show.

'Sandy, love.'

She felt his fingers move slowly on her. He was touching her lightly but her skin was alert, the tiny hairs in the pores stood up.

'Sandy . . .'

There was a mouth on hers but it was tight like a ring of rubber.

'No, Nick.'

'What can I do? What is it you want?' His mouth was wide like an open bin, his eyes like glass eyes in a row.

'Nothing.' It was an old routine.

He lost his temper. 'You fucking cow, you really store it up. Christ! You cunting bitch!' He felt better, banging round the house. She kept out of his way.

Later he said, 'Lover, let's be friends.' He spoke nicely,

75

but still it was like seeing him through the wrong end of a telescope. He'd become a strange person, like someone she didn't know. His eyes were furtive. His skin was pale and unhealthy. She thought, did I love this man? Anything like love had run clear away, like water down a plughole, she felt nothing at all.

'I'll take off,' she said, but she couldn't believe it. Alone in the house she played over their fights, she said to the walls, 'Bastard, you bastard, you bloody bastard!'

When he came home she said flatly, 'How were things?'

'OK, OK.' He was uneasy.

'There's sod all for dinner.'

He wasn't angry. 'I'll lend a hand.' Good as gold he went to the pantry and took out some potatoes and started to scrub them.

Oh yes? she thought. Who have you been screwing? Bloody fucker!

He got out beer and told jokes from the depot. She laughed and forgot. The dinner burned, they ate it soot and all.

She was watching him eat. When he ate he turned into a shovelling machine, he didn't speak or look at her.

They sat on at the table.

'Where are you, Nick?'

He was miles away, he was thinking of some bint.

'Bastard!' she thought, and the next day, 'I'll split.' There was satisfaction in saying it over. It was words at first, but she could see that with time the words would turn into the thing. Except that it wouldn't happen, she hadn't the nerve.

She'd find Davey grizzling in different parts of the house. 'Shut your row!' She couldn't quiet him.

In room after room she walked round in tight circles. 'I'm off. I'm going.' The words rolled through her head, then Nick came home and she said nothing. She lay awake in the night: I'll never leave here. I'm coming to bits.

She banged his dinner on the table.

'I'm going, Nick.'

She'd said it. It was hardly different from saying it to herself, but Nick looked up gawping from his spuds. His mouth hung, his face was yellow.

'Come again.'

Her voice was a whisper. She was on a cliff-top.

'I'm clearing out.'

'What do you mean?'

'I mean I'm leaving. Are you sodding deaf?' It would be easier if she got angry.

'Sandy. Lover.'

'I'm not joking, Nick.'

'Let's sit down.' He meant her, he was sitting. She wanted support, her heart was slapping like an open-heart on the telly. She didn't sit.

'I can't take any more, Nick. It's how I feel about you. You've put the tin lid on me.'

She'd thought he'd shout and hit but he only stared.

'What'll you do?'

'I don't know.'

'Where'll you go?'

'London maybe.'

'Yeah, London, right.'

He looked at the wood of the table.

'Sandy, I know things have happened, but, I've tried to say sorry. I'm sorry, lover. I really am.'

'It's not just that, Nick.'

'No.'

His eyes were bloodshot.

'What is it?'

'I want to have my life.'

He shook his head.

He sat back.

'If you go out that door you don't come back.' He looked red as if his head was cooking.

He got up.

'You can't take Davey. Davey stays with me.'

She thought, Davey's the stick he'll beat me with.

'That's all right, is it? You're ready to leave your kiddy?'

'Davey doesn't like me, Nick.'

He bawled out hoarse at the top of his voice, 'Well you could sodding well be natural with him, couldn't you?'

He was big and red and shouting, she was frightened. 'I tried with Davey, Nick, I really did.' She stopped speaking, she wanted to cry.

He stopped shouting. He stood munching his lips in and out as though his mouth would eat itself.

'My mind's made up, Nick.'

'Go on then, go, get out you fucking cunt!'

'Right.' She'd go now, she wouldn't wait. But she was confused, the room swam. Bastard, she said to herself. She went upstairs. Her head boomed. She started packing but she was confused, she kept forgetting things. She felt about to faint. Bastard, bastard, she repeated to keep momentum.

She went downstairs with her bags. Nick was still standing, staring, struck comical. He followed her vaguely as she hurried round the house, snatching anything she found that was hers, tea-cups, a lavender-girl in china. She shovelled them all in a plastic bag.

'Right.' She stood by the door.

'There's Davey. Won't you say goodbye to Davey?'

She stared at him. She went to Davey's room and opened the door quickly. Davey gazed up at her, terrified.

She stared at him. His eyes nervously went to Nick's. She was frozen in the door.

She flung round, eyes smarting. She was out the door and up the road, small with her bags.

Nick ran after her.

'Sandy! Come back!'

She didn't stop. He got in front of her, and stood there blocking.

'Come back, Sandy. Give it another try.'

'It won't work, Nick, I know.'

'Please, Sandy.'

'Get out of my way, Nick.'

'Please.'

THIRTEEN

'Mum.'

'What, Sandy? Oh, hello love. How are you?'

'Mum, I'm at the bus station. I've left Nick.'

'You haven't. Oh Sandy. Oh dear. What will we do? Stay there, love, Dad'll come and get you.'

The little car pulled in between the buses.

'Good to see you, love.'

Away from home he wasn't shy, he hugged her in the middle of the bus station.

'You'll tell us at home.'

As they came up the path she saw her mother bob nervously in the lit-up window.

'Love.' Her mother hugged her.

They sat, she told. Talking made her more angry and wild, but they both sat looking as though they'd just heard she'd died.

'I'll never go back to Nick, not ever.'

Her mother said, 'These things happen in a marriage.'

'He only tried to knock out my eye.'

Her father said suddenly, 'I'll bust his face.' He was crimson, his eyebrows bristled like horns.

'There, Alan.'

He went quiet, he stayed red.

'What about little Davey?'

'He hates me.'

'Oh Sandy.'

'He hates me, Mum, he does. Don't ask me why. Ask Nick if you like.'

They hadn't more to say. What could be said?

They were all tired.

'Stay in your old room, love.' Her mother went with her to it. 'I've made it nice.'

'Where are all my things?'

'Oh I put them out. You didn't want all that stuff. And look, I got Dad to paint the walls. That's marigold.'

The empty room was yellow and cold, like stepping inside a yellow fridge.

'It's made a difference,' Sandy said.

The only sign of her living there was a little Santa from a Christmas cake stuck on the mantelpiece.

'Sleep tight, dear.'

'Good night, Mum.'

Spending the night there was more like sleeping outside a room than in it.

'Morning, love.'

Her dad had brought her tea in bed, her mother was making a big breakfast.

'Have a sausage, dear. Some tomato?'

They smiled to her but didn't speak. Last night she'd told them everything, but today it was as if she hadn't, and they didn't want her to.

'You rest, Sandy.'

Her mother could not rest, she started vacuuming as soon as she got up.

'I'll help you, Mum.'

'Thanks love, but why don't you help your dad? Do you hear, Alan? Let Sandy help. Why don't you try for the parador?'

Her father looked up from the kitchen table, where he was arranging a neat sheaf of papers.

'Do you do the competitions now, Dad?'

81

'Your mother's a busy woman, Sandy.'

She was. When she'd done the house, she went on the phone, it seemed there was no end to the calls she must make. There was some row in the world of competitions.

Her father smiled to her, he wanted them to make up slogans together. But bastard, she was thinking, you bloody sod, Nick. She couldn't sit.

'I'm off out.'

'All right, love.'

But it wasn't better out, the old town was dull. She was swearing at Nick wherever she walked.

'I'm not going to stay with you, Nick, no way. I'm shut in a box.'

She'd got to the high street without realizing. Her head was like a pot where bits of Nick, glimpses of Davey, things she'd said, things Nick did, all churned together. She looked round the shops and went home.

The phone was ringing. She panicked, it was Nick.

Her mum answered, and continued talking. It was another competitor.

Bastard, why doesn't he ring?

Each time the phone rang, the sound hit her like a hammer. Each time it was another competitor.

'What's up, Mum?' she asked at lunch.

'Oh Sandy, you don't know half.'

Someone had found out that all the competitions were being won now by employees of the firms who set them.

'That's expressly prohibited,' her father explained. Her mother wrote to the *Competitors' Journal* each month. He read out some of her letters.

Her mother smiled cheerfully. 'I haven't been so busy since I was in Complaints. Can you manage some more, love? I got braising steak specially.'

'I'm not ill, Mum.'

'No, love.' But they looked sidelong at her, and spoke quietly again so she felt like an invalid.

'What do you think you'll do, love?' her father asked. She thought he was wondering when she'd go, then she saw he was afraid.

'Let's not talk now,' her mother said.

'I'm going to London, I'll stay with Pearl.'

'Oh don't do that.'

'I'm not going back to Nick.'

'Don't say that, love.'

The next day her mother sat down beside her and talked hours about the competitors, then suddenly said, 'Sandy, why don't you go and talk to Nick?'

'No way, I never will.'

Her mother frowned, her chin looked big and white.

'I don't know, Sandy.' She shook her head and went away.

Things had changed since she left home. The house didn't use to be so clean. The only soft things left were the woolly cardigans her mother still wore. They'd be bright jazzy colours, and all soft and furry, a different bit of her mother from the rest of her. She wanted to stroke them and curl up in them like she used to, but she couldn't, her mother would never be still. She'd say 'Sandy' in a falling way, like a word going downhill, and there'd be a bit of love in it but she was unhappy as well.

Her mother came back.

'You should give it another try, really. Talk to him, love, try to make up.'

Sandy thought, you're not my mum. 'I'll see what I do.'

Her mother looked at her in an unhappy way, as if she were some animal that had come out the wrong shape.

Her mother tried to wind her watch.

Sandy could see her father in the garden not moving.

A floorboard by the radiator creaked.

'I'll get some tea, dear.'

Sandy got up to help. They made a cosy tea and lit a fire.

'We only want what's best for you, love.'

Sandy's face crumpled. Two tiny tears like pinheads came to the corners of her eyes, but that was it.

'I'll see what I do, Mum.'

Things didn't get better. She thought, why did I come? She'd thought she'd go straight to London, but somehow she came here instead. She wanted a bolt-hole. But these people couldn't help her, they weren't her real mum and dad.

The woman couldn't sit down, all her world was competitions. Who was she trying to beat?

The man was kind and he hated Nick. If they came together in the hall, he would put his arm round her and hug her as they walked to the kitchen and she wanted just to snuggle in that arm. But in the kitchen the arm came away, and there was only the arm, he didn't speak. His brows were bristly, his eyes were kind, sometimes he looked as if he wanted to love her and cry; but he couldn't help.

The weekend came, they went shopping together. Her father pushed the trolley but otherwise was helpless. Her mother discussed the prices loudly, she kept track of how they changed from one week to the next. Sandy dawdled, she couldn't think prices.

In the evening her parents dressed up for the Social Club.

'Won't you come, Sandy? It'll take you out of yourself.'

'I'm not in the mood.'

'Oh come on, love, it's the draw tonight. Look, I'll give you these tickets. You might win a hamper.'

'Leave it, Mum, please.'

'Oh Sandy. Sandy oh. I don't know.'

They went, she sat thinking, they're not my parents. She didn't look like them at all. Her nose was quite different, firm and curved. Her hair was different. She was like a bomb exploding in slow-motion, while they tried to be nice and live their lives. Her mother threw flowers out as soon as a petal dropped. The competitors were in uproar, all the prizes and holidays were going astray, all the wrong people were on Tenerife, it was higher than the Post Office Tower.

'I'll go mad here,' she said aloud to herself. Why did I come? I haven't a home.

At breakfast she looked at the man and woman.

'Have you seen the train timetable?'

They looked at each other. They looked big and they looked little. The room was cold. She felt she was a stone in a giant catapult, God had pulled it right back so the rubber stretched to breaking.

FOURTEEN

Nick started, hearing the bell. He hurried to the door, there was a large dark person behind the glass.

'Wup, Nick!'

'Barney! Great to see you, man. Come in.'

Barney took a big step, and was inside.

'You're in the money, then, Barney?'

'A coin or two, Nicholas.'

He wore a huge overcoat of dense green-black stuff. It fitted roomily round all his curves.

'Good, isn't it?' He showed it off.

Nick took him into the living-room.

'Fuzz been round, then, have they?' The room was a slum, Nick's shirts and clothes lay over the furniture.

'Right, mate, I'll clear up.' Nick gathered his shirts off the sofa. 'Have a seat.'

Barney seated himself kindly. He didn't take his coat off, evidently he liked it too much and preferred to sit with its wide skirts round him.

The fire of plastic coals was on. Barney made a performance of warming his hands. Round the fireplace orange shapes turned slowly.

'Barney, do you want a cuppa?'

'Cuppa what?'

'Tea, mate. I drink a lot of tea.'

'You on the wagon, man?'

'No way.'

Nick went into the kitchen, and rinsed two cups from

86

a heap of dirties. He put the kettle on. The house was silent.

Till Barney shouted through the door.

'Sandy not here?'

'She's gone.'

'What? Gone where?'

'She's gone, man.'

Barney came into the kitchen. 'That's tough.'

'Yeah, it don't feel right being in bed by yourself.' Nick flashed his sharp grin of teeth.

'She just went off, like that?'

'That's right, mate. She didn't give notice.'

From habit, Barney made goggle faces.

'Drink your tea, Barney.'

They went and sat. Barney sipped his tea, his lips forward, his brows raised, his eyes half closed, like a maiden aunt. Nick gulped the tea scalding.

'Where's Davey?'

'He's with my mum.'

'Well. Does that work?'

'Yeah, she thinks it's great.'

Barney sat back, sombre. He seemed to get smaller inside his big coat.

'Where's she gone, then?'

'Search me. She's disappeared.'

'She hasn't disappeared, Nick.'

'She's disappeared! Christ, Barney! Do you think I don't know if my wife's disappeared? I spoke to her parents. They said she wasn't with them, they weren't to tell me where she was.'

Barney pushed his legs out, then worked his face. Gleams of orange light wheeled across the walls.

Nick sat up. 'Here, do you know any birds, Barney? I want a bird. Let's go up Doug's, see what's doing.'

'Yeah.'

'Let's hit it, man!'

'Let's get there.'

They sat.

Nick sat forward, and made a cat's cradle with his hands. 'The thing is, Barney, I have to be careful. If Sandy heard I was doing anything, I don't know, maybe it would give her what she wants. She could get a divorce for all I know.'

'She doesn't want a divorce.'

'Oh yeah? Well, that's good news then.'

'She needs a break. Anyone married to you would need a break.'

'That so, Barney? Because the way I see it, she'd only be happy if she got a thousand miles away.'

'Yeah but Nick, she wouldn't leave her kid.'

'You don't know her, man. She's off.'

Barney rearranged himself and his coat.

'Anyway, you want her back, don't you?'

'Me? She could come back tomorrow, as far as I'm concerned.'

Nick's head drooped over his cup.

'Here, don't do that, old mate, you'll get salt in your tea.' Barney stood up. 'Nick, I'll tell you what. I'll buy you a drink.'

Nick sat straight, he'd recovered his sharp look. 'You said it, mate. I'll get my coat.'

Nick went to the bathroom. Barney investigated the clothes on the chair. He took a pair of Nick's underpants and put it on his head like a knitted hat. The legs made funny ears. He stood by the door, serious and preoccupied, waiting to go.

'Oh Christ, Barney! Are you going to the pub like that?'

'I like to be noticed.'

'What are you doing to me, man?'

They drove to the pub, where several old men, all like

Adam the Gardener, stared with aged eyes at Barney, collapsing this way and that on a pub stool.

Barney leaned back, all the pub eyes on him. 'Hey mate, do you remember that time we went up Vic's and he'd hocked his clothes and had nothing to wear but a pair of Y-fronts?'

'Yeah, right.' Nick grinned.

'He's with Olivetti now.'

They chatted and reminisced, but after two pints, Nick had had enough.

'I must get back, Barney. Got to get up early.'

'Right, man. One for the road, then.'

'No, mate.'

'A short.'

'I must get to bed.'

It was half-past nine.

Barney drove Nick home. At the door Nick called, 'It was great to see you, Barney.'

'Good luck, Nick. She'll be back, you see.'

'Yeah, of course she will.'

Barney drove off, at a loose end.

FIFTEEN

Sandy turned and returned, she had come and she had stopped. The vast glasshouse echoed, queues blocked her way, beyond them were more queues, arches, more space. Behind railings and gates the trains lay in green cylinders. They were iron snakes, they'd plough forward through platform and people.

All round her people streamed, or knew what they were waiting for. They banged dead telephones, and tried others angrily.

Outside was white sky and grey buildings. Taxis, buses, churning traffic. She stayed in the canopy, lost. Why be frightened? But it was like being born, going out in that space and crush.

She rang Pearl.

'Pearl? I'm here. How do I get to your place?'

She felt safer on the Underground. Over the heads she looked at the job ads, Ann Pettingells, Kellygirls, Alfred Marks.

She emerged from the station in a road of trees. There were tall houses in a row, with black windows.

'Sandy!' High above was Pearl's round face. 'I'll come down.'

Pearl burst from the doorway, big and friendly like a mum.

'Great to see you, Sandy. How ya doing? Come up.'

They climbed through the unpainted, uncarpeted house.

'Sit down, Sandy. A drink? Rum 'n' Coke?'

'Great.'

'You don't sound great.'

The room was plain and not dusted much, but had big cushions to lean on.

'Tell us then, what happened?'

'What? With Nick? Oh let me say later, Pearl. It didn't work out.'

'No?'

Pearl waited.

Sandy looked at her and looked down again. She sat huddled like a tortoise putting its head in.

Pearl lay on the floor smoking, and watching Sandy through the smoke. Sandy's shoulders made little jerks.

'Pearl.'

'Yeah?'

'Are you sure it's all right for me to stay?'

'Yeah, yeah, the room's there. I spoke to Art.'

Pearl smoked, Sandy didn't drink her drink.

Pearl put a record on and made them joints. Later, desultorily, Sandy talked. Pearl nodded or shrugged.

'Do you think you'll go back to him?'

'What, to Nick? I'll never go back to him.'

'What about Davey?'

Sandy picked at the rug. Finally she said, 'I don't like children, Pearl.'

Pearl nodded, they sprawled.

Later Pearl said, 'Let's go out. Coming?'

Sandy looked at her glazed. 'I can't get off the ground.'

When they came outside, Sandy blinked, dazzled. Faces, clothes, cars, everything flashed.

They turned into an endless street. In bright sun and shade, the market stalls curved away under the railway bridge and up out of sight.

Sandy woke up, they moved down the line. Pearl held frocks to her chin.

'Hey this one's lush. Hide me, Sandy.'

Pearl dodged between the racks of dresses.

'Oh. Oh. I don't know if I can make it, Sandy.'

Sandy said loudly, 'Come on, Pearl, you can make it.' It was what they used to say.

Out of her clothes Pearl did not look so fat, she had a big white lovely body. But still the dress was difficult, her belly and breasts pressed tight the thin material.

'No, I need a bigger.'

Sandy had found a dress, she held it up in the sun.

'Christ, Sandy, that's someone's bloody petticoat, dyed blue.'

'Well I like it.'

She changed, but in the mirror it didn't work. The dress was a crumple. She looked at her face. She didn't look like London, she didn't look like a woman, she looked like a kid ready to cry.

'Um,' said Pearl. 'That's good with your hair though, Sandy.'

'Sure?'

Jerkily Sandy smiled and slowly the petticoat-dress came right. She looked younger, like someone who hadn't been married.

'You've got to get it.'

'Yeah, but I'm skint.'

Pearl got it for her.

'You shouldn't, Pearl. It's lovely.'

They found a park, all sun. It was crowded but still they stretched on the grass. Together they watched the sky.

'Oh Pearl, I'm so glad I've got away. You don't know. I was in such a hole. I can't tell you, really.'

'Yeah. It's nice, London.'

'It's nice getting out. Do you know, Pearl, we never went out, not ever.'

'What a pig.'

'Yeah. Well, he tried to pull his socks up, at the end. It was too late.'

She got up on one elbow. 'It's funny really. Because at the start it was Nick who didn't like marriage, and in the end it's me.'

Pearl chewed on a grass.

'Do you reckon you'll find someone else?'

'I won't look. I'm not going to get married again.'

It was evening, shadows reached them from the far side of the park. They strolled, then took a tourist bus to see the lights.

A clock-face rose like the moon. Fountains played between lions, Nelson stood one-armed high in the sky.

Sandy stretched back on the open bus seat. 'Pearl, I can't believe I'm here. I'm all over the place.'

'Yeah, you need to settle.'

They went home, they were tired from the shopping and the sun.

Monday morning Sandy said, 'Well I'm off job-hunting.'

'Come in with me. I'll ask round mine.'

They went to the hairdresser's where Pearl worked. Everything was new and smart, the radiators and pipes were painted grass-green, there were big ferns growing up the wickerwork. The hairdressers wore clothes like martial arts pyjamas and had close-cut unisex hair. The girls had big features and spoke with accents. The boss himself spoke common but ever so gently, as he padded round in soft slippers, stooping to dry the hair of his clients with little puffs of his breath.

Pearl introduced her.

'Earl, this is Sandy.'

'Hello Sandy.'

Pearl showed her round, and showed her the styles they did.

'Do you see that woman?'

She pointed to a customer.

'She's only thirty-five, and she's got to the top in the Civil Service. They let her come here in office hours.'

They looked close, and saw that the attractive woman in maroon was working even now, she was talking non-stop into a small cassette while her hair was pulled with tweezers through tiny holes in a rubber cap.

'You know, Sandy, this is a real top place.'

Sandy gazed at the woman, and studied her in close-up when she went to pay. Her voice was husky but clear, and businesslike and confident like a man's. When she smiled, her nose sharpened. She walked away straight-backed.

Sandy nodded. 'That's the life.'

'Yeah well, it's not for us. What you reckoning on doing, Sandy?'

Sandy still gazed after the woman.

'I don't know. There was a sign in the Tube about careers for women.'

'Yeah? They don't mean you and me. It's a real problem. Just a mo!'

'What?'

'You could be a bunny.'

'What, a bloody bunny girl?'

'Yeah. Oh, I'm sure Earl could fix it.'

'I dare say he could.'

'Hey!' Pearl had a brainwave. 'Just the thing. You could be a girl croupier. Oh no really, it's not what you think. And they're really in demand, a girl croupier in the Playboy, oh no you'd be away then. I wonder if Earl could fix that.'

She went and asked him.

'Earl says it won't do. He says you have to speak educated, to be a girl croupier.'

'I speak all right.'

'Oh no, he says you have to speak educated. He says you could be a little bit of fluff that a fart would blow away, but if you spoke educated you were in. But isn't that funny, Sandy? Because here it's all classy and they want you to speak common, and the other place is a sleaze-pit and you have to speak toffee-nosed.'

Sandy shrugged.

'Yeah, it's difficult now, Sandy. If you'd come when I came, that was the time, you could have done anything. But now there's nothing. No really, there's nothing at all.'

'There'll be something.'

'Reckon? I know! Now we're there. You could be a travel girl.'

'What in a travel agent's?'

'Yeah.'

'Christ, Pearl! I didn't leave everything and come up here, just to be a travel girl.'

She left the hairdresser's, and spent the morning at agencies putting her name down. She wasn't what they wanted. There was nothing in the airline offices, nothing in the big stores, nothing in the City. She couldn't even get a job on a jewellery island.

'What about ITV?' No chance.

'Can't I even answer the phone? That's what I used to do.'

'We'll let you know.'

We'll let you know, we'll let you know. Her ship of hopes was sailing from her.

She sauntered down the pavement, there were no cards with vacancies in the shop-windows.

She sat in a little park to rest. The day had clouded, a

dustbin lid blew off. The houses were huge and closed like forts.

She saw an ad for a waitress in the window of a steakhouse. She shrugged and went in. The young manager studied her with his horny-lidded pop-eyes.

'I want you to say "Hi!" to me, like Americans say it.' He sat down and pretended to be a customer.

'Hi!' Sandy said.

'Not like that, for crying out loud.' He was a real cockney.

'Hi!'

'What?' He put his hand to his ear and leant her way.

'Hi!'

'I give up. And look how you stand! Americans don't stand like that. Your posture's awful, you look like someone's bloody grandma.'

'You rude sod.'

'Come again?'

'I said you rude sod.'

'Fair enough, I can't argue with that. Still.' He got up and stood looking at her, shaking his head. 'I don't think you're a steakhouse girl.'

'No I'm bleeding not.' She left.

She walked up big streets all afternoon.

The rush-hour came, everything swung at her. There were too many people, too many buses, London was nothing but enormous confusion – hairdresser's, boutiques, offices, shops, different bright bits going round in a cyclone.

She arrived home exhausted and wanting to cry.

'Sandy, hi! How'd it go? Got anything?'

'No way. God, Pearl, I don't know why I came. There's nothing for me here.' She sat down heavily on the bed. 'It was all a bloody dream, wasn't it? A jump in the dark. Crazy. I've made a big mistake.'

'Yeah, well, maybe. Still, don't forget, we're going to the jazz club.'

Pearl was already made up, she had a dead-white face and staring black eyes with lashes like paint-brushes.

'Come on, Sandy. You'll soon get with it.'

'I can't, Pearl, I feel so depressed. I feel everything I had has gone.'

'Yeah, well.'

Sandy took a bath, Pearl brought her a Nescaf. Afterwards she put on the petticoat dress.

'Oh you look great, Sandy. You've really got it.'

In the mirror she looked tired, but still the dress suited her.

'Course, you'll want a bloke.'

'That's all right. I'm off men.'

'I know what you mean. But look, I'll ring Alaric.'

Sandy made up, with big blue eyelids that went with the dress.

'Who are you going with, Pearl? Vic?'

'Oh not tonight, no, it's Ed tonight.'

'Ed? How many boyfriends have you got?'

'Yeah, well, you see that's me, I like to be taken out. I get low if I have to stay in.'

Ed came. He brought Alaric, who was large and fair and slow.

When Ed's car stuck in jams Sandy gazed through the window. There were crowds and lights, the people now were couples and groups. Everyone was going out.

They waded through the jazz club and sat at a table. An elderly negro was playing, people were quiet like a concert.

Sandy looked round in heaven. The people were smart and relaxed and cheerful. It took her time to attend to the music. It was deep, throaty, breathy, not like a record: it filled the club with a thick sad-happy mood.

The audience was applauding. She shouted, 'Isn't he great!'

Alaric said, 'Yep. He can say it with a sax.'

Pearl was being rude to Ed. It was her style and he liked it.

'Oh look, there's Sam!'

She got up and rocked between the tables calling, 'Sam!' in a loud voice.

'Who's Sam?' Ed said. No one knew. But Pearl stood talking to him and laughing loudly.

The two men watched her. Sandy watched them, Pearl had them on strings.

Pearl came back.

'Ed, get me a Bacardi.' She didn't say anything about Sam.

Ed went quiet, and didn't get the Bacardi.

Alaric put his arm round Sandy.

The club-owner came on, a grey-haired man. He introduced a blind man who played several instruments at once.

Alaric touched his cheek on Sandy's. After a moment she sat up alert, this wasn't what she wanted.

The blind man talked to the audience, and gave out whistles so they all joined in. Sandy looked round at everyone then piped loudly. She thought I'm free, I've got away.

She looked at Alaric, he had a broad face, quite strong, with little eyes. He was kindly and didn't press her. After a little she rested on his arm. Her tiredness came back. The arm was comfy as a bed, she could go to sleep there.

'Ed, give me a light!' Pearl was impatient. Presently she wanted to go and they went.

In the car Alaric held Sandy close, his fingers moved on her nervously. She thought, it's funny, I don't feel anything. The fingers stopped.

Ed stopped outside Pearl's.

'Will you give us a nightcap?'

'No, I'll give you a kiss,' said Pearl. It was a quick kiss, and she was out of the car. The men had to go.

'See you, Sandy,' Alaric called uncertainly.

'Bye.'

Their car drove away, she found she was relieved.

'You are awful, Pearl, leading them on. How can you do it to them?'

Pearl cocked her head and said nothing. She looked a sight in the street-lamps, her eye make-up was like a road-sign. She was pleased.

They went upstairs.

'Did you like Alaric?'

'He's nice but I don't know.'

'Yeah, you're right, he's not an executive. I mean, Nick was better looking than Alaric.'

'Nick! Why do you bring him in? Thanks a lot.'

'No, but it's true. He was good-looking, Nick.'

'Yeah, from a distance. From close up he was a bastard. God, Pearl, you just don't know how far away all that seems. You know, it's funny, it's like it was years ago. I wouldn't have believed it.'

'That's odd.'

'Yeah, it's all gone. Still I wish you hadn't mentioned him. God, but I'm tired. I'm turning in. Thanks for everything, Pearl.'

As she curled to sleep she tried remembering Nick, but she couldn't see him. He could be in America. She wondered about Davey, but he was like a dot. She tried to remember Alaric but he'd gone too. The jazz club had gone. It was weird, London, everything raced.

In the dream she was in the cottage, she and Nick were just married, they sat in front of the electric fire. The door banged open and Davey came in.

'Hello Mum, hello Dad,' he said loudly.

She fell awake in panic. Which house was she in, her mum's house, the cottage, Pearl's house? Davey. Nick. She wanted to howl, someone was leaving her for ever and ever. The bricks in the wall shivered as they separated.

She reached out and touched cold emulsion. Her bed and the room came solid, but the panic didn't go. She was between lives and falling, she had given up everything.

The morning sun poured on her bed, she woke blinking in its warmth. She murmured to herself, it's all right, I can live alone. It's what I want.

She found a job in an office, it was not much more than office-girl. But it was in the centre, half-way up a tower. It was a little firm with two bosses, one was Development and one was Finance. Finance took her on, he was like a handsome uncle, he looked out a minute room she could make her own.

'We'll see you on Monday.' His big boy-face smiled.

She sat in the open, on a bench outside a pub. London was still a dazzle and she was confused, as if she wasn't all here yet, parts of her were still *en route*. But she had a place. She raised her face to the London sun.

Opposite her a new boutique was opening. There were mannequins in the window like pretty robots, chrome all over, standing naked. Even the paving stones were being re-laid. A man with rubber knee-pads rested stones on a bed of sand-and-cement, then watered them like a gardener. With his rubber mallet and a chisel he split a brick exactly in half. She liked the busy way he went on, while round him people came and went. Voices chatted and called in the distance and music came from the shops. She could smell new leather from the new boutique. The pavement-layer stood up, his face was all curves like a lorry-load of jokes. He went to a hut of corrugated metal, and sat in its doorway having his sandwiches, watching what she was watching, the unstopping stream of happy people, all in bright colours. You never saw the same person twice.

SIXTEEN

On Saturdays Nick would take his mother and Davey out. If he could, he went in the truck, Davey loved it. As he came up the road, he'd see his mother near the window and Davey at the glass.

'Wotcher mate!'

Davey hurled headlong down the path. Nick snatched him and turned him upside-down.

'Hello mate,' he said to his mother.

'How are you, Nicholas? You're looking thin.'

'Yeah, I'm not sleeping well. How are you? Is he giving you a hard time? He's a rascal. He's a tearaway.' He made to chase Davey, who ran back laughing.

'He's all right. It's true, I'm not as young as I was.'

'Go on, look at you. You're a girl.'

'Cut it, Nicholas.'

They went in, where she sat comfortably describing Davey's pranks. As they talked about him, Davey squirmed in Nick's lap, and twisted in contortions and went almost inside out. He fixed his eyes on Nick, full of daring.

'But he's good as gold really,' she said at the end, she always needed to say both things. 'You're a good boy, Davey, aren't you?'

'Goo boy.' Davey twisted like a corkscrew on the floor. He got up and ran bang into Nick's knees.

'Clockit Picket!'

'Clockit Picket! Who's he when he's at home? The union boss.'

'Clockit Picket!' Davey shouted, giggling at the name.

Nick brought out the chocolate biscuits.

'Not in the house, Nicholas. It gets everywhere.'

They went out, his mother grumbling. 'You can have your lorry all chocolate if you like.'

As they got in she said sharply, 'Lorry driver! I never thought my son'd be a lorry driver.'

'What you want me to do?'

'Anything would be better than this, Nicholas.'

'I'll go down the bus depot if you like.'

She frowned, he wasn't serious.

'I know, I'll be a chauffeur. How'd you like that? I'll look like a bandsman, and go round in a Daimler. We could all go for rides in it.'

She smiled tightly, it was a lovely idea.

'Here, slow down, mate. You'll have us in the ditch.'

Davey, in Nick's lap, swung the steering wheel violently. His feet thrashed for the pedals. Nick sat him to one side.

The engine coughed, they started. Nick drove fast and smooth, swooping through roundabouts while Davey screamed and his mother made a pantomime of being shocked. She was happy, too, her face was young and pretty. They were like a funny family, sitting in a row in the buckled and dented cab.

They stopped at the park.

'Boats!' said Davey.

'Hang on, mate.'

Davey trotted to the paddling pool while Nick loped after. There was a noise like hornets, objects circled on the water.

'Boats!'

Davey stood on the edge, bending at the knees and

103

waving both hands, while the radio-controlled boats zig-zagged and swerved.

'Let me, let me,' the children next door cried, while the father worked the controls and the small destroyer turned a corner. All along the pool-side fathers or children pushed little levers.

'Oh please let me.'

'I want a go.'

'Wait, will you?' The man fiddled the knobs. 'Damn and blast! Go and get it, Henry.'

The boy waded through the pool to the disabled ship. Nick and Davey moved to other groups.

'That's a tug-boat. That's a submarine. Do you know what that is, Davey?'

'Ot.'

'It's a yacht.'

Their eyes on Davey, Nick and his mother sat on a bench.

'How is he?'

'He's a good boy mostly. Sometimes he's in the dumps.'

'Of course he is, poor kid. He misses his mum.'

'He misses her. But it's a funny thing, Nicholas. He never says her name, not Mummy or anything.'

'Well, he's a kid. And what about her? I've heard nothing from her. Have you?'

'No.'

'Davey, you stay there where I can see you.'

'She must miss him, Nick. She's a mother, can you imagine what she's feeling? To be without your child – you can't run away from your child.'

'I don't know.'

'You can't, Nicholas. A woman isn't like that.' Presently she asked, 'What is she doing?'

'Search me.'

Davey was bored with the radio-controlled boats. They moved to the iron horse, which Nick heaved back and forth, so the machine jerked noisily while Davey hung on chuckling.

At the slide, Davey climbed up the steps by himself. He gave a shout as he came down, and immediately hurried and climbed up again, as though all he wanted was to slide and climb up again non-stop for ever.

He tired of the slide and went on the climbing-frame. He was higher up than Nick. He'd chuckle and laugh, and do things Nick told him not to.

'Davey, don't go there. You'll come a cropper.'

But out Davey went along the thick bar, looking back as he climbed, full of roguery.

'Christ, Davey! Come back!'

He wouldn't, so now big Nick climbed the frame.

'Davey, stay there!'

Davey stopped. Looking back, he smiled, saucy-roguish. It was Sandy's look exactly.

'Oh sod!' It was the first time he had seen Sandy in Davey, he felt as if odd hands were wringing his stomach. Quite roughly he brought Davey down to earth.

'Let's have tea.'

He piled them in the lorry. They drove to a chippy and had a fish tea and ice-cream after. It was friendly and easy after the park, and odd with Nick's mum there instead of Sandy. It was like a good dream where things were mixed up.

'Davey, you'll never eat all that.'

'You've got room for another, aincher mate?'

'Nicholas, don't do that. You shouldn't do that to the child.'

'Go on, have yourself a ball, Davey. You're only young once.'

He took them home. Gradually Davey calmed, and

went to bed. Nick went up to him, but he was already asleep.

'Thanks for the out, Nicholas. That was good.'

'Thanks for looking after him. Christ knows what I'd do otherwise. He must be a trial.'

'He's a good boy, Nicholas.'

He gave her from his pay. They had a bottle of Guinness, then she was tired and he went.

'You're sure it's OK?'

'I love it. I've not felt so good since before your father died.'

It was a strain, none the less. Once when he spun the lorry round a bend, his mother was shaken. She was really hurt and frightened, and all a tremble and panting. She made nothing of it, but he said to himself, you're a bloody fool, Nick, she's not a young woman.

He went more carefully, and watched more. He could see she was strained, Davey was a handful. In the end she said, 'I don't know how long I can keep this up, Nicholas. I'm not as young as I was.'

He nodded. 'Don't worry, mate. We'll find something.'

'I know, Nicholas.'

But Nick didn't know. He couldn't have Davey through the working week. They'd come to an impasse.

In the end Nick's cousin Harry offered to take Davey. They couldn't have children, they had talked about adopting.

'We'd like to have him, Nick.'

Nick's eyes felt hot. He and Harry had never got on, Harry was always a play-safe character. He wore glasses with thick rims, and was fleshy and talked slowly. He worked in an insurance firm. His wife Grace was serious, with a pale, waxy face. Nick didn't see much of them, except he advised Harry when he wanted a new car. That was boring, Harry only wanted Volvos.

'That's good of you, mate. That's good of you both.' Step by step he was losing Davey.

'We'll make him welcome, he'll be ours.' Grace was wet-eyed.

'You're going to stay with Uncle Harry and Auntie Grace.'

Davey's face was blank but he saw Nick smiling so he smiled.

Davey passed into their care. Nick saw him at weekends.

A job came up with more long runs. He said goodbye to the tip-up trucks, but still spent most of his evenings at the cottage.

He came to, sitting in the armchair. Hours had passed and he hadn't moved. He couldn't think what he'd been thinking. Used clothes and crockery surrounded him.

He was walking between rooms, this evening he had been seven times round the house. He was looking for something but he had forgotten what.

He was restless in the night and went out in the garden. He wandered through the black, feeling his way. The house, the house, he wanted to get out of it and he didn't want to leave it.

He stood in Davey's room, there were toys still there. He picked up a model racer and revved its flywheel on the window-sill.

He was sitting in an armchair when he started to cry. The sobs came like fists that clenched in his throat then opened. He gasped and sobbed loudly. My marriage is over. My marriage is over.

He was in bed, it was too cold to sleep. He woke suddenly from a dream that Sandy was going.

He was in the armchair with his head raised. Silently

and again and again he was saying, Sandy come back.

He thought, I shouldn't go on living here. He thought, if I let the cottage go, it shows I don't expect her back.

I'll keep everything good. She'll be back.

She won't be back, I should get a bird. He couldn't be interested in other girls.

I'll move into town and get a bedsit. I'll do drives abroad and get some money.

He stayed in the cottage.

She didn't come back, she didn't ring or write, he had no idea where she was.

He let the cottage go, and moved into a bedsit in town. He lived the same life there, sitting in in the evenings, in the low-lit room. He got a portable telly and sat in front of it hours, coming to in the middle of different pro-grammes.

I must get out, shake it up.

Next time he went north, he visited Barney in Brum. He left his load in a lay-by and roared into town in the cab.

'We'll make a night of it. Christ, I need it.'

Together in the throbbing cab, which was all engine except for them, and light on its wheels with no load behind it, they drove to the Bullring. It was shut up and dead, a crater. They drank from pub to pub in a circle round it, and ended up at a club.

'Now see here,' said Barney in a loud voice as they came in, 'I want the best cunt money can buy.'

They sat down at a little pub table and looked round the velveteen room. Girls sat on the wall-seats in different get-ups, looking at them or away. Nick was eyeing a girl who from here looked a kid when Barney started clapping his hands over his head.

'The madam, if you please. I want to see the madam.'

Nick leaned over. 'Mate, mate. You'll spoil the pitch.'

A middle-aged woman had come to the table, but Barney clapped and shouted in the other direction, 'Where is the madam? I wish to see her.'

Nick gave him a sharp nudge, so he had to turn round. He did one of his double-take blinks and stares.

'Ah, madam, good evening. We're looking for the best two tarts in town. Nothing less will do.'

'Steady, squire,' Nick murmured.

The woman looked at him and moved away. Presently a girl with a wall of face but breasts like hills came over and sat by Barney.

She got up at once. 'Do you mind? Bloody fuck!' To Nick she said, 'Tell him to keep his hands in. Bloody fuck!'

'It's all right, darling, sit down. He's out of it.'

Nick sat her down and sat himself, and tried to focus his eyes on the girl with fair curls who from here looked fourteen. They'd drunk so much, he had to feel good. He couldn't think of Sandy. He lolled at ease. Across the room, two tall girls in leather stood talking to each other while a man at another table watched them. He was still as a waxwork, his black eyes didn't blink.

Barney's girl shot to her feet. 'Oh bleeding fuck!'

Nick called out, 'Don't mind him, love, it's just his way.' She'd already gone.

'Barney, I don't think we're going to score this way.'

But all Barney could do was sit with his head back, his eyes closed, his eyebrows high, vaguely kissing the air.

'What's with you, mate?'

Barney's head turned towards him like something falling over.

'I want my girl.'

'What, the laughing woman?'

Barney rolled a heavy eye.

'Right, Barney, where is she?'

'It's like you, man, we've split.'

'Old mate, you never said.'

'Yeah, you and I, Nick, we're in the same boat.'

They shook their heads. Barney's eyebrows looked as though they were leaving his head.

'You see, you're married. Sandy may come back to you. My laugher won't come back.'

'Sandy.'

Nick sat forward at the table. His face was sharp and down.

'You'd think she'd fucking write or something.'

'Easy, man.'

Nick looked round with large eyes, bloodshot. They'd been in a great mood, he'd got away from everything. Now he was dropping back in his hole.

The middle-aged woman was looking their way. Near her, the man watching the two tall girls had not moved. His elbows were on the table and his hands clasped up together; his mouth and nose pressed on his hands, as on a wall he was looking over. His eyes didn't look like eyes with whites, they looked like two currants thumbed into his head.

'A connoisseur,' said Barney.

The girl Nick had eyed came and sat beside him. She was well through her twenties but with a tiny face. She sat forward and stroked his wrist, leaning close.

'Hello there.'

'Hello darling.'

She shoved closer on the bench.

'What's a big handsome man like you doing in a place like this?'

'It's the luck of the draw, innit?'

'Come with me, then. I'll change your luck.'

'Yeah right.' He didn't move. He leaned over to Barney.

'Shall we cut it, man? I'm not in the mood.'

Another girl was coming to Barney.

'Hello sailor. Mind if I join you?'

'Be my guest.' Barney got up importantly and dusted the seat.

She sat beside him nestling close while his puffed face stared past her at the corner of the ceiling.

She stood up sharply. 'Bloody hell!' She strode across the room, exchanging looks with the madam.

Over at his table the watching man moved. He went and talked to the two leather girls, who seemed to know him. They stood tall over him smiling. He moved closer to one of them, who led the way upstairs.

As he left, Barney hollered, 'Er, madam, do you have such a thing as thongs?'

The man stopped and turned and looked at Barney: his eyes were like pellets. He turned back, and continued with his girl.

'Or tongs if that's easier,' Barney shouted. 'I'm not particular.'

The madam looked at Barney. Two serious men in black seemed to have grown out of her. One of them was the shape of a door. The two came over.

'Gents.'

They looked up.

'Hit the road, gents.'

Barney sat back screwing fat eyes at them, his arms stuck before him making fists on the table. Nick said, 'Old mate, let's move.' The men didn't wait, they'd already grabbed Barney.

'Leave him be.' Nick staggered up. He heaved the man heavily off Barney.

'Leave him bloody be!'

For answer, the man punched him in the face. He saw the fist growing, the big white knuckles in front of his eyes.

111

He swayed from the punch, and while he swayed they shoved him. Barney in the distance sang, 'Why were you born so beautiful, why were you born at all?'

They were in the passage to the street when Nick's head cleared. A ripple of heat ran through him. He wanted it, the fight. With all his weight he pushed his fist through the bouncer. The man's head jerked back like a head on a spring. The other came for him. Nick brought his knee up hard in his groin, and fisted his face as his head came down.

They were both on top of him, he didn't care. He lashed and kicked continuously, while he saw their occupied faces and felt blows land on him somewhere. Nothing hurt, he was glad punching.

He was turning in slow circles and slanting over.

The bouncers were stepping back indoors, giving each other match reports.

Barney's voice was coming closer.

'Nick!'

'How's that?'

'You OK?'

'Ace, mate.'

'You don't look it.'

Nick got up with difficulty, and climbed up his cab so he could see in the wing-mirror.

'Christ! The living dead.' His face was green in the street-lamp, the blood was black and everywhere. Maybe his ear was torn. He didn't hurt.

'Let's hit it.'

'Man?'

'Let's go for a spin, mate. We're on the town, aren't we?'

'Sure.' Barney hauled himself into the cab.

'Take her away, Nicholas.'

The huge lights came on like search-lights, Nick

112

crashed into gear and they started. High up in the cab, with the wide screen of window before them and the lit-up road sliding below, it felt like flying.

'Slow down, man.'

'No way.' Nick was demon-driving.

Nick took bends breakneck but held the cab steady. They were soon through the flyovers, devouring motorway in the dark outside town.

Barney mumbled, 'Show 'em, Cisco.' He had his hands up in front of him. He moved them like a steering wheel and made driving noises like Davey.

'Get with it, Barney.'

They wobbled but held the road. Car-lights going the other way flashed in their eyes.

Barney gasped, 'Man, I need air.'

Nick drove on to the shoulder and stopped. He felt only now what shape he was in.

They staggered out. Nick rolled in the earth on the verge of the road. When he tried to lie still the world sank and corkscrewed. It spun over, he was falling off it.

He vomited a bomb. Sick filled his head so he couldn't breathe. He coughed to cough the foul taste out.

When he came to and raised his head he saw Barney out on the central reservation, swaying as he tightroped down the crash-barrier. Every so often a car shot past, in the flash and zip Barney flared up and faded. He rocked crazily as he fumbled in his pockets. He struck a match, and held it at arm's length flickering and guttering, trying to illuminate the space he was in. A car slipped past, blowing it out, but he lit another and held up the shivering flicker.

Nick passed out. He lay in damp grass retching, slipping in and out of consciousness. Sometimes, when he looked up, Barney was sitting astride the crash-barrier, at other times he was in the middle of the road while cars burst past him. Still he had his match, in the middle of the black.

Nick's head cleared, he sat up. Across the road Barney was crawling down the gutter, shouting to his match-box to come back to him.

'Ahoy!' Nick called.

'Hello captain,' Barney shouted.

With care Nick levered himself vertical.

Barney called, 'I'm sinking.'

In staggers, runs, stops and starts, the odd car exploding by, Nick zigzagged till he landed on the reservation.

'Come on, Barney.'

'Hello Dad,' Barney said from the gutter.

For some time they rested talking on the crash-barrier. Distant lights grew suddenly big, cars roared and left them.

'Do you know something, Nick?'

'What's that, Barney?'

'I don't reckon we'll make it back. I mean, a man could starve here. Have you thought of it? Starved to death on a traffic island. There's a headline.'

The convoy of cars continued. Barney stared at them bemused, as though they were a wall. Each time a car left there was pitch dark all round them.

Nick's voice said, 'Barney.'

'Man?'

'You know Sandy, and that?'

'Yeah.'

'I finished it. I mean, she loved me, man, and I killed it.'

There was no sound from Barney.

'I've got nothing in my life.'

Barney didn't speak. Nick sat looking nowhere. Cars racketed past.

Nick got up.

'Let's move it.'

In a shamble, not like two people but like a bundle of any old arms and legs, they staggered in a zigzag across the tarmac, and collapsed against the side of the cab.

'Let's go.'

Eventually they did. At the next junction they came off the motorway.

'Where are we heading, man?'

'Don't worry, mate. We'll make it.'

'Right.'

They were coming on to smaller roads, that went up and down as well.

'It's closing in on me, Barney.'

Nick seemed not to have lost speed since he left the motorway. He only slowed when he came to a corner he didn't see, and impacted on a dry-stone wall: which, as they stopped, continued on, so that as they took breath they heard rocks and boulders rolling ahead of them down the steep slope. There was a clattering, lights below were coming on, they had sent an avalanche through a village. And then, as in the past, a dog barked, and more dogs, in a dog-avalanche spreading further.

'Mate,' said Nick, 'this is our scene.'

They drove on a little further and parked in a field. They fell out of the cab. Mumbling to each other, both on all fours, they crawled away to be sick again and passed out in deep grass.

In the distance the yapping dogs settled.

The sun rose in birdsong over the Welsh hills and found them spread-eagled on a steep flank of grass. The air was fresh and sweet but their heads were clubs of lead. The bright red lorry-cab tilted at a crazy angle on the steep sward. Mist was in the valleys, a swallow dipped close by them.

'Mother!' Barney mumbled.

'Hey, Barney, you know where we are?'

'Where's that?'

'The end of the road, man. We got there.' Nick rested his head down again in the tickling grass, the trickling dew.

SEVENTEEN

A warm voice crackled through the offices. 'Morning, Ros. Morning, Is. Morning, Sarah Ann.' It was the finance partner, he loved the sound of his voice in the morning.

'Could you come through, Sandy?'

'Yes, Mr Rowe.'

They went to his office. Outside the window the dome of St Paul's was blue and bright.

'Oh Sandy, sit there. It's more comfy.' He had her sit where he could see her.

'The sun's lovely in your hair.'

She dipped her head quickly.

He began dictating. The letter sounded like a letter to her.

'We should be grateful for an early reply.'

His large eyes looked at her, it was her reply he wanted. She met his look briefly.

'I'll read it through, Mr Rowe.'

She read out the letter, with a slight chirp of music like a business birdsong. Her old self was back, the excitement of life in the offices, the bosses. And he was handsome, the finance boss, though middle-aged. She watched him play his game, she watched herself join in.

He got up and went to the window. Looking through the plate glass, he breathed deeply.

'What a morning!' He slightly rose as he flexed his feet. 'It's too good a day. Sandy, what do you say to – lunch in Le Touquet?'

It was one of his lines they mocked in the office, forcing their voices down, 'Had lunch in Le Touquet yesterday, actually.' But it was star treatment.

'That would be nice.'

She was fluttered, she felt like two people at once: an excited fresh girl, and an older person looking over her own shoulder.

'Thank you very much.'

'Good thinking.'

He took his cap.

'We'd better start early. Ready? After you.'

She walked springily down the corridor, his tread behind her. An affair with the boss – was that her dream? Still she was happy, a kid dancing in its father's eyes.

It was funny in the lift, standing beside him as if they were a couple. She snuck glances at him. He was so close she could only see bits of him, his breast pocket, his chin that looked less plump raised up, his handsome nose. Oh yes, she thought, he'll want his reward.

Going out, they met the other partner coming in. He was the technical man, young, pale in glasses, he was a worrier.

Her boss didn't worry. 'Hello Ray – off to a meeting, need Sandy. Toodle pip.'

'Bye James.' He had a soft voice, Scottish, like a bit of peat crumbled in a pot. He watched them go.

They turned into the reserved bays, between the building's legs. He went to her side of his sports car, and opened the door for her like a gentleman for a lady. It was a different kind of car from Nick's, it had fat curved wings, and old leather seats that looked worn and friendly.

'Thank you kindly, Mr Rowe.' She pulled her legs in elegantly.

'Don't call me Mr Rowe.' He didn't say what he was to be called.

The engine was powerful. He drove smoothly and fast, they soared down an avenue. She sat back luxurious.

They were soon out of London, on the open road. They left it for roads that divided smaller, running into the orchards and switchback hills of Kent. She said to herself, this is something extra – and I dare say I'll get my reward.

They were in a lane with high hedges. He hopped out, opened a five-bar gate, and drove into a meadow. At the far end was a black hump of building, like a big Nissen hut going down in a swamp.

'We keep her there.' It sounded like a wife that he kept in Guildford. They wallowed spongily to the hangar and got out. The grass was still wet, and broke in fragrance as they trod it.

'Lovely morning – it's a beauty, isn't it?' He made the day sound like another sweet girl.

She remembered sunny days, alone in the cottage garden.

He looked round. 'Something on your mind?'

'Nothing bad.' She shook her head clear.

Grunting he heaved back the scraping doors. Inside in the dark she saw the plane, reared up on its front wheels like a dog sitting up, with a propeller in front like a sycamore leaf. She thought, I don't call this an executive jet. He was tinkering with it, she watched him fill the petrol tank with the help of a funnel.

'Give us a hand, there's a poppet.'

A poppet?

Together they pushed the plane out. She shoved vigorously, laughing: the effort was fun.

'OK. Hop in!'

But it was not so simple. There was a footstep in the side but after that she had to step across the wing.

'Not there, not there – over there, that's right.'

'Are you sure it's solid enough?'

'Pardon?'

'Will it hold us up?'

'Hold us up! Don't you worry. But you must step on the right spots.'

She fitted herself in the tiny cockpit. It was a snug trap. He was too big when he got in beside her, she was shut in a hole with a bear.

The controls looked like any car dashboard.

'O-kay. Contact!' He turned the ignition switch. There was a big iron gargling, black smoke poured from little vents. The propeller jerked its arms like a tick-tack man, then turned to a transparent disc.

They bounced across tussocks. The runway when they got there was a strip of mown grass down the middle of the field.

'Hang on to your hat!'

Slowly they gained speed. She thought, we're not going faster than a bus. The plane tipped up, they were going headlong upwards. Her stomach dropped away: this is me going up.

The plane came level. Carefully she looked out. The trees had turned to cauliflower sticks, the hillocks of Kent had rolled out flat. The engine made a noise but she couldn't see movement.

'I feel I could fall.'

'What? You're on top of the world.'

Soon she got used to it. They were flying east, ahead the haze was shining. A railway track caught the light, in sharp lines curving to the horizon.

He talked about the plane and the different things it did.

'Don't you know what stalling is?' His eyelids tightened, it sounded dangerous and exciting.

'Don't be scared now.'

She could see he was pleased. He steered the plane

upwards till she lay on her back, they were going straight up into space.

'Don't do that! We'll fall!'

They did, the plane lost hold and crashed. Her eyes and mouth gaped, she couldn't shriek.

As they fell, the front of the plane tipped down till it was diving. The propeller got purchase and he levelled them out. Her body and soul came back to each other.

'It's all right, you see. I say, you're all right, aren't you?'

Inside she still crashed, she heard the rushing of the passing air.

'Sandy?'

She gazed at him, ashen. She thought, he's just the same as Nick, Nick would play a trick like that. And he'd seemed such a different sort of man. What's with these men, they're big kids playing dangerous games.

He sat nearer and his hand clasped her hand. His breath was hot.

'Don't worry, Sandy. I wouldn't let any harm come to you.'

Will he try it in the plane? she thought – we'll fall out of the sky. Neatly she lifted her hand clear.

'What's that?' She pointed to a blue-grey shadow ahead.

'That's the Channel.' He sat back in his seat and began talking through a microphone to people on the ground.

He left her in peace as they flew over the sea. The waves were distinct and looked as though they were just underneath them, till she saw a tiny ship.

It was warm in the sunlit cockpit, she began to feel sleepy. The stall had left her with a funny feeling, as if they'd sidestepped out of life. They were in a little bubble high over the world, and there they hung motionless in the golden air. The bubble slightly shook, and made a noise, but they were still. She thought, it's lovely, this is

121

what I wanted. I've got away from everything. It was like a happy dying and going to heaven.

'Do you want to drive?'

She blinked awake. 'What do you mean?'

'It's dual control.'

There were two steering sticks in front of them, one for her and one for him. They were connected and moved in unison: the stick in front of her gently stirring and leaning like something disreputable. She touched it warily, and put her feet on the pedals.

'That's right, that's all you do.' He explained how it worked.

'Well, I've never done this before. Don't blame me if we go for a swim.'

Gingerly she held the stick and moved it slightly. Nothing happened, the plane continued just as it was.

'Come on, a bit more.'

She moved it in little jerks but still nothing changed.

'Pull it over.'

'All right, then.' Laughing she pulled the stick over, and pushed one of the pedals down with her foot. Abruptly the plane tilted on its side, turned sharp right, and careered towards the sea.

'Ai!' she screamed, but at once he pulled the plane steady.

'Are you all right?'

'I'm OK.' She wasn't frightened this time. She looked at him with spark, there was a secret between them made by the danger.

Through trial and error she continued. She got the hang.

'You're flying high, Sandy.'

He put his hand on hers to guide her movements: and the hand was helpful, this time she let it be.

They crossed the French coast. She was disappointed, it looked no different from England.

'Is that Le Touquet?'

122

He nodded. The little town looked like any resort. What had she expected – casinos, palms?

The runway grew into a giant white road. They bumped and were on it.

They climbed out and walked to the airport buildings.

'*Parlez-vous français?*' she enquired.

'*Un peu.*' He seemed as he walked to take more space, as if he felt bigger in France than in England.

'*Bonjour, messieurs!*' He waved travel documents to the officers, smiling. They nodded, and looked at her. She was wondering where in the town he would take her.

He said, 'The airport restaurant is very good at Le Touquet.' She thought, what, are we only going to the bloody airport restaurant?

The room was full of windows and light. She sat stooping shyly and looked round the big room: there's no one here but us, this place can't be much cop.

'Let me tell you what's good.' He looked elderly, studying the menu with his glasses on.

The waiter brought her a black egg in black sauce. For some moments she inspected it. She laughed.

'Whatever's this?'

'Try it.'

'I don't know if I should. I don't know where it's been.'

It tasted odd and fancy.

'Have some wine.'

'I don't mind if I do.' She took little sips, the wine was strange, like cloth that's nice to the touch.

As they ate his face grew bigger. He was like an old relative giving her a treat, she thought this man's too old for me. But she felt easy, she felt French herself, gay and insouciant.

He asked about her as he hadn't before.

'You're adopted, are you?'

'Yes, that's right. Found on the doorstep.'

'You don't remember anything from before?'

'Oh no, nothing. And my mum and dad haven't told me anything. And I don't want to know. It isn't anything to do with me now.'

He looked at her with an interested face.

'That's true I suppose. That's not all about it, though, is it?'

'I don't know. I don't know anything about my real dad. And my real mum? I know I don't care about her.'

'Perhaps you do really.'

'It's true my dad probably did worse than my mum. Probably he ditched her. And she ditched me.'

He nodded and smiled kindly. She felt unsteady.

'It's funny, I never talk about this. I don't think about it ever.'

Somehow he had made her weak. She brought them quickly back to London, she talked as if she'd lived there always.

He agreed and nodded but wouldn't stay in London.

'Where did you live before?'

'Oh, you don't want to know about that.'

'No, really, where are you from?'

'I don't want to think about it.'

'A mystery woman.'

She asked, 'What about your past?'

'My past? It's not good. To be honest, it's bad.'

'You mean girlfriends?'

He paused. Maybe he was counting, and lost count. He shook his head.

'I used to think I was looking for Miss Right. But I don't know that Miss Right is looking for me.' He looked up, laughed, and made a funny face. She laughed too, she liked him more.

She asked, 'Have you ever been married?'

'No. Have you?'

She stuck on the question.

'Are you separated?'

She nodded jerkily.

'You didn't get on?'

'He was murder.'

'Any kids?'

She thought, I'll say nothing. 'Yes, a little boy.' She thought, what a dead way to speak.

'Do you miss him?' His eyes were large and doggy, she saw he'd like to be a father.

'I don't think about it.'

He put his head on one side. 'You think of him sometimes, I bet.'

She met his eyes. 'No, I really don't. Almost never.'

He started to look like a schoolmaster. She thought, he thinks I'm hard as iron. So bloody what? I am. That's me. All her good mood disappeared, she felt sour as old vinegar years in a jug.

'He didn't like me, my little boy.'

'No?'

'Sometimes I thought he hated me.' She blinked quickly, then looked round hard-eyed.

He sat with his head down, making lines with his fork on the cloth. His face was flushed, his eyes were moist, she saw he was feeling sorry for her. She didn't want that. Sympathy poured from him like warmth from a too-hot fire. It was too much, it made her want to cry. If she started, she wouldn't stop. It wasn't for Davey, it was for her, she wanted to cry and curl up like a child.

He looked up and round and called the waiter, and talked about coffee.

'Cream?'

The moment had passed.

'Would you like a liqueur?' He was sleepy and gave a big yawn.

125

She was drowsy, she felt full and good. 'Thank you very much. It was a lovely dinner.'

Afterwards they left the airport. They sauntered down a leafy road, looking at big houses standing back among the trees.

'Ah!' he said several times, inhaling. He walked with his hands in his jacket pockets, thumbs out. It was a sporty way of walking that wasn't quite right, it made his paunch and bottom show.

'Sandy.'

His arm came round, she accepted it. They walked on between trees. He didn't pull her, he was kindly and tender. She nestled closer. His kindness turned hotter.

'Sandy.' He stopped. His chub face grew hard-edged and handsome.

'Hello James.'

They kissed and he was not like an elderly man. She liked him.

'Come with me.'

He led her into a spinney. It crossed her mind, he knows this spinney. She was excited and drowsy and confused. And this is high life, love in the bracken?

He stroked her hair and kissed her hair and moved his face around in her hair.

'Oh Sandy, I love your hair.'

He caressed her nicely but her excitement died. She had moments of panic but he didn't notice. Though her body lay there she wandered away. She hovered in the branches looking down at herself: look at those two, look what they're doing. Was this the big time? She had nowhere to go.

'We'd better be getting back.'

She fiddled her clothes on.

They crossed the runway in yellow sunlight, and got in the plane. She heard him in the distance, crackling the

126

radio. She felt funny, as if she'd been going round a big house, and she opened a door to the best room she thought, but after all it was the back door, that was it. She looked out on trod earth.

They flew back. There was an odd mist over the Channel. When they flew low, with the waves just under them, they could see the English cliffs quite clearly, but if they climbed they were blind in a weird white haze.

On the drive back to London he was kindly but said nothing. She was fidgety, she felt she rattled.

Outside Pearl's he stopped, and came round quickly to open her door. He snapped it shut as she got out.

He kissed her nicely.

'Bye,' he said.

He drove off quickly, she was relieved.

'Sandy! A black egg! I don't believe it!' Pearl shook her head. 'Oh Sandy, you're away.'

'Do you reckon? I don't know. Is that all I am, Pearl, a secretary getting screwed by the boss?'

At intervals she had sex with Mr Rowe. He took her for drives in his beetleback tourer. Once or twice she spent the night at his flat. It was chintzy and nice, with dimmer switches everywhere.

Each time as she left he'd say, 'Bye' quickly. But she got promoted.

'Sandy, that's great! You're really getting there.'

'Mm.'

'Christ, Sandy! You're never satisfied. You've got a good number there, don't knock it.'

But Sandy was restless. She brought home brochures for the Open University.

'God, Sandy, did you come up here just to do a correspondence course?'

'I don't know. I don't know what I'll do.'

EIGHTEEN

He'd lost wife and kid, he couldn't stand his room, he wanted to get away from wherever he was. He drove now and drove, on the road at all hours. Any overtime going he took. And in a way he was satisfied, spending all day eating tarmac. He drove on auto-pilot, watching traffic dead-eyed, his cab filled with music and his mind switched off. In the evening he was exhausted, he just pulled off the road and dossed in the cab: he slept on these trips as he never did at home.

But always he came back, after one day or two, back to his bad nights, grieving in the dark. He had to go further. He put in for a run to the bottom of Italy. He needed to get into a different world. He could stop off at Monza, see a race.

The night before he left he hardly slept, not because of Sandy, he was excited like a kid. He was up at the earliest and, while birds twittered, he looked his lorry over. Its aluminium sides glowed in the dawn-light.

He crossed to France and drove fast south. He hadn't been abroad before, but soon he felt at home. The scenery was like a travel brochure: châteaux and forests slid by in the distance. He took a detour to a vineyard to try the new wine, and stacked the back of the cab with bottles.

He picked up a girl hitching. She was fair with candid eyes. They hardly talked.

'*Voulez-vous un pique-nique*, love?'

He had a basket of French bread, cheese and wine, which he'd bought earlier at a Services.

They parked by the bank of a fat French river, like a Mississippi with willow trees. They ate and drank and lounged in the shade.

She slightly squirmed as she made herself comfortable. They were surrounded by the brushing fronds of willow. Her white hand was plump but with slender figures. Her frank eyes were soft too.

On the outskirts of a city he set her down.

'*Merci beaucoup*, darling.'

'*Au revoir, Monsieur Nick.*'

His mood, as he drove on, was full of sun. The world was big with lots of chances. The end with Sandy wasn't the end of his life.

Falling asleep, he thought of the girl happily. She was already vague, her open eyes grew faint.

The following day he came to the Alps. For hours he ground upwards. He crouched forward, his stomach knotting, the engine was going to seize solid.

On a side of mountain he stopped for a breather. Goat-bells clinked, there weren't any trees, the air was keen as broken glass. He sat on lichen, gazing into several valleys.

He came down cruising with his engine as a brake. His ears went funny, he was travelling in silence, swinging and swooping, curving and looping, coasting tight bends and hanging over cliffs like a bird on a draught. He had crossed a great wall: at last he flew clear.

In the late afternoon, when he paused at sea-level, the air was warm and sweet, he'd not known such air.

In Milan he met the fat tanker-driver who was behind him when he crashed.

'They let you back on the road then?' the man bawled out to him.

'Couldn't keep me off it, mate.' Nick went and sat with him. 'Hey, do you know the way to Monza?'

'What, the race-track?'

'Yeah, I was reckoning to take a day off and go there.'

The driver smiled. 'I know the way.'

'Do you want to come along?'

'Sure.'

Nick relaxed. 'What's that, then?' The driver had a beaker in front of him with a green-black liquid in it.

'That? That's the aperitif of the house.'

'It looks like formaldehyde.'

'Yeah, it tastes a bit that way and all.' The Italians looked round at his loud English laugh. 'Get one.'

'Yeah, OK.'

They went to the bar, where Nick lost count of the different ingredients. As he sipped it, it felt as though the sun, which had just gone down, was rising again.

They sat to two vast plates of spaghetti.

'You'll end up like me, mate,' the driver said, devouring.

'No way, man. I can eat a horse and it disappears.'

'Ah, I see a man with worries.'

Nick blinked, the aperitif of the house had weakened him. Out of nowhere all his marriage came back. He told his story. The driver only nodded. 'Yeah, that's how it is if you're on the road. It's sad about the kiddy. You're feeling smashed up, are you?'

'Reckon so.'

'Of course you are.' The driver sat back, giving space to his belly.

'I wish you hadn't said that. I came away to forget.'

The driver raised his brows.

When Nick got to his room, he wanted to weep. His hope of escaping from sadness dissolved. He had got away from nothing, he couldn't get away. All he could think of was good days in the cottage. They had come home from the hospital with Davey. Ever so gently the Lotus paused: even so Davey woke and started to cry. They carried him together into the house, patting him lightly, soothing him to sleep for the first time in his crib. They stood over him together, like the little plaster Holy Families he had seen for sale.

Outside Italians made a noise, it seemed they never slept. He lay stretched on the sheet, smoking. He couldn't weep, he couldn't curse Sandy, all he could do was lie awake in the dark. His grief was getting bigger not less: time didn't help as people said.

In the morning there was Monza, he had waited for this day. The fat driver joined him and they set out for the race-track.

When the car-park came in sight, the driver interrupted Nick.

'No mate, take this way.'

They cruised the perimeter of the track.

'What's going on?'

Bands of young Italians walked up and down the fence. *Carabinieri* in black jodhpurs stood by.

'I reckon they don't know if they're coming or going.'

'You'll see.'

One of the groups huddled quickly together, and began to disappear.

'Hit it, man!'

They sprinted from the lorry, and joined the others pressing through a gap in the fencing. Other men came running, *carabinieri* were blowing whistles. They were the last two through.

'*Grazie*, Jack,' '*Arrivederci*,' they said to the *carabiniero* who almost caught them. His flushed face, with tufts of moustache, with hot round eyes, stared through the hole after them. Then he stood up and the seat of his jodhpurs filled the gap as he stood guard, while the men still outside

131

resumed patrolling, looking for other weak points.

They were safe inside, bright grass sloped to the track. But the men they'd come in with headed elsewhere.

'Where they off?'

'Grandstand seat, look around you.'

Nick saw that on every building, on every small concrete block-house, people had climbed. Further off, huge hoardings looked over the track. Men clung to their bony framework, and stuck out on top like Punch and Judy.

They'd come in near the pits and pressed up close. Through the people they could see the cars, hard-coloured, dazzling, their new paint looking like wet paint. There were sudden revs of engine, mechanics ran shouting, everything was more alive than at Brands. One driver, all in silver, stood up in his cockpit, shouting and holding both arms forward to a bulldog-faced man who stood some paces back, with a white jacket round his shoulders.

The tanker-driver chuckled, 'I reckon he's the gaffer.'

A brunette half his age was attached to his arm. With her nose up like a bird she looked round bored.

'Nice piece, eh? Gor!' He nudged Nick hard – then shrugged like an Italian, disgusted. Nick ignored her, he was looking at an engine a mechanic was tuning. It was vast and hidden in paraphernalia, its ducts and wiring shone through hot oil.

The loudspeakers crackled, all the teams moved, engines spat and revved. The cars left the pits and crawled to the grid. The heat sweltered, the crowd pressed close, cars shimmered and trembled in the scorch.

The flag went down, engine noise deafened, the cars stirred then zipped out of sight.

'You have to laugh,' the driver said. 'You go to a race, and what you don't see is the race.'

They heard the engines far away, and the loudspeakers

132

shouting, frantic. Then their voices were drowned, the cars had returned. They closed up on the curve, jockeying and pressing to slip past quick. They were gone in seconds, but Nick still saw his glimpse of the two lead drivers, neck and neck. The inside driver, just ahead, sat rigid, braced to the turn. The one on the outside leaned forward, challenging. Nick was with him from now on, straining to pass the leader: he'd marked his car, it was rainbow coloured with different ads while the leader was white and red.

'It'll be a two-car race.'

Again they waited, just catching distant gear-changes. Nick looked round frustrated, and realized that the men up on the hoardings were able to see everything.

'Coming up?' he said.

The tanker-driver shook his head grinning. 'You're joking.'

Nick shinned up the wooden buttress at the back of the hoarding, and came out on top among the Italians. It felt much higher than it looked from below, but he could see everything: the grey track looped away between trees. Far off it was hazy but the car-colours flashed. Right in front it was blinding, his eyes hurt to look, but here the cars came again, like bullets down the straight. The red-and-white car was still in the lead, with the rainbow car on its tail, they manoeuvred as they slowed but still cornered breakneck, slewing round. After two laps more they started to lap other cars, they whistled through the stragglers like an express train.

The next lap, the red-and-white was still in front. The rainbow car swung behind it – but only to gather speed in the shelter of its wake. As they slowed for the bend it jumped alongside, and cut across in front and was away up the straight. The red-and-white was already far behind it.

'Viva! Bravo!' the Italians hollered.

'Ace, mate! Nice one!' Nick was shouting. The Italians nearby gave him the thumbs-up.

The car-colours blazed, his head began to ache: but the race went on, it would go on for hours. From all round the track came the screaming of engines. He had the best view of a race he'd ever had.

Right under him a car went into a spin, the next car swerved, missing it by millimetres, another car, braking, swung across the track. And the rest were on top of them, there'd be the worst pile-up: but the cars that had snagged were already away, the others streamed after. There had been a great gasp, the hoarding trembled, they had all held on tight. But at once the crisis vanished and left no trace. A breeze passed the hoarding, carrying the castor-oil smell of exhaust.

The afternoon sun had begun to descend. Nick's eyes were streaming, his skin was scorching, even up here it was so hot he could faint. The rainbow car was still ahead. The red-and-white was spent, and dropping back.

At the finish, the rainbow came first. The Italians cheered and waved, the hoarding drummed.

Nick and the driver walked out through the gate, in the thick of the huge slow satisfied crowd. Nick's face was burning, he shone from the sun and the race.

They climbed into the lorry.

As he started, Nick said, 'I wanted to do that, once.'

'What, racing?' the driver said, comfortable and sceptical.

'Yeah.' He sighed.

He took the lorry off at a lick. In his mind, still, he was on the track, challenging and swerving as the corner widened and opening up on the straight.

*   *   *

He lay down that night still hearing cars race, but woke in the early hours thinking, where's Sandy? How could he forget the nice things they had? If after a time he tired and forgot, this was only a rest till he hurt again. How long this would continue there was no knowing, as there was no way he could sweeten his grieving.

He drove on through Italy, but the cottage, now, was with him in the cab. He remembered Sandy saying one morning as he left, 'Don't be late, Nick. Come as soon as you can.' She said it with such sweetness, frowning, her mouth small, that it hurt him sharply that he had to drive off.

The motorway was endless, traffic thickened in an angry swarm. Famous cities slipped by in the distance. He made no move to turn off and see them.

He drove into increasing heat. The sun became blinding, the sky was harsh blue, the men driving tractors had big straw hats. When his cab became an oven, he stripped and drove on in his underwear and driving boots.

He left the motorway, and took long roads that became ever emptier.

'Where are they all?' He had started to have imaginary dialogues with Barney.

'They heard you were coming, man. They got off the road.'

'Right, mate. It shows respect.'

Isolated in the burning cab, he was glad to have the imaginary Barney for company.

'They'll put you in the bin, man,' the silent Barney said, 'if you talk to me when I'm bloody not here.' Then the cab was full of his goggling face, and his eyes rotating, and his finger wobbling to tap his head and missing.

'Good on yer, Barney,' Nick murmured aloud.

The lorry had problems. It was hard to start, there was a knocking in the engine he had never heard before.

135

Far in the south, in the middle of a dead-empty dead-straight road, he broke down.

He climbed out slowly, and looked all round with hurting eyes. It was the midday scorch, about him was nothing but brown earth and brown stones. The exhaustion of the long trip overwhelmed him.

He sat down and took breath. No other traffic passed. Every person in Italy must be having their siesta.

He set to work, touching the lorry carefully: its sides and bonnet were hot as an engine.

After an hour he had made no progress. He went underneath and as he worked there, on his back in the dust, he severed an oil-duct. A sump-full of black poured on him. It was hot and thick. He couldn't breathe, he choked oil and swallowed oil and spat oil. He couldn't see, he was oil-blind.

Slithering and swearing he clambered out, and wiped his eyes as best he could. He was tar from head to foot. He got a wrench from the tool-box and climbed down again, but there was no need, all the oil was on the road. Dust stuck to the oil on him.

He was angry and careless, as he crawled out he bashed his head on the running-board.

'Oh fuck and Christ!'

He hurled the wrench into the tool-box, and walked a quick circuit round the lorry, muttering, exclaiming, kicking his feet.

He paused and surveyed himself. His knuckles were bleeding where he'd barked the skin, his forearm had a gash he hadn't noticed. There was some cut over his eye so he blinked red on one side: he was like a smashed boxer. And all over him dripping, in rivulets like fibres, was the winding black oil mixed with sweat.

He rested his head hot on the lorry door. Slowly, from all sides, the different troubles of his life came together.

136

He was watching Sandy leave, and he was shouting at her and hitting her. He was chucking his job in the boss's face. He was cursing his father for leaving him helpless. His lorry was crashing, no way could he save it. He couldn't stop seeing Sandy's bruised face. His different fights were occurring again, with men and with women. Sandy, the bouncers, his dead dad were there. He shut his eyes and stretched his head back. His pipes of blood would burst like the oil-pipe.

He took hold of the wrench and ran at the lorry. Shouting he crashed the iron in its side. The shock shot up the steel haft, he staggered yelping, his hands felt smashed.

It was himself he wanted to smash. He punched his head with his hands, and reeled and sat down in the dirt. He punched his head again, and sat looking at his hands, they were black-red lumps of oil and meat. Small tatters of skin waved to him.

He crouched before his lorry in the sun, almost naked and black with oil, bleeding and weeping.

High overhead was a round tiny cloud. He blinked at it through the black-red haze. The sky stayed hard. At the road's end a mirage shimmered.

He got to his feet. To himself he said, 'Great, man. Great.'

A passing *carabiniero* sent a breakdown lorry to him. Finally, in the foot of Italy, he reached the depot and unloaded.

At the entry to the main road he stopped. Hurry home to England? There was nothing for him there. He felt light-headed and free.

He turned back and continued down the coast. The stony hills knelt in brown light. When twilight came he pulled off the road, he could sleep in the open down here.

The evening seemed peaceful, till he realized he was

hearing a clatter of bells. A shepherd was bringing his flock up the road. Near him the sheep turned off the tarmac, and slanted across the hillside. The flock was enormous, it seemed to well up for ever, spreading over the ground like a flowing white field. The bells made a racket. The shepherd was an aged man, lean and bent, wiry and dry. A black and white dog barked at his calls.

On the hilltop an old woman with thick legs waited for him. She was squat and stout: in silhouette she looked colossal.

They all disappeared, he still heard the bells. That's the life, he thought, I should stay here. Melt into the landscape, get away from everything. I'll do it too, they can fly someone out to take back the lorry.

He was well tired and fell asleep easily, lying on a rug from the cab.

He woke in the early hours, and got up and stretched. The air was keen, the sea was appearing in whiteness. For a moment he was surprised to see it so close, at the foot of the low dirt cliff. It lay quite still, stretching away till it blurred in the dim. He could see no horizon. Just below him the water was clear as a stream.

He climbed down, stripped, and walked straight in. He shivered in the chill: but it was not like an English chill. He plunged, and swam steadily out to sea. He took breath and swam a time under water. This was his wash. All kinds of dirt and strain and grief could slip from him into the sea.

He paused, and flapped his limbs in the coolness. His cuts stung. He swam on slowly. He was far from shore, if a cramp came he'd drown: so what, it was an end.

As he swam, he saw something he saw once in his life. The vague light ahead of him brightened. Far off, an edge, a horizon appeared. A red eye blinked, then a bronze wheel

138

rose: he could see it move, till it hung complete at the bottom of the sky and steadily brightened to blinding. When he turned to face the opposite way, every stone of the coastline stood clear in pink light. His lorry, tiny, shone like a big slab of silver.

The sun had emerged like a person being born. The world was new, but he wasn't new. But he felt as if somewhere a door for him opened.

The closer he got to England, the more he had to see Davey. How could I go so far away? He even, on the motorways, wondered if there would be a message from Sandy.

'Can we try again, Nick?'

'Well, I need to think about it.'

Maybe she'd written, asking for money. Maybe she said she just had to be with him. He began to be sure the message was there, waiting at his bedsit, or round at his mother's.

There was no message. He went to see Davey.

'Hello Nick.' Old Harry was solemn, as if he'd come on the wrong day.

'Hey up, mate.'

Grace came down the hall. She looked tired but pleasant, not like the old Grace. 'You're brown, Nick! Doesn't he look good, Harry?'

He could see it in their hall mirror. He was sunburnt, lean, he looked like a cowboy in a film.

'Where you got Davey?' He was as impatient to see him, as if Davey was his lover.

'He's in the back room.' They opened the door. Davey was wading in paint-splashed paper.

'David, guess who's here.'

He came across in a waddling run.

'Driver!'

'Wotcher cock!'

He hit Nick's legs so hard, Nick almost fell.

'Steady on, captain! Whoa!'

Davey was attacking him, his short arms flailed. He grabbed both of Nick's legs, and tried to push him over. Nick stared down at the energy threshing him, Davey was as glad as he was to see him.

'Hold it, mate, you'll have me on the ground.'

He stooped down and tickled Davey till he wriggled.

'There we go! Who's a scoundrel?'

Davey lay on the floor, looking at Nick with challenging eyes.

'Driver!' he said again.

'What's all this driver stuff?'

'Oh, that's what he calls you, Nick,' Grace explained. 'He calls me Mum and Harry Dad, and he calls you Driver.'

Seeing Nick's face, she said, 'It's not that we taught him to, he just fell into it.'

'By accident, like?'

'Driver!' Davey shouted, flat on his back on the floor.

'I'll driver you.' Nick snatched Davey angrily and held him at arm's length. Davey, dangling, looked shocked. Nick brought him close, and sat down with Davey in his lap.

They both went quiet. They were tired as if they'd worked hard together, Davey sank against Nick with all his spring gone.

'That's OK, captain.' He enjoyed feeling the weight of Davey and the warmth, while the minutes passed and Davey still rested, with a funny glum face and empty eyes, as if he were slowly refuelling. Nick settled steadily deeper in peacefulness. It was best to be home, he didn't need travel. He felt as much like a mother as a father, he wouldn't be able to let Davey go.

'He's sticking to you,' Harry said.

'Yeah, it's like a battery-charger.'

They didn't laugh.

At last Davey stirred and was ready to move.

Nick gave out his presents. He had an embroidered blouse for Grace and some thick slippers for Harry.

'Oh that's lovely,' said Grace.

'Thanks a bunch,' said Harry.

For Davey Nick had a special present. Together they opened it.

Grace said, 'Oh Davey, what a present!'

It was a robot that walked on its own. It had lights that flashed and made a space-noise, a laser-gun fired from its stomach. Nick knelt down setting it going.

'Let me, let me!'

Nick showed him the switches and where the batteries went. Davey sat as if hypnotized by the sound of Nick's voice. He explained again.

He stood up. 'Sandy been in touch?'

'What, Sandy? No, not a word.'

'No. Right.'

Grace said slowly, 'I don't understand it, Nick. You'd think she'd want to know how David is. I don't see how a mother can just – forget her child. I don't see how it's human to do that –'

'Sandy's not a good mother,' Harry said slowly.

Nick grunted and scowled, he didn't want it from them. They were talking as if Davey were theirs. He glanced at Davey, who had his back to them. His head was raised, he was completely still.

'It's great the way you've looked after him.' He thanked them at length, to keep his claim on Davey.

Davey released the robot, which walked about the room. It rattled its noise and fired its laser, and walked into chair-legs and their legs. Davey chuckled, repeating, 'Driver!'

'Switch it off, David,' Grace said suddenly, 'it's getting on my nerves.'

Nick fixed to take Davey out the next day.

'I'll come at ten.'

They nodded, and continued to look at the clock. They stopped talking. Davey started saying, 'Mummy, I want tea.'

'Later, David. Do be good!'

'Time I went.' Nick stood.

They trooped to the door in a little procession.

'Goodbye, Driver!'

'Cheers, mate.'

He wanted to snatch Davey and run.

He sat in his bedsit, thinking, they've got my kid. His trip abroad seemed years away.

Later, for hours, he thought about Sandy. Even now, she hadn't written, she hadn't rung, she'd done nothing for her kiddy. Grace was right, she was bad, it wasn't human to be like that.

He thought of her all night, he couldn't get off it. At moments he'd recover the clear mood he had, swimming in the sea as the sun came up. Then he'd think: Sandy! – He'd hurt her if he could. How could he get to her?

NINETEEN

Sandy shook awake in the middle of the night. They were battering the door, they were breaking in.

'Pearl!' someone hollered at the top of his voice. It was Pearl's door they were hitting, not hers. Pearl didn't answer.

'Pearl!' the man shouted. He was nearly crying.

'Go away,' she heard Pearl call.

'Pearl, let me in!'

He stopped, waiting. Sandy waited, she could hear him panting and shuffling in the passage. It was one of Pearl's boyfriends, she couldn't tell which one.

Bang! He was kicking the door. He'd break it down. It could be her door, the noise was so loud.

'Pearl!'

'Go away! I'll scream out the window. I'll call the police. Bugger off!'

He stopped, presently he tramped up the landing. There was silence. He stormed back and banged again. 'Pearl, let me in!'

'Leave off for Christ's sake!'

'Pearl!'

She didn't answer.

He left. He banged downstairs and slammed the street door.

Sandy huddled. Should she go to Pearl? But Pearl was all right. Probably she was with someone, that was why she didn't open the door.

143

Inside her head the banging continued. It was at her door, it was Nick breaking in. It was her father, her real dad, she didn't know what he looked like. She lay in bed shaking. She was made of ice, the ice was breaking up.

It was cold at night. She lay not sleeping. Something very sad was knocking at her door, it wouldn't stop till her house fell down.

'Who was it, Pearl?' she asked in the morning.

'Didn't you know? That was Sean.'

'Who's Sean?'

'You don't know them all, Sandy.'

'I don't know half.'

'But he's really bugging me, Sean. He's at it at all hours. He rings me at work and all.'

'You know, it scared me, Pearl. I thought it was Nick.'

'Next time it may be Nick.'

'I hope not.'

'Don't you want to see him?'

'I never want to see him. I thought he was a million miles away. I felt good like that, now I'm all shook up.'

Pearl smoked.

'Don't you want to see Davey, though?'

'I don't want to know, Pearl.'

'Christ, you do take the bloody cake, Sandy.'

'What you mean?'

'Well, Christ, never mind, I mean.' Pearl returned to her thoughts.

Sandy sat nodding her head. 'It sounds bad, I know. You think I'm weird, not wanting to see Davey.'

'No way. Forget it. That's your business, Sandy.'

They were quiet.

Pearl sat up, 'Hey, you know what? I've only just thought. But isn't that funny? You've done what your mum did. I never saw that before.'

144

'What do you mean? Do you mean my real mum? I never knew her.'

'No, that's what I mean. She left you when you were a kid. Now you've done the same thing to your kid. Isn't that funny? I never put the two things together before.'

Sandy was staring.

'No, but isn't it strange? It just shows. It must be genetic.'

'I never thought of it, Pearl.'

'Go on, you must have done.'

'No really. I never did.'

Pearl shook her head. 'Yeah, it's in your stars, I reckon.'

Sandy sat glum, then went to her room. She felt hopeless. She was stuck in a groove and she'd never known it, it was like Fate. She couldn't change, she couldn't like kids, she couldn't love men, she couldn't be married. That was it. That was her. She wasn't ice, she was a stone.

She tried to think about her real mother, but nothing came. She knew nothing of her, she felt nothing for her.

'I feel dead,' she said to the room. She'd made it a nest, with coloured scarves knotted to the radiator pipes. The colours were dead.

'Well, but I'm here,' she said next morning.

But London had changed as if the sun had gone in. It all continued, busy and bright, but set at a distance. She remembered her dream of the big spinning top. London was like that, everything spun, the restaurant on the Post Office Tower went round. The rich went round on a casino wheel, the smart set fell round, half out of cars, the traffic went round in a big dragging wheel.

There was a racket in front of her, and a blur of windows, yellow, crowded, stopping. The doors breathed open and ticked as the sardines hurried inside. She stayed where she was, watching the train accelerate inches from her face. Eventually the same train would come round again, she was on the Circle Line.

In the evening they sat in the flat.

'Let's get out, Pearl. I've got to keep moving.'

But Pearl was depressed about Sean. They sat like cadavers, getting half-way down a bottle of brandy saying hm and ah and yeah to themselves.

The weekend came, but Sandy felt nervous as if the man went on banging. She looked at prospectuses she'd got for courses, and shovelled them aside and went out for air. Outside she felt exposed, as if she were walking on a wall and the bricks were loose and wobbled. She looked at the Serpentine and the people walking. The big park was pretty but it shook like a migraine. She felt so like nothing, she could blow away.

Pearl stopped on the landing. It was early evening.

'Sandy?'

She knew Sandy was in but she heard no sound, no music, nothing. No light showed under the door.

'Are you all right, Sandy?'

There was no answer. Pearl shrugged and moved off, then came back to the door. She listened.

She tried the handle, it opened.

'Sandy.'

The room was empty. She went in. In the dim she saw Sandy. She was lying on the floor with her head jammed into the corner of the room.

'Christ! What you doing down there?'

She went close. Sandy looked up at her with dull eyes, stupid.

'Are you stoned?'

Sandy slowly shook her head. She said something quietly.

'Come again? Are you feeling bad?'

'Pearl, I'm on the bottom.'

'Yeah, love, I can see that.' Pearl stood over her like a giant, looking down. 'Move over.'

She got down, and lay at an angle to Sandy, so her head also pointed into the corner.

'God, the room looks big from down here.'

They lay looking up at the grey square of ceiling. Very slowly the room darkened.

Sandy looked at Pearl and sighed palely. 'It's all right, Pearl. I'm not going to cut my throat.'

'Christ, Sandy.'

Colour had gone, the room was deep grey, Sandy's clothes hanging up looked black. Sandy's posters had gone black and white and serious. The mirror caught a window and was bright.

Pearl slowly shook her head. She had nothing to offer, she had fallen in Sandy's hole.

Above the radiator Sandy had hung a Stones poster, and in the draught of warm air it slightly flapped. Pearl watched it stir and fall. She heard the soft push of water through the pipes.

Sandy was saying, 'I'm happy in a way. I could slip through the floor, and go.'

The room was black but the ceiling was bright. It was a hot grey, brownish, from the street lamps outside.

Sandy moved her hand till she touched Pearl's. She took Pearl's hand and held it. Pearl shut her eyes tight. They lay still.

Slowly the crisis came on, like a season. All day at the office she was on the edge of tears. At night she woke in terror, someone was leaving her, they were going for ever.

She made people shy, the boss held away from her. If they met in a corridor, he wouldn't see her till the last moment.

'Sandy.' He'd nodded and gone, walking faster.

147

'Bastard!' She hadn't thought of him for days, now she wanted to cry. 'He's ditching me. He wants to get clear.' At her desk she closed her eyes, I don't care about him, he's nothing to me.

He'd been nowhere, now he filled her thought all night. I have to get clear of him, we're not going anywhere, and, he's ditching me, he's steering clear.

Her eyes were sore in the morning, she made up specially. She fluffed her hair till it looked like copper feathers.

'Hello you!'

He looked up, caught: and saw she was cheerful. He smiled, his eyes shone, he was excited at once. She thought, men – it's like pressing a switch.

He stood up looking shrewd. His big face was handsome and strong. She went close, she wanted him to hug her to nothing.

They went to a locked room. He stroked her and gave her little kisses. She held his head hard on to her mouth. He pulled away and went back to his little kisses, but he caressed her strongly as he held her.

Their legs naked, top halves dressed, they made love on the hard-tufted carpet. She clung hard to him as he came to her.

As soon as they'd done, she wanted to dress and go. She'd finished with him entirely. That was nice, here's a penny to take yourself off. He hauled his trousers round his middle as if he were shaking up veg in a bag.

'See you!' he said breathlessly. His new-tied tie held him tight by the neck, his head bulged out as if it had grown too big.

She didn't nod. She felt nothing at all except that she felt free.

For a day and more she was calm. She'd finished with the boss, he was just a fat island behind her. She'd stopped being depressed, she'd found somewhere still, a quiet cove. She didn't want anyone, she was all right by herself.

It was evening and confused. She felt like an empty bottle, falling at the pavement. It grazed stone, in the splinter of a second it would be in pieces.

'There, Sandy, there.'

Crying, she was howling. The tear-storm had caught her, she was crying so she couldn't stop. When she paused exhausted it was only like elevenses, then the crying poured again.

'I'm sorry, Pearl. I'm a bloody monsoon.'

'It's OK, love. Go with it. Let it come.'

'I feel I've got a reservoir inside my head.'

'Yeah. If you marry again, it'd better be a plumber.'

'Pearl!' She gave big gasps, that were sobs and laughs at once. 'Marry a bloody plumber!'

She cried again. Pearl stayed with her while her crying became frightening. She hurled herself through each sob as if her chest, her stomach, would turn inside out.

Finally the crying became a snuffling. Sandy wiped her swollen eyes.

'I don't know why it happened today, Pearl. Nothing's happened today.'

'I know what it is.'

'Yeah?'

'It's delayed shock. We should have expected it.'

'Reckon? I don't know. I feel like a bloody kid.'

'You are like a kid, Sandy.'

Sandy stared. Finally she said, 'It's true. I am. I don't want to be anything else. I don't want to be a mum.' She clutched Pearl's big arms and buried her face in Pearl's big breasts, while she burst out crying again. 'I want someone to look after me.'

'OK, love. There, there.'

Sandy cried steadily holding Pearl. Finally she raised her

head. She frowned as if she were making out something in the distance.

'You know, Pearl, I seen something.'

'Yeah? What's that?'

'It's my mum and dad I want really.'

'You didn't get much joy off them.'

'No, not them. I mean my real mum and dad.'

'It's a bit late in the day for that, isn't it?'

'No, I could look them up.'

'What do you mean, look them up?'

'I could go to Somerset House.'

Pearl gazed at her.

'Could you? Yeah well, why not? Yeah. Why not? 'sgood idea.'

'I'll go in the morning.'

'Sure, you do that.'

Pearl put her to bed. Like a mum, she tucked her up. With her plump hand she moved Sandy's hair clear of her face. Sandy smiled to her, snivelling, her face had gone like a baby's.

'You are nice, Pearl.'

'Get some sleep, love.'

She slept solid. In the morning she felt brighter than she had for weeks.

'Are you going, then?'

'What's that?'

'To Somerset House.'

'Oh. That's right. Yes I'm going.'

The sun came in the room, the plan felt different.

Pearl was saying, 'It's a good idea, I was thinking last night. It might be what you're looking for.'

'Yeah, I suppose.'

But on the Tube she was in two minds. She began to be frightened. The train was taking her somewhere she didn't want to go.

She came up to street level and walked the pavement nervously. Were people watching her? Her mother was lying in wait round a corner, a woman with no face, just blank skin.

She looked at the outside of Somerset House: the windows were blocked with shelves. A stout statue stood in the courtyard. Instead of going in she wandered to the middle of Waterloo Bridge. The white balustrade stretched far to either side, the river reflected the sky. Behind white buildings she could see St Paul's. She thought, what am I looking for? There's no one there waiting for me. Suppose I found some woman and she said she was my mum. So bloody what? She wasn't there when I wanted her. Really it's like as if I came out of nothing.

She looked round at the big sky, the big river. She was in the middle of the city and she was in the middle of space. Other people crossed the bridge but the pavement was wide. What have I come out of? The question was like a big wall painted white: it went up like a cliff, it was white like snow. That was it, it was blank. You can't fill the blank in now.

She looked round at London, clear in the sun. She'd seen something clearly, but nothing was different. She didn't feel desperate, she didn't feel sad. She'd faced a big hole, she could leave it. She walked from the bridge.

At home she tried to explain.

'But don't you see, Pearl, there isn't any point. Say I found some people, what do I say to them – hello Mum, hello Dad? That wouldn't mean anything, they'd still be strangers. I couldn't like them really.'

'Well, I don't know, Sandy. It might have helped you get it together.'

'I don't see it, Pearl. If I haven't got anyone, I haven't.'

'Gosh, Sandy, that is sad.'

'Is it? I don't feel sad. At least I don't any more.'

151

'Of course, you've got Davey.'

'What?'

'It isn't true you've got no one because you've got Davey. He came out of you.'

Sandy said quickly, 'Davey doesn't like me.'

'Well, if you say so, girl.'

Sandy sat. She looked to one side then looked to the other.

Pearl said, 'I mean, Davey, he came out of your inside. If you should go back to anyone, it's Davey, not your mum.'

Sandy looked up. All at once her throat hurt.

'I suppose I could ring and see how he is.'

'Why don't you? You could have done that months ago.'

Presently Sandy said, 'But I don't know, Pearl. Nothing's changed really, has it?'

'Ring anyway.'

Sandy nodded numbly. Her face said nothing would come of it. She thought, I'm in no state to think of Davey now.

She didn't ring, and Pearl let the subject be. She tried sometimes to think of Nick and Davey, but they were faint as old photos.

One evening she thought dully, I suppose I'd better ring. Pearl was out, she went to Pearl's room.

But who could she ring? Nick's mum? Barney?

She looked at the phone. It was like a black crab crouched on the table. Was it listening for her moves?

Christ, what am I afraid of, I'd better get it over with.

While she dithered, the phone rang. Oh I must answer that. The bell was hysterical. She knew it was Nick, it couldn't be Nick. It was like Sean banging, it was a man breaking in.

The bell drilled her nerves, she unravelled in the noise.

152

She was alone with a goblin, it had a black shell. She crouched in Pearl's chair.

It had stopped, the ringing was in her head. She panted slowly, loosening her limbs.

She looked round the flat, nothing had changed. She thought, I was a telephonist, whatever's wrong? I answered phones all day.

She thought of Davey crying. What if he's ill, and they're ringing to tell me? Be all right, Davey.

She picked up the phone, the line hummed to her.

It isn't Davey, they wouldn't ring here. I'm all over the shop.

The hum broke to a high note, she put the phone down. But she had to ring. She dialled Nick's mother.

She looked at the receiver, out of its mouth came the little thread of sound. It was nothing but the dialling tone, going on for ever. She rested it down.

The other number she had was Barney's, probably it was out of date. Barney was funny, she could speak to Barney.

An old man answered. 'Hello? Barney? Barney who? Oh him, he moved out. Sorry, can't help you, love, don't know where he went. He didn't leave a number. All he left was old clothes that were bloody ridiculous. No, I burnt them. Bye.'

She sat breathing out. She thought I'm exhausted. She had tried her best, she had no more numbers. She felt one thing, relief. It was good that she rang and good they didn't answer. The time was past when she could speak to them.

She went back to her room. She was tired, she was empty.

She went with Pearl to a carnival. Why had she rung? She had opened a cupboard and it wouldn't be easy to shut it again.

153

TWENTY

Nick was tired of long haul driving. He travelled Europe but what he saw was road, coming at him in an endless belt. He didn't get away from Sandy or his trouble, he could be unhappy anywhere. He'd strung himself thin from one end of Europe to the other.

He saw Barney.

'I'm jacking it in, mate, I want a change.'

Barney blew his lips out. 'Yeah, man, but where'll you go?'

They went through the ads. A farm was advertising for a driver.

'Get away. You need straw in the brain to go in for that.'

Still Nick applied, and got the job. It was what he wanted, he could bury himself.

The farmer was a young man with a chapped face, a hoarse voice.

'You've come, then, have you?'

'Did you think I wouldn't?'

The farmer eyed him, he was shrewd and shy. Nick could see him thinking, Will he siphon my petrol, will he steal my grain?

The farmyard was cement, tidy as a garage floor. There was no one else, no animals, no noise.

'You reckon you can drive a combine then?'

'Sure, mate, I can drive anything.'

'I certainly hope so. They cost a penny or two, combines.'

154

He inspected Nick.

He licked his lip. 'I'll drive you there.'

They went to an endless field of grain. The combine stood at the edge like a yellow factory on wheels. Nick soon got the hang, and the farmer left him.

'Got your lunch? I'll come at five.'

High in his cab, Nick engaged the engine, and was away in a thin cloud of chaff.

The day stretched endless like the field. The machine slightly swayed as the ground rolled.

He saw blood on his blade, and got down.

'Oh bloody fuck.'

He'd scythed a rabbit, there was nothing he could do. He cleaned things with straw and sat down in the stubble.

'Bloody fuck. Bloody fuck.'

He started again, but kept watch. When he saw a patch of brown, he stopped and climbed down. He could walk up close to the animal. It crouched flat, its sides quivered, its feet didn't move. A shining eye watched him come.

'There, mate, there. Easy as you go.' He reached out and touched it, its hair was bristly. He stroked it, amazed.

'It's OK, captain.'

It jumped and ran off, he could see its pads and bottom, its ears up like fingers.

He got back in the cab and drove on carefully.

The sun strengthened, the air burned, the combine heated red hot. He stripped but still baked, sweat ran in his eyes, his throat itched breathing straw.

He lunched in the machine's hot shadow. The horizon danced, he could scarcely make out the edge of the field. He remembered southern Italy. He was really on his own, he could forget Nick and Sandy and all their mess.

When the farmer came in the evening, Nick was tired, sunned, contented. He'd covered acres and the farmer seemed pleased.

'You can drive a straight line.'

'I reckon.'

The farmer dropped him at a cottage where he'd rented a room, the couple there gave him cooked dinner. Afterwards he wondered, shall I go to the pub? Instead he lay down, and slept sound and solid as a boulder.

The next day it rained. Nick sat in a barn door watching it pour. Two other men who worked there sat on boxes beside him. Only one of them would talk, an older man, stooping and scrawny like a crooked piece of pipe. Nick told him how he kept stopping for the rabbits.

'You're pretty new to country ways, old boy.'

'That's as may be.'

'So what are you then?'

'I'm a driver. Long haul.'

He talked about Europe but the others weren't impressed. The older man interrupted him.

'Can you drive an articulated?'

'Piece of cake.'

'Ah, that's easily said. Can you reverse it, though?'

'Course.'

The other man spoke at last. 'Well and what about it, that's nothing at all, that's no more than getting a tractor and cart and backing up to the muck-heap.'

'OK, mate. Sure. Will you have a swig?' Nick passed him his beer-can.

The man looked at the tin, then took it and sat back. He was hard to fathom. He was short and close, he had a sly hook-nosed head and lank black hair.

The older man resumed, 'What do you get paid for that, then, what you do?'

Nick told him.

He whistled. 'You know what we get, don't you?'

'More than he's paying me, I hope.'

The man said.

'Christ! And I thought there was money in muck.'

'And that's in a good year.'

'What's your union say?'

The man broke out in a hacking laugh, like rooks in a creaking tree. 'Union? What you talking about? This is farmland, boy.'

'Yeah, but you got a union, don't you? They should do something for you.'

'Union?' He laughed again.

The other man looked sidelong at them. 'No, you don't come here for the money.'

'No? Why d'you come?'

'I wanted some peace and quiet for a change.'

'You a driver an' all?'

He closed his eyes and shrugged like a man who was something better.

'I'm the mechanic here. Eric Lloyd.' At last he held out his hand.

The older man stood up.

'Money, eh? Money.' He croaked his laugh, and crossed the yard.

Nick shared another beer with Lloyd. Now they were alone, he talked more. In the past he'd been all over, another restless man, changing jobs from one works to another. He'd started his own garage and gone bust. There had been a marriage which also went bust. Drily he listed his disasters, Nick liked him more as he went on.

'You done anything in racing?'

He'd done that too, he'd been in the pits several seasons with a car one of his bosses sponsored.

'Man that's great! That's just my dream.'

'Yeah? I gave it up.'

'Why d'you do that?'

'I couldn't take the smashes.'

'No?'

'No. The driver we had, he was a good friend of mine.'

'Yeah?'

'He broke his back and his head too. He's flat out now, and he's like a two-year-old. If you show him a racer, he knows what it is. He just cries, like a baby.'

'Christ!'

They were silent.

Lloyd looked up. 'That's your idea, is it? Get behind the wheel, out on the track.'

'It was once, at any rate.'

Lloyd looked at him. He shook his head. He had a funny quizzical look. Nick wondered.

'Do you still have contacts?' Almost painfully the old hope stirred.

'No I don't. I'm right out of it now, and you're better out of it too.'

Lloyd got up briskly and went about his business. Nick sat watching the rain.

The next day the farmer stopped him in the yard.

'Where d'you work before?' He'd evidently heard his views on wages.

'Ace Haulage. I told you.'

'Why d'you leave?'

'I was always away. I didn't see my kiddy weeks at a time.'

The young farmer scraped his boot on the concrete.

'Do they have a good union in road haulage, then?'

'Nah, it's just a club. They arrange things so everyone can flog the same amount of tat off a load. If you're in stook they do bugger all for you.'

'Perhaps you should have been convener, maybe you could have done something for them.'

'What me, mate? That's not my line.' He could see the farmer's ill-will, and kept just ahead of him.

The farmer shrugged. 'Can't stand here all day.'

Nick went back to the combine. He kept off wages, and the farmer let him be.

Mainly he worked alone in a field. When he was at the farm he would hunt out Lloyd, among the barns.

'Eric?'

'Over here.'

Lloyd was always in some nook of machinery. Nick liked watching him: he was a perfectionist, he got every part clean and working perfectly. They'd talk engines, all sorts, but when he could Nick would get him on to racing. Nick crouched the other side of the motor Lloyd was deep in, so they talked across the distributor leads. In Lloyd's talk his dream returned, crowds milled at the circuits, cars jockeyed for place and swooped into the pits. Lloyd saved an engine, and in seconds the car was out again winning: or spinning from the track.

He didn't talk further about his friend who was injured, but every so often he'd murmur, 'Drivers!'

'What about them, mate?'

'Oh nothing. It's just, they've got a bloody funny attitude to being alive.'

'Yeah, well, they got it in the blood, haven't they?'

'They've got something haywire in the head, and all.'

Nick frowned, Lloyd glanced at him slyly.

He worked on.

'But I've had engines come back in that state – it's a shame. I mean, drivers, they think it's their car, they think it's them making it go.'

'Well it makes a bit of a difference who's driving.'

'What! You take the engine out and see how fast they shift.'

'Anyway, it's something when a car comes in first.'

Lloyd stopped talking, his hands worked in a net of wires.

159

'You're really caught up in it, aren't you?'

Nick nodded.

'Have you been on a track?'

'Yeah, I went to racing school. I've been along to be a marshal. I did everything I could without having a car.'

Lloyd looked at him through the engine. His face was kindly, as if Nick were a relative he liked.

Nick said what was on his mind. 'Could you help me get into it?'

'What, racing?'

'Yes. Could you?'

Lloyd looked at his leads with concentration. For some moments he adjusted them. Finally he said, 'Maybe.'

Nick was in a daze but Lloyd wouldn't say more. He started cursing the engine.

Nick looked back through the barn. There were tractors and combines and cars and trucks, and harrows and ploughs, and bailers and elevators from the olden days. They were all in their places on the concrete floor, as if they were on a grid. The huge doors stood open, when the flag went down they'd all take off, the farmyard would rev and move. The machines were waiting for the day.

'Does he mean it?' Nick asked, walking home.

It became clear the next day he must wait to know, Lloyd was not willing to be hurried. Nick found he could live with the question open. His dream of racing had waited so long it would be a shock if something came of it.

When the harvesting was finished, the three men and the farmer went out to fire the fields. It was something new to Nick, standing at the edge of a Sahara of stubble, while the men called to each other, judging the wind. The small fires spread to a line of fire, then the line began to move. They supervised it at an easy pace as the flames and thick smoke blew mainly away from them. Black smuts collected on their clothes and skin. If need be they walked through the blaze, protected by thick boots. The yellow smoke swallowed them in a blinding choke.

Evening fell, they went back to check progress. The line of fire had broken into many fires, there were big fires like bonfires and small fires catching or dying, while runs of flame trickled ahead. Burning pieces of straw moved forward on the air, there was a huge heat all round them. Like Daniel in the furnace Nick trod through ashes. He kicked burning straw. His skin hurt, he was tired and exhilarated. He felt bigger than himself. All the stuff inside him was laid out and burning at large. It was dark night and like a war, it gave him comfort.

When the fires had burnt out Nick ploughed the black field. The tractor wallowed in a furrow, dragging its shear, turning over by force the compacted earth. He'd never driven with a load like this. If the plough stuck in a shoulder of clay his front wheels lifted, the whole works reared up, he nearly had a tonnage of tractor on top of him. He was glad there was risk.

After, he was put to plough a hill. He laboured up a slithering slope of earth, thrashed by a gale that scattered the trees. He was caught in a downpour, the slope turned to mud, in spite of their huge tyres the tractor-wheels sank.

'Why the fuck did I come here?'

The weather was never still. When he drove home down the shining lane the meadow grass glowed rich green and the tree-trunks were dark like peat. As the storm-clouds cleared the birds broke out full blast in the tree-tops.

'Straw in the brain? This is a great life.'

In the dusk of a fine day he came down the lane, his balloon-wheels trundling, tractor-engine thudding. Midges dodged by him, bats flew round an oak, fireflies switched on and off in the hedge. He glimpsed an owl,

161

ghostly grey in the twilight. It was like a cut-off head, its ears gone into wings, flying by itself; it had strange eyes that looked over its shoulder. Across the meadow hares stood up. It was all grand, he was driving slower, he switched off the engine and lit a cigarette. He sat motionless smoking, till he was a firefly himself as the dusk turned to dark. When he came to he felt he'd been nowhere, it was like deep sleep, he'd never before been at peace.

'I could stay here for ever.'

At the weekend he visited his mother.

'A farm labourer? My son a farm labourer?'

'Right, mate. A yokel.'

'Oh Nicholas, how could you? If your father knew. A farm labourer. Right in the dirt. Oh.'

'It's OK, mate. I like the work.'

'You can't like being a farm labourer, Nicholas. I've never been so ashamed. I'm just not having it.'

'Thanks, Mum.'

And Barney when he came said, 'What do you mean, peace, Nick? You're off the track. You're in a siding. You're nursing yourself.'

'Ta, mate.'

The farmer explained quietly. 'You see, I don't need an extra man in the winter months.'

'Cheers, mate.'

Nick went round the haulage firms, and fixed to get back on the road.

On his last day, Lloyd asked him round for a drink.

'You keep it neat, mate.' He looked round the tiny cottage. It was bare and painted white, and like a workshop. On the window-sills were small pieces of engine, which Lloyd had polished to brilliance. Nick fingered them, Lloyd tested him on what they were.

Lloyd gave him a whisky. They sat down on two hard

wooden chairs, which seemed to be all the furniture Lloyd had.

Lloyd raised his glass. 'One for the road, then.'

'That's about it.'

'So it's back to long haul.'

'Yeah, I suppose. It's a pity.'

'How's that?'

Nick reflected.

He said, 'You know, Eric, I had been hoping kind of you might help me you know to get into racing and that like.'

'Oh that. That's not so easy.'

'Yeah I know.'

Lloyd looked aslant at him. 'Course, we could give it a try.'

Nick glanced at him, but Lloyd's face was still serious.

Nick shrugged. 'Can't do it really. I've got no money, I've got no car.'

'OK. But I know a man.'

'What do you mean?'

'I mean, I know a man. That's the secret of everything. He's got three garages, he wants to sponsor.'

'Is this the bloke that sponsored the other guy?'

'Never mind that. But he's got a car now – well, he wants to drive it himself.'

'So – if it's his car?'

'Oh he's tried, that's no good. He wouldn't ever win. He isn't mad enough.'

'You reckon I'm mad enough.'

'You remind me of some mad guys. But that's not the main thing. You need control.'

'I reckon I've got control. I can keep cool. I can heel and toe OK.'

'Heel and toe? There's more to it than that.'

'All right, mate. But you're saying maybe I could drive the car?'

163

'Well, I'd have to give it a rebuild. It needs it badly.'

Nick sat back. He let himself feel his pleasure.

'Oh Christ!'

Lloyd went on. 'You know what I'm saying, do you? If there's any prize money, it'd go to him. Except that I'd expect a cut.'

'What would I get?'

'Depends what you put in, doesn't it? Still, that's in the future.'

'Yeah?'

'Yes. I need to see you on the track. I need to see if you're any good at all.'

'Oh man.' Nick shook his head. He wanted to weep.

Lloyd said, matter of fact, 'You may get killed, you know.'

Nick said, matter of fact, 'Oh sure.' He swallowed the remaining whisky.

The rest of the evening they talked races.

Nick got up to go.

Lloyd said, 'I'll be in touch.'

They shook hands.

The next day Nick checked in at the haulage depot. He clanked into gear.

'That was never for me, farming. I'm a man of the road. Pity.'

He pressed down his heavy boot and pulled away.

TWENTY-ONE

Ever since she rang she had felt unsettled, as if in some shut place, like a cellar or an attic, a phone were still ringing. She wondered, should I ring again? But time had moved on. At night she'd think, why don't I care?

I'd better start to enjoy my life: but somehow not all of her was there to enjoy it. It seemed she'd left bits of her behind on the road, like a lizard leaving its tail behind. There was a bit of her that Nick still had, another piece that Davey held. Even the boss had a part of her, somewhere in his Alvis. Some of her was still in the cottage.

Still why worry, here's the new life. She had an all right time with Pearl, in a sort of OK nowhere land. She thought, God I need excitement. There was no excitement going.

A designer joined the firm. He was young and tall and pretty and pale, he had fair hair he shampooed every day, and baggy white canvas clothes. He didn't speak but sat around looking good, knowing that people were looking at him.

Sandy shivered as she passed him. Her hair was new-dried and felt like a halo.

'Hello Philip.'

He nodded, but that was all. He hardly ever looked at her.

'He's so rude, Pearl, but he's pretty. He isn't like anyone I've ever known. He looks like an angel.'

Pearl raised her eyes to the ceiling.

Sandy decided, I'll make him see me. She lay in wait, it had become a hunt.

'Oh is that yours?' There was a huge drawing on his desk, part in pencil, part coloured with paints.

He looked at it with her. 'Do you think it's all right?'

'It's lovely.' She turned to him. 'I like your work.'

'Thank you very much.' He blushed and his blue eyes were nice in the blush.

'Morning, Sandy,' he said now.

'Hello Philip.' She was cooler, she thought, he'll ask me round.

After work one day he asked her round.

'Would you like a cocktail?'

He made her a drink with grenadine and cream in it.

'This is a Pink Mist.'

She sipped it, it was mainly gin.

'I like your drinks.'

They had several cocktails, later they made love. He was funny in bed, he seemed to know he had a beautiful body, and just let it lie there for her. It was white, hairless, beautiful, boyish.

She turned round in the bed. 'I like to do this to you.' The sheet draped over her like a big low tent.

Afterwards she lay thinking, he leaves it all to me.

She told Pearl, 'It's so exciting when I'm with him. Other times I don't think of him at all.'

Pearl made a face. 'I know the sort.'

She thought, Pearl's jealous, I've never been so thrilled. 'What do you talk about?'

'Oh we don't talk. I just do it then I go. I like it like that. And I only go when I want to. He's moody too. It's funny really, because he's not my type. Perhaps that's why I get excited.'

'Yeah, well, it takes all sorts.'

166

She'd leave it to the day's end to see if they got together.

'It's a lovely evening,' she said outside the offices.

He was sheepish. 'I've an ad to get done.'

'Forget it, Philip. Bye.' She stepped straight on to a passing bus.

'What a man!' She stumbled upstairs, and found a seat on the crowded top deck. It was nice watching the first-floor windows go by, and people in their offices packing up. She quickly forgot him.

'Come back! Oh stop him, please!'

Sandy stared. Davey charged down the bus straight at her. There was so much nappy and plastic round his legs that they stuck out at right angles. His eyes and mouth chuckled as if Nick were coming after him.

'Stop him! He'll fall downstairs.'

The child was next to her. A panic-person inside her jumped up. She jerked her arm out. At the same moment he stumbled headlong, he was like a big doll on the floor. Sandy lifted him at once. His face looked up at her, goggle-eyed, astonished. She was terrified he'd shriek, but he was still winded, or taking breath.

'There, there. You're all right.'

His eyes looked in her eyes, they were the same blue as Davey's.

'You naughty boy, you gave me such a fright!' The mother had come, she grabbed him from Sandy and strode back to her seat. The child's eyes showed over her shoulder, then his face screwed up, his mouth made an O, as she smacked him hard.

At the front of the bus, between other heads, he looked back at Sandy. He'd stopped crying and stared at her steadily. She met his eyes: then she had to look down, she couldn't look where he was.

'Here, love.' The woman next to her passed a tissue.

'Thanks.' Sandy sobbed a bit and made coughing noises,

which died. She thought, no, I can cry for myself but I can't cry for Davey.

She looked up, the child was looking at her. He smiled. Walls in Sandy fell.

'Have the box, love.'

'I left my baby.'

Everyone looked at her as she coughed her big sobs.

She crawled to her flat and sobbed the evening through. Pearl was out, she had to talk to someone. Why cry? – If I don't like children I don't. Davey doesn't like me. Finally she slept, and in her dream she ran from Davey through the field of rape. It wasn't clear who was crying, he was crying and she was crying.

She thought about Davey all day at the office. She was alone with him and they weren't at war. They crawled racing on the cottage floor, then they curled together laughing.

Snap! The fingers clicked in front of her.

'Where are you, Sandy?'

'Oh! Oh, I was miles away.'

'It was somewhere nice.' The Scottish boss smiled.

'Nice?'

'Perhaps it wasn't.'

Her face had gone sad. 'Sorry. I was feeling sorry for myself. Stupid.'

She started typing, still shaking her head.

For days she was quiet, shut in herself. She stopped seeing the designer, she wanted to see no one.

'Oh but it's too late. I'm not going back.'

The mood passed. Her eyes dried. It's a long time now, she said to herself.

She took up again with the designer, but she had grown impatient.

He lay back in bed, in a pool of soft light. His eyes were half-shut, glazed and happy, his mouth was a little bit open as if he had been sucking something. She thought of babies.

Her eyelids tightened as his drowsy eyes turned to her. His little lips mouthed, 'Did you like it?'

'Like what? You didn't do bloody anything!'

'What?'

'You heard. Do you call that loving someone?'

He turned his back and sulked. For a few moments she looked at his slender white shoulders, his hair like blond feathers. She got out of bed.

'Christ! I'm off out of here!'

She got dressed as she was, while he kept his head turned away. His shoulders looked as though they could weep. She left without saying goodbye, banging doors, clattering stairs, tramping up the road like a burly person.

'Sandy!' he called after, like someone on a flute. She hadn't the patience to turn round.

Afterwards she was pleased, this was a new her, she ddn't use to take a strong line like this.

She told Pearl what she had said.

'Oh, good one, good for you, girl. You're wising up, Sandy.'

'Right. I mean, I didn't leave my kid to look after big babies.'

She saw a child and its mother on the pavement of Oxford Street. It was a little boy in a tiny duffle coat, all square. He was laying down the law.

'Mummies should not hold little boys' hands when they cross the road.'

'You've got it wrong, love.'

As she watched them, Sandy's eyes pricked.

'Pearl, I don't know where I am.'

'I can see that, love.'

'It's just, I don't know. I see a child in the street and I can't stop crying.'

'It takes you that way sometimes. Fix a rum 'n' Coke, will you?'

'It's ever so funny. I wonder what Davey looks like now. They grow very fast.'

'You wouldn't know him.'

'Don't say that, Pearl.'

'Christ, Sandy. I should get you on the water rates.'

'I'm sorry, Pearl. It's just –'

'Yeah, I can see you're obsessed.'

Up the East End she saw a woman stick her finger in a pint of beer, and pull it out all froth and put it in her baby's mouth. A woman with her laughed.

'What! That's goodness,' the mother said.

Stupid fucking cow, bloody cow, Sandy muttered. She said, 'Christ!' to the woman as she passed, the two women stared after her. She wanted to hit them, she wanted to run.

She saw a little boy in harness trotting in front of his mother like a pony. Children were everywhere, she was hunted by children, the thought of them grew like a new baby inside her.

She came out of the supermarket at Saturday midday. It was crowded in the street, she hovered in the entrance blinking. In the corner there were three babies in push-chairs, left there by mothers shopping inside. She stopped and stared at them, it was the funniest thing. They were wrapped up like parcels and slouched down in their seats. They were lined up for the taking like the goods in the store.

She had a spasm of anger: how bloody stupid, leaving kids alone like that.

She tried to move, but they were looking at her. She couldn't pass them.

'Hello.' She smiled, and one of them smiled back.

'You're a good boy.' The child looked up at her, he seemed perplexed. The child next door started rocking his pushchair, the third one looked away, screwing up his eyes at the brightness of the street.

'Is your mum inside, then?'

His look was serious. Her look was serious. She thought, does he wonder if I'm his mum? They stared at each other, till it seemed that just through staring a change was occurring. Each second they held each other with their eyes, she was a little more his mother and he was a little more her baby. If she stayed long enough, he would be her child.

This pushchair was right at the end of the line. It would be the easiest thing to slip off the brake and hop up the street with it.

She was very close to the child and its round face looked up at her. Its eyes were huge and blue, she could fall inside them. Then the supermarket had gone, she was alone with the child, there was just its face like a world and she over it like God.

She looked round: people streamed by, worrying, fatuous, no one watched her. Her shopping was breaking her arms. A headache had started inside her eye. Her foot was beside the pushchair brake.

The child jerked suddenly, she was thrown off-balance, her shopping went over the pavement. As she stooped the pushchair slipped sideways and she looked into the dagger face of the woman taking her baby. She wanted to cry, You're taking my baby, but already it was too late, she saw only the woman's back, and the little wheels to either side of her ankles.

She teetered lightheaded down the pavement. She expected any moment to come to on the ground, looking up into a circle of faces.

She felt OK when she got home, and collapsed in front

of the telly. But in the evening as they went out she said, 'I'm going to see Davey.'

'Yeah?' said Pearl.

'No, I mean it. I will.'

TWENTY-TWO

Sandy rang Nick's mother and found out where Davey was.

'But Pearl, I don't know what to do. I can't just go round. And I can't ring, Nick's mum was shit.'

'Mm. Well. You could write, I suppose.'

'What, write a letter!'

Pearl shrugged.

Sandy wrote, asking how Davey was. She found she couldn't say more than that.

She waited days. She was frightened of the reply, she was frightened they wouldn't answer, she was frightened the reply would come from Nick.

Grace wrote back. It was a tiny little letter saying David was very well thank you.

'Isn't that awful! Isn't that cold, Pearl? I *am* Davey's mum.'

'Yeah, well.'

For some days she couldn't do anything, then she wrote saying she wanted to see Davey. She'd come on Saturday.

They didn't answer.

She waited for each day to end, the people and the office were only half there.

Saturday came. Before she left home, Sandy stood with her eyes shut, like a person saying a prayer.

'Good luck!' Pearl called after her.

At the station she had a moment of panic: I got away,

173

why go back? It was like stepping back into a box she'd got out of.

The train was fast, she sat in a hazy drowsy mood. Things had been wrong but they could all come right again. As the train came into the station, she stood: this is the day I get my life on the rails.

The wind outside the station was cold. Her view was blocked by a big factory building, square with tiny windows, grey as the sky. Her good spirits left her, she found she was frightened.

Near the house of Harry and Grace she thought, what will they say to me? I haven't done anything about Davey. How could I be like that? Her legs swayed as she came up the path.

Harry opened the door.

'Come in, Sandy.' His voice was at the back of his throat.

He took her coat solemnly and led her to the sitting-room.

'Sit down.' He sounded as if someone were dying next door.

She sat in a brown armchair, he sat on the sofa.

A bird in the garden made a noise like a telephone.

'How's Grace?'

'She's well.'

She looked round for toys but there was nothing in sight. She looked at her hand, her little finger shook jerkily.

'How was the trip?'

'All right.'

A door closed, quiet feet descended.

'Sandy.'

Grace came in. She looked as grey-faced as Harry, she sat beside him.

'We haven't seen you for a long time.'

174

'No.'

'You're managing?'

'Yes.'

'What do you do?'

'I work in an office.' The room was getting smaller. 'Where's Davey?'

'David is having his rest. Do you want some tea?'

'Yes please.'

'I'll get it.' Harry went out, they heard him running the kitchen tap.

Grace looked down, she looked tired and strained. Everything in her said, You're a bad mother, Sandy.

'How is Davey?'

'He's very well. Oh, he was crysome at first but he's good now.'

'You don't know how much I want to see him.'

Grace looked up and looked through her.

Harry brought in a tea-tray nervously tinkling. He served.

They drank their tea looking at her: it made her feel weak, as if they were parents and she were Davey's sister. She thought, I've cut myself out, I've given them my baby and they won't give him back.

She said, 'Can I see him now?'

They shuffled on the sofa. Harry said, 'You know, Sandy, it would be better if you didn't see him. It would do so much harm.'

'What do you mean?'

'We think he's forgotten.'

'Forgotten what?'

'Forgotten you.' He swallowed.

'Don't you tell him about me?'

'Oh no, Sandy,' said Grace, 'we never mention your name.'

'Doesn't he say anything about me?'

175

'Not a word. And he calls Nick "Driver".'

Sandy's tea-cup danced in its saucer.

Harry said gently, 'He's forgotten, Sandy. It's for the best.'

'But I came to see him.'

'We couldn't stop you coming, Sandy. But think about it, do. We've made a new home for him. Leave us be.'

Sandy curled up. 'I want to die.'

'Really, Sandy.'

The telephone-bird rang.

Sandy sat up. 'I want to see him.'

Grace said clearly, 'It'll make him unhappy.'

'I must see him.'

'No,' said Harry.

'What do you mean no?'

'I mean, I won't have it.' Harry got up, his face was bloodshot. 'You've left him ages, without a word. You haven't asked how he was, you haven't sent him a present, you've done bloody nothing for him. You don't come back now.'

Sandy stared up at him. 'I am his mother. I want to see him.'

'No!'

Harry stood big, leaning over her.

Grace said, 'All right, Harry.'

'Please Grace, let me just look at him.'

They turned to each other.

'Of course you can look at him.'

'Thank you.'

Grace got up. 'I'll see if he's asleep.' She went upstairs, then came down and whispered, 'You can take her up, Harry.' She turned her back to them.

Harry led Sandy up the stairs on tip-toe. Her heart clenched quickly, she couldn't wait a second. They went

176

into a small square room. The curtains were drawn but an orange light came through them. Sandy stepped to the small bed on softest feet. She saw brown hair like a nest, and a curling ear. There was a faint moan in his breathing, then he sighed and heaved and turned on his back. Sandy's heart stopped, she heard Harry breathe quickly. But Davey lay still, his face pale, his mouth just open. Sandy gazed, he'd changed so much. He was a boy, a little man, he had a nose not a button. He lay back breathing quietly, he had no troubles.

There was a whimpering noise, Harry took her arm. Sandy knew it was her noise but she couldn't move back, she must hold Davey.

His lashes were so delicate she almost saw his eyes behind them looking. She saw his eyes, he was looking back. Without a sound, without a stir, his eyes had opened. Perhaps he still slept but he was looking at her.

Harry pulled her arm hard. Could they get away, while Davey still thought he was dreaming? Harry tugged, she was confused, she did step back, Davey murmured. They looked at him. He gave a cry.

'Out!' Harry shouted, forcing Sandy through the door while loudly he hollered, 'Grace!' but she was already there, leaping up stairs, because Davey's yell was at the top of his voice.

'You see what you've done!'

'My baby!' Sandy waved her limbs but Harry shoved her downstairs off-balance. In the bedroom Grace was saying things but Davey didn't stop, his shrieking was bigger than the house.

Sandy shouted, 'I must go to my baby!'

Harry filled the staircase.

'Harry!' Grace was calling, Harry looked upstairs. The crying went on, everything they had built was falling to pieces.

'Harry!'

'You get out! The damage you've done! You never come back here! You don't see him ever!'

Harry's face was huge, he pinched her arms through, she was struggling and shouting but he'd shot her out and banged the door. She heard him clump upstairs shouting. She heard their voices, she heard Grace crying, and Davey shrieking still.

She looked at the house from the gate, and heard Davey shrieking. Crying herself, her hands at her head, she wandered in the road. Her head fell off, an arm fell off, she came in pieces in his shrieks.

TWENTY-THREE

Nick braked, a van had blocked the road. It was trying to back between the stalls of the market, it must be a stall-holder packing up for the day.

He quietly swore, he was starting out on an all-night run.

It was a good old market van, dented, patched with different paints, no name on it; and it was in trouble, it couldn't fit between the stalls. It came forward suddenly and banged a parked car. The stall-holders nearby shouted. It reversed, stopped, then advanced and banged the car again.

The van door opened and a woman, a girl, got out. She looked at the car she'd bruised.

'Oh Christ! Fuck it!'

She had ginger hair and a small pointed face. She wore an afghan dress, all mirrors and emboidered bits, crimson, mauve, yellow. Nick clambered down from his cab.

'Is it bugging you, darling?'

She looked up sharply, she had a jutting pointed chin.

A stall-holder called out, 'Yeah, well, like as how I reckon she's trying to get a quart into a pint pot there.' The stall-holder next to him laughed across his lettuce.

Behind Nick's lorry cars honked and fretted.

'Can I run it in for you?' He used his kindly voice, mature, like a dad.

'Would you? I'd be so grateful.' When she smiled he saw she had a wide mouth, attractive.

179

Nick got in the van and reversed carefully between the stalls.

'Stop, stop, thank you. Oh that's just right.'

He squeezed out. She'd already opened the back doors of the van.

'Thank you so much, that was tremendous.' She flashed a smile, radiant-eyed, then she got on with piling shoe-socks in the van.

'Pleasure's mine.'

Over the stall-tops he saw his lorry. Behind it people were shouting and hooting, the tailback stretched to the end of the town. At his leisure he got in and moved off.

When he had a day off, he looked round the market till he found her stall. It was all afghan goods, joss-sticks, tassel skirts, little jackets. He watched her at the back, fitting out a plump girl. When she turned from her customer her face went peevish, then was all smiles as she turned back again. He liked her wide mouth, and the birdlike way she darted about.

When she was between customers she came out front, looking tired. She stood hugging her quilted jacket round her. She didn't recognize him, then she did.

'Hello!'

'You've got nice stuff.'

'It moves.'

Their eyes kept meeting, as if they were people who knew each other, who had been apart a long time. She brushed her red hair back, showing her forehead so her face looked neat.

Quite quickly she got impatient, but he kept her talking deliberately. Her eyes swivelled busily but she didn't send him packing. He could see it annoyed her, being obligated to him.

He released her, and strolled by Women's Institute

honey jars. Presently he was back, he'd timed his visit carefully. She was peering down the line of stalls, and looking at her watch. No customers came. She started folding blouses.

He passed, nodding briefly. Like an afterthought, he said, 'Do you want me to bring the van in?'

She stared a moment, then smiled like a light switched on.

'Oh would you, that would be marvellous.'

'Where is it?'

She explained. She jingled the keys some moments, then gave them.

He slid the van through the market and opened the back.

'Pass them across.'

He stowed the dresses neatly.

'Oh that's wonderful.' She smiled her wide smile. He showed his strong arms, his careful hands, he knew how to pack a van.

The stall was nothing but wooden boards and metal pipes.

'May I drive?'

'Why not?'

'Where to?'

She told him. The van had clutch-slip and no brakes, still he drove smoothly.

'Are you there every day?'

'You're joking. No, I get two days a week. I need more than that. And the stall's no good, it's the tightest place. What I need is a stall on Saturdays.'

'Why don't you get one?'

'Oh, people queue up years for a Saturday stall.'

'There'd be a way.'

'You know all about it then.'

'What's your name?'

181

'Teresa. And yours?'

'Nick.'

She looked at him shrewdly, with curiosity.

'You're a driver. You drive well.'

'I'm hoping to get into it. On the track.'

'What, racing cars?'

'We're getting it together. We've got a car.'

She didn't care about racing. They went back to the market and how she needed a better stall.

They stopped at an old terrace house. He helped her unload and stack everything in her hall, till there was just a narrow passage going through to the kitchen.

He closed the van doors. She came out on the doorstep. He could see she wasn't sure whether to say goodbye or come in. He stood out in the road, as if about to call goodbye and go.

'Would you like a cup of tea?'

He paused for moments. Her distinct face became uncertain. He said, 'All right then. Thanks.'

As he went in, he shut the front door.

In the morning he helped her set up. It was beautiful in the empty market. The air was chill, the stone fountain in the middle splashed sparkles. The first buses passed, driving fast. Other market traders were laying out stock, chatting loudly over their goods. The drunk, who sprawled all day on the fountain steps, was also setting up. He pulled bottles from his overcoat pocket and stood them in a row.

'Morning, Jock,' Teresa called.

'Morning, dear,' he said in a sober voice.

'Nick, can you reach to put this up top?'

'Give us it here.'

They worked together cheerfully.

'Now that is a stall.'

They stood in front of it. The stall was bright as a bazaar,

182

and shone all over where the stitched-in afghan mirrors caught the sun.

Teresa glanced all ways and fidgeted. She was impatient to do business.

'Must hit the road,' Nick said.

She looked at him. 'Thanks very much, Nick.' She stood in front of the all-colour stall, her sharp face white.

They waited.

He said, 'Going up-country. Be in Brum tonight, then it's Glasgow. Don't know when I'll be back.'

She turned to her stock.

'See you,' he said.

She glanced quickly. 'See you.'

TWENTY-FOUR

The gin fizz jumped out of Sandy's glass in long spokes that wet Pearl's hi-fi.

'Bloody Christ, Sandy, get a grip on yourself. No I'll wipe up, just try and sit still.'

'Pearl, I have to see Davey.'

'You won't get near him now, girl. Oh look, Sandy, it's all over the record, we'll hear gin fizz every time we play it.'

'How could I leave him? How could I do that?'

She woke in the night. The world was a landslide, bricks and dirt slipping.

She wrote to Harry and Grace, they didn't answer. She rang, they put the phone down.

In the office they told her, get a solicitor.

'A solicitor? I couldn't do that.'

'Why not? You'll have to, if you want custody.'

'Custody?'

It was all too new.

'I could never afford it.'

'Go to a surgery. Go to Citizens' Advice.'

That was a dream, instead she wrote again to Harry and Grace.

Again they didn't answer.

The lawyer's waiting-room was little and dark, with magazines on the table about battered wives and CND.

Across the room, an elderly man stood up.

184

'Sit down, George.'

He sat again beside his wife, but still kept looking at his watch.

She looked into an office through an open door. A fat man with frizzy hair talked loudly to himself, then a voice answered him through a partition wall. The voices were confident, she was frightened, they'd tell her she had no hope, she'd given up all claim.

Eventually it was her turn to see the solicitor, who was a slender woman in a black suit with a long slender turned-up nose.

'So, Sandy, tell me all about it.'

As she described her marriage, the solicitor shuffled folders. She put on glasses and took them off, the nose bobbed up and down peering at papers.

'He left you alone all day?'

'Yes, and what he did!'

'Did he strike you?'

Sandy nodded. The solicitor was wise, she seemed to know all the story already. For a moment Sandy woolgathered, she was walking down the lane with Nick, they saw a hare standing up in a field.

'It was exciting when we first got married.'

The solicitor's face pointed. 'How much does he give you?'

'What do you mean, how much?'

'Does he give you any money?'

'No.'

The solicitor was looking at her watch. 'So what shall we do?'

'What I want is to see Davey.'

'No problem.' She picked up a small microphone and spoke a letter into it.

She turned back to Sandy and smiled.

'OK?'

'Is that it? I can see him now?'

'We'll see what they say. But they have to let you see him.'

Not to seem surprised, Sandy murmured, 'Of course they do.'

The solicitor studied her, her funny nose smiled cheekily. 'We can do much more than that, you know.'

Sandy looked back at her: she had come to an edge.

'I just want to see Davey.'

The solicitor made a mouth.

'Thank you very much,' said Sandy.

'See you soon,' said the solicitor.

Sandy walked away sunny. She could see Davey, the solicitor would fix it. Still she had an unsteady feeling, as if she had pressed a switch which set a quiet motor going, what it would do she did not know.

Sandy waited suspended to hear from the solicitor. Outside work she couldn't see people, she couldn't go out with Pearl. At weekends she couldn't stay home, she sauntered London back-streets.

She wandered Sunday in a little brick courtyard, where an old man was peeing without hiding himself. All the floor of the court was cardboard boxes, and tissue paper different colours, rustling and stirring lightly. There was yellow paper the colour of rape, she waded through it, thinking of Davey.

The old man left, she had the court to herself. She liked the old buildings and the bright-coloured paper, somehow they put her in mind of the cottage.

It started to rain. She burrowed among the papers in a corner of the yard, till she nestled warm in tissue. It was a gentle rain, like a happy crying. It would stop and start and pelt and slacken. The light in the courtyard dimmed and brightened. The wet tissue-papers round her were colourful as flower-beds. For an age, at peace, she watched the rain.

The rain became a downpour briefly. It stuck her hair to her head and soaked the papers: then stopped. A yellow brightness filled the court and in the distance someone laughed. She emerged from her corner: only her shoulders were wet. She found dry papers underneath the wet, and dried her hair and left.

At last the solicitor wrote to her. It was arranged with Harry and Grace, she could go to see Davey at intervals.

She paused at the gate. Clouds came pouring over the housetop as if there were a bonfire at the back. In the wind-noise she half-heard Davey crying.

'Come in, Sandy.'

Harry stayed in the shadows, his cheeks had red patches.

'How's Davey?'

'He's ready for you.'

They were motionless in the tiny hall, there was no sign of Grace.

'We look after David, you know.'

'Can I see him, please?'

Harry breathed in, and held his breath. He left through a glass door at the end of the hall.

He returned. He held by the hand a well-washed little boy in a small funny overcoat. His face was round and pale, he advanced slowly holding Harry's hand hard. He had hair like fine wood-shavings.

'Hello Davey.'

He looked up at her sideways, askance. He was white and frightened, his mouth hung open. His eyes flickered between her and Harry. This wasn't the child that shrieked to have her.

'What have you been saying to him?'

'Nothing, Sandy. We've said nothing about you.'

187

She knew that was true.

She knelt down. Their heads were so close they could bang together. He hid quickly in Harry's leg. Slowly his white face emerged from the trouser-folds like the moon over hills. His eyes were big as lamps. His body made slow willowy motions, swaying towards her then away.

'Oh Davey.'

She sobbed.

He looked up at Harry. 'Sandy's unhappy.'

He reached his hand nervously towards her face. The tiny pads touched her cheek. She took the hand softly and kissed it, still the hand drew back.

She was uncomfortable crouched, and stood.

'Do you want to come out, Davey?'

She held out her hand. He looked up at her, still gripping Harry's hand. He swayed and coiled and in funny curling movements slowly worked nearer to her. Very shyly he let go of Harry's hand and took her fingers. He looked anxiously back to Harry.

Harry sucked his cheeks as if he had false teeth and couldn't make them fit.

He opened the front door. From the gate Sandy saw Grace at a window.

As they walked up the street she felt, oh, freedom, as if a big roof lifted, her wish came true. She looked at him with appeal, he looked at her frightened.

'Where shall we go, Davey?'

He said something she couldn't catch.

She let him lead her. They went to a park not far from the house. It was gusty but bright, there was a sprinkling of parents and children, wrapped up.

'Oh this is nice. Do you remember, Davey, we had a home in the country? I used to take you in the fields.'

'Yes.' His eyes were scared, she didn't believe him.

188

'You remember me, don't you?'

'Remember you.'

She couldn't tell. She sat on a seat and held both his hands.

'My baby.' But he was a cold baby.

'Come to me, Davey.'

She pulled him to hug him but he swayed and fidgeted and levered himself clear.

'You're cross with me, Davey, aren't you? Oh you must be cross.'

He looked past her shoulder, at the lorries in a traffic-jam outside the park.

She gazed at him helplessly. They weren't mother and child any more, she had let it die.

'Shall we go to the swings?'

At the play area he dawdled. He took his hand out of her hand but stood beside her.

'Won't you play, Davey?'

There was a framework of iron pipes like a cage inside a cage. He squirmed to the centre and sat there. She could hear him quietly talking to himself, every so often he said his own name.

'Won't you come out, Davey?'

He gazed out at her through the squares with an expressionless face.

Presently he came out and climbed the steps to the slide.

'Come down, Davey!'

He sat still at the top. Other children milled, he wouldn't budge.

He came down head first on his back.

'Oh that was clever. What a funny way to do it!'

He lay on the slide-end, gazing up at her.

'Come back, Davey. Where are you going now?'

He hung upside-down like an odd monkey creature, like

something with claws, looking at her through the thick rope net.

'Hello, Davey. Won't you talk to me? I am your mummy.'

He put his arms through the ropes and clawed tighter on them. He froze there, like a tree-creature in vines, gazing at her with serious eyes.

'Speak to me, Davey.'

He slightly swung.

'I'm your mummy. Please call me mummy.'

She put her arms through the ropes and held him. They were all in a tangle with the hard hairy ropes.

'My darling.'

His body seemed paralysed, stuck to the ropes. His pale face looked up at her, with eyes like a refugee photo. Starved eyes, they made holes in her.

He clung on the ropes and she hugged him through the ropes.

'Oh, Davey, I don't know what I've been doing. I've been so stupid.'

He began to look frightened. She went the other side of the net. He waited motionless. He let her prize his fingers loose, and lead him down.

They started for the gate, then he ran to a large round rotating platform. Standing on the rim, he pushed with one foot.

'No, you get on, Davey. I'll make it go.'

She yanked on the hand-bars and pushed it round. The spindle in the middle clanked loudly.

'You want it faster?'

It was rocketing round, bars difficult to catch. Davey had climbed to the middle and lay there. Each time he came past, he met her eyes. He caught her and lost her, caught her and lost her.

'What is it, Davey?'

He mouthed something each time he passed, his lips closed and opened again. It must be mummy, she heard him say mummy.

The machine was going slower, he sat up in the centre.

'You get on, Sandy.'

He spoke clearly. She saw the back of his head.

'Oh, I can't, Davey.'

Here was his face.

'Get on, Mummy.'

She saw his back.

He appeared again. She caught hold, got on, and clambered to where he was.

He greeted her with big eyes, sharing a secret. She clasped him as the machine rotated.

'My baby.'

The wheel clanked, as it turned and they turned with it. The long frieze of park and people and climbing frames passed continuously in front of them in a strip of trees and parents and children as he sat snug into her and she held him close. She wanted them together to turn for ever.

The platform creaked as it stopped. They stirred.

'Oh Davey, look at the time.'

On the way back he seemed exhausted and fragile. As they neared the house he grew crysome and at the gate he dropped her hand.

'David!' Grace was wet-eyed with pleasure to see him. He went quickly to the kitchen. Sandy saw no one wanted her there.

She left like a howl but in the train she was happy.

191

TWENTY-FIVE

'Nick, could you look at the van?'

He saw Teresa often, and often when she wanted something. Then her voice, her eyes, would smile, at other times she was impatient. He didn't mind, he liked it when she needed him. She was a person of class, she was a dentist's daughter, he liked her educated voice.

'Nick, there's a Footware Fair at Torquay. Could you take me?'

Her voice was full of rustles, the words nestled in his ear.

'Yeah, why not?'

They set out in her van. He drove comfortably, as if they were married. They sightsaw in the Cotswolds.

At Torquay they checked in as man and wife. She wriggled close to him, cold in the unfamiliar sheets.

In the morning they walked on the prom. She clung to his elbow like a funny bird.

'Nick, I've got a thing about your arms.'

'What I like's your shoulders.'

'Nick! They're fat, my shoulders, they're terrible.'

'What do you mean, fat? You're not fat anywhere.'

She made a face. She swung on his elbow. The big sea crashed the pebbles.

They approached a hall of shoe-people and shoes.

'Do I look all right?'

'You look great.'

She wore a green dress and had her ginger hair tight back

in a bun. With her white pointed face she was smart like a fashion photo.

They paused by the soft shoes. There were turn-up toe slippers and slippers that were like a bed for each foot. There were open-work shoes, and sandals that clung by an ankle, by a toe, by an instep.

'You know, Nick, I think I should get into espadrilles.'

'Yeah? They don't look afghan to me.'

'I've got to expand, Nick.'

The salesman joined in. 'Right you are, madam, you must think ahead. The future is rope-soles.'

Teresa's face was taut and shrewd. 'I think so, yes.' She picked and chose, they carried boxes of espadrilles out to the van.

In the evening they danced at a footware party. She danced in a jigging bouncing way, swaying quickly from side to side.

They drove home, it was a good two days, but it was clear when they were back that she wanted to be left. It suited him. After work the next day, he rang Lloyd.

'How's it going, Eric?'

'Not so bad. I've got the car here.'

'What, on the farm?'

'Of course. Come over.'

Nick drove there in the old saloon. They walked to a shed, Lloyd unlocked the doors.

'There you go!'

'Christ, Eric! Where's the rest of it?'

What they saw was a car-frame, just a few metal stems, rested up on metal trestles. The fairings were off, the wheels were off, the engine block was out and rested on a bench.

'I've been checking it through.'

'I reckon you have.'

They felt their way round the skeleton slowly, fingering welds and bearings.

'You'll run smooth in that.'

They went to the engine.

'When I've done the rebuild, by God that'll shift.'

Nick shook his head. 'I just hope I'm up to it. Maybe I need a rebuild.'

'Oh, you'll do. I can tell.'

They stood either side of the engine admiring it. It was like a powerful heart wanting its body.

'I never thought this would happen.'

'Oh, things happen. Too many things happen.'

'Yeah well, they haven't happened to me yet.'

'I'd wait if I were you. You're the sort of guy things happen to.'

'I guess.'

They went over to the wheels, stuck up in a column like quoits on a stick. Nick stroked the fairings which would make him streamlined.

Lloyd explained, 'That's only one set. There's others back at the garage, but these are what we need right now.'

As Nick's hand moved on the smooth curved surface, Lloyd's hand came forward and rested on his.

Nick pulled back. Lloyd talked on quickly as if nothing had happened. He kept his face down.

Nick said loudly, 'I'm sorry about it, mate. Not my line. No hard feelings?'

Lloyd looked up. 'No, course not.'

They talked competitions, and the best race to start at. As they left the barn, Lloyd asked, 'How's your kiddy?'

'What, Davey? He's great. He's dying to see the car.'

'Another mad driver, is he?'

'He's a tearaway.'

'I reckoned he would be.'

Nick drove back thinking, at least Eric asks. Teresa

194

never mentioned Davey, and she was blank as a wall if he talked about Sandy. Still he was excited when he saw her next. He had the afternoon off and spent it at her stall, playing at being a market trader. They went home together tired and contented.

All evening they talked markets.

'There's only one problem, Nick. I have to get a stall on Saturdays. And I can't.'

'There, darling, there.' He put an arm round her. 'Maybe I'll help out.'

'Oh if you could, Nick. But there's no way.'

'No, baby?'

After his next long run he decided to act.

There was a little alley behind the Town Hall, and an office with no sign to say what it was. He went in.

He blinked, it was chaos and full of dust. All anyhow there were papers tied up in sisal and others stuck on spikes. There were broken trestles and bales of canvas and stacks of old receipt books with carbon papers like tongues sticking out. Sitting on a swivel chair rocked very far back was an elderly fat man. Horn-rim glasses sat askew on a chapped face of bust veins. He smoked a cigar like a film millionaire. He wore an old trilby which he pushed back to see Nick.

'And what can I do you for, sir?'

'Oh, I'm a friend of Mrs Dow. I wanted to ask about the market.'

He leaned back further. 'Right you are. You're a friend of Mrs Dow. How is the good lady?'

'She's great, man.'

'I'm glad to hear it. And what might your line be?'

'Me? I'm on the road. Heavy goods. Containers. Trucks and such.'

'You're on the road.' He became more cheerful, Nick sat down. For some time they talked goods in transit, the old man reminisced. When he was a trader he'd run several vans, they compared notes on different makes.

'So, you were saying, you wanted to ask about the market.'

'That's right, yeah. It's to do with Mrs Dow.'

'That's all right, I like Mrs Dow.'

'Thing is, she'd like to have a stall Saturdays.'

'I believe you.'

'Is there a chance?'

He drew on his cigar, the atmosphere got like a bonfire.

'I'm sorry to say it can't be done.'

'It must happen sometimes.'

The man took off his glasses, spat on the lenses, and wiped them with his brown thumb.

'Do you know the waiting list on Saturday stalls?'

'Mrs Dow's been waiting a fair old time.'

'Ah, there's whole families waiting to get a stall Saturday. There is a man that has been waiting five year and more.'

'That's pretty good. Still, wouldn't you say Mrs Dow's a good trader?'

'Mrs Dow? She's a businesswoman.'

'And she's there in all weathers. Sleet, hail, Mrs Dow is there with her afghan goods. Frost, snow, whatever, she's there.'

'That's true for sure.'

'She's got her own van. She's not one of these characters that brings stuff in a car. Nor on a bike. She's not a hippy. She's a real trader. Would you say that's fair?'

'That's fair. I think you could say she's one of us. I like Mrs Dow.'

'Still, if it can't be done . . . Here, it's twelve, I must hit the road. Can I get you a drink before I go?'

The man thought. 'The Spread Eagle's open.'

At leisure, cumbersomely, he locked the office, and

196

they crossed the alley to the bar of the Spread Eagle.

'What's your pleasure?'

Nick bought drinks. They talked roads and goods while the man worked his cigar, bringing the pub's atmosphere to a thickness he could breathe.

Nick prepared to go, then had a thought. 'Oh by the way, I've a tip for the races. Newmarket this weekend. Do you fancy a flutter? I'm putting something on. Can I put a bit on for you?'

The pub-chair creaked, the cigar puffed like a chimney.

Nick went on, 'Let's give it a run. Leave it with me. If it comes in, I'll let you know.'

Nick stood up. 'OK, I'm on my way. About Mrs Dow –'

The man cleared his throat like a foundry raked out.

'Look, if she comes to see you, and asks about Saturdays – will you just think about it, you know, consider it?'

'Yes I'll think about it.'

'Cheers.'

Nick left, and went to Teresa's. He waited a few days, then he sent her along to ask herself.

'It's no good, Nick, nothing will come of it.'

'Just go and ask. But be nice. Be your nicest. You know how to ask for something.'

She frowned but she went, in her prettiest afghans. She came home.

'It's really true, Nick. He'll let me have a stall on Saturdays. I can't believe it.'

'He was in an OK mood, was he?'

'He was nice.'

'That's good. Maybe he had a win on the nags.'

She looked at Nick. 'This is thanks to you, Nick, isn't it?'

He smiled.

'Oh that's wonderful, you don't know.' Her eyes were enormous, her wide mouth grinned.

The day of the new stall approached.

'You'll help me, Nick.'

'Sure, baby. There'll be other help too, my mate Barney's coming down.'

'Who's he?'

'Oh, he's great, you don't know him.'

She pulled a face.

The day came and Barney, in a wide-hipped green Italian coat like a woman's smock.

'Hello there, friends. I don't know your name, darling, but I wish I did.'

Teresa didn't answer. Barney chatted, delaying them as they loaded the van. He did the same thing when they got to the square and set up the new stall.

'Do you want to have a look round the market, Barney?'

'Thank you, Nick, I can take a hint.'

The goods were set out, shoppers filtered through the market. People fingered the shoe-socks and put them back.

'Business slow, is it?' Barney said.

'Takes time,' said Nick.

'They're not used to me being here,' Teresa said.

'No problem, I'll give you a hand.' Barney stepped in front of the stall and started to call out in a strong voice, 'Walk up, walk up, get your afghannies here. Shoe-socks and rope-soles, Spanish espadrilles. Skirts with mirrors in 'em. Ladies' waistcoats! Madam, have I got shoe-socks for you! Guaranteed hand-made, every stitch out of true, made from the softest wool of the yak. Look at the workmanship! Feel the texture! Smell them, madam, that's pure ozone from the high Himalayas. Afghannies, afghannies. Afghannies for the family! Afghannies for the kids! Give granny an afghanny for Christmas!'

Teresa looked strained.

'Turn it up, mate.'

198

Barney goggled, 'Can't stop now, man, got the bit between my teeth.' He raised his voice. 'Sir, can I interest
you in a pair of afghan mittens? Or take just one, sir, it'll
hold both your hands and the hands of your best friend
too. Ladies, we have bags. We have bags for nicknacks
and bags for your toiletries and bags to hang on the wall
with nothing inside them. You name it, madam, and if
it's afghan we got it.'

'Do stop him, Nick.'

'Can it, man.'

'Sure, Nick, sure.'

Barney moved to a sheepskin stall that was temporarily
untended. He got behind the trestles as if he were the
owner and started shouting, 'Teresa's for afghannies!
Don't shop here, madam, we have no afghannies. Teresa's
the name, afghanny's the game. Third stall on the left,
beside the fountain and the bottle display. Beg pardon, sir,
is this your stall I'm standing behind? I mistook the way,
excuse me please. Nice weather for the time of year, don't
you think? I wish I could say the same for the political
situation.'

The inflamed stall-holder saw him off. In the distance
they heard him calling, 'Teresa's for afghannies! Guaranteed no synthetics, all fresh-made from pedigree yaks!'

Nick was busy at the stall, then went back to the van
for more. Teresa traded continuously.

Barney came back, full of false meekness.

'Good takings, then?'

'It's been a great day.' She smiled and flashed her eyes
at Nick.

'Oi oi,' said Barney.

'I'll take you out.'

She took them to a cocktail bar.

'She's nice, Nick,' Barney said as he left. 'Bit of a tartar,
though. Watch your step there, boy.'

'Never a dull moment, anyway, mate.'

'Yeah, well, you'll get some funny moments with her. See you, Nick.'

The days passed, Nick helped with the stall. But presently again Teresa tightened and pinched.

'You don't know how to say thank you, do you?' he said one evening to the back of her head. The small bun of red hair was held tight with a large wooden pin. The white thin back of her neck went tight.

'What do you mean?' She was sharp at once.

'Nothing, man.'

'I've said thank you, Nick. I can't say it every day afterwards.'

'Right on, girl. For myself, I like saying thank you if I get a favour. I enjoy being done favours.'

'Lucky you.'

'Christ! You think I'm a common bastard, don't you? Middle-class fucking cow.'

'Good night, Nick.'

Still they went next night to a party. She danced in her funny jigging way. Later she was hard to find.

On the way home he said, 'Did you screw at the party?'

'And why not, I'm not your wife.'

'Cunt!' He turned about-face and walked away fast.

When they next met she was impatient to make love.

He didn't know where he was with her, they agreed and disagreed all the time. When he was away from her, he would think he saw her if he saw someone like her. He would abruptly smell her scent when he was alone in his cab.

Always after upsets they met again, and made love as if they would eat each other.

TWENTY-SIX

Coming for Davey this time was a treat. But when Harry let her in, she found Davey shrunk in shyness. He sat crouched on the bottom stair, his face in his hands. One eye would glance at her then quickly hide again.

'Come on, David,' Harry said impatiently. He shook him into his miniature overcoat. Davey bit his lip, sucked his mouth, looked everywhere but Sandy's way.

'Well I hope you can handle him. He's in a funny state these days.'

They were on their way quickly. Harry breathed out as he shut the door.

'Are you glad to see me, Davey?'

He didn't answer. She wondered, are we back where we started? But he took her hand and began to pull her along the pavement.

'Wherever are we going?'

He said something quietly.

'What was that, love? I didn't catch it.'

'Volvo.'

'Come again?'

'Ford.'

He was saying the makes of the cars they passed. She joined in.

'What's that one, Davey?'

'Austin.'

He was right every time.

'Davey, however do you know them all?'

He stopped and looked at her, with sly excited naughty eyes.

'Does Nick tell you?'

'Driver!' He walked ahead of her. Cars, lorries, he named everything.

'That's very good, Davey. Oh but do slow down.' She thought, here's another king of the road.

They walked from street to street, till he tired of the car-names.

'Let's sit down, love, I need a rest.'

They went into a park. There were swings in the corner but he didn't run for them, he sat beside her under the big trees. He had grown quiet, his eyes had heavy lids like an older person.

He moved against her like a cat after food, then took her hand and clung to it.

'Love.'

They sat, his body pushed into her body, her arm round him holding him close. They watched the other children play, they watched the gardener, a lanky man, follow a motor-mower across the grass. They watched the branches of the trees swing back and forth in big heaves while all their leaves fluttered like papers on a board. The wind made a rushing noise but they were sheltered. It was the first time ever they were quite still together.

When they came to a long time had passed, as if they had fallen asleep and woken when they were ready.

'Shall we go and have tea, Davey?'

'Yes,' he said happily.

They left the park.

'Look, Sandy.'

They had stopped on a small bridge. Underneath was not a river, but a narrow sluice, and beyond it a deep pool of water, covered with bushes that grew from the bases of buildings. A youth sat on a wall, fiddling with a fishing line.

'Oh look, Davey, he's caught something.'

'What is it?'

'I don't know. Isn't it a funny thing?'

It wasn't like a fish, it had a silver shell, and little thin silver legs. It writhed and curled on top of the wall, then slipped down on to a concrete shelf.

'Look, it wants the water.'

It flapped and squirmed on the concrete.

'Won't you put it back?'

The youth looked up at her and shrugged. Later he reached down for it.

'I wouldn't want to pick it up, though. Would you, Davey?'

'Yes!'

The youth chucked it in the water.

Next to the bridge there was a tea-shop. They went in.

'But whatever was it? I've never seen anything like it.'

'It was a Davey-fish!' He laughed with zest.

'Davey, you are funny.'

She couldn't get the creature out of her mind, all silvery and twisting by itself on the stone.

They looked together at the menu.

'Oh they look great, Davey! What'll you have?'

He looked up huge-eyed.

'Ice-cream.'

They ate together at leisure.

Watching him, she hurt, as if a thread round her insides were pulled tight, cutting her.

She found she asked him, 'How is Nick?'

He looked up at her uncertainly.

'He takes you out?'

In a rush he said, 'I can see his car.'

'What car is that?'

203

Through a mouthful he cried out, 'Racing car!'

'He hasn't got a racing car!'

'He has!'

'Uh! If you believe what Nick says . . .' She watched him closely: what does he know about Nick and me? What have they told him?

'Harry and Grace – they're nice to you?'

'Oh yes they're very nice. They give me space toys.'

Perhaps he saw she was unhappy. 'Where do you live, Sandy?'

'I live in London. I work in an office. I've got plans, though.'

'Plans? What plans?'

'Well, it's called a course. It's like going to school.'

He stooped right down, like a hunchback at the table.

'Are you clever?'

'Oh Davey, I don't know.'

The girl said to them, 'We're closing now.'

Sandy turned, surprised. 'Is it early closing?'

The girl nodded at the clock, and banged their plates together on a tray. The other tables were empty.

'Davey! Do you see what the time is? God, I had no idea! We're very late.'

He gave a funny quiet smile, they were naughty together.

'We must get back, we must run. Get up, Davey!'

But he took his time. As they came into the street she thought: I've got Davey. I've kept him beyond time. I could keep him for good.

'Look, Davey!'

A lorry of cars, a car-transporter, slid slowly in front of them. They took the same direction.

Presently he said, 'This isn't the way.'

She walked on firmly; she held his hand harder.

'Are you a naughty mummy?'

She didn't answer, and he kept up with her. They passed rush-hour cars, the people in them were relaxed as they waited. The day was sunny and tired, she was going home and Davey was with her.

They could see the station at the end of its road.

'Where are we going?' He stopped where he was.

'Shall we go to London, Davey?'

They looked at each other, uncertain. The pavement broke in two.

She drew him up the road. Over the station a door opened in the sky.

They stopped outside the ticket hall. Taxis passed them, cyclists fountained from the side of the station.

'Are you all right, Davey?'

'I'm all right.' He couldn't stand still, his legs kept twisting. There were small movements in his cheeks.

She said quietly, 'We'll go there another day.'

They felt very tired, walking home. The buses were full or gone.

It was twilight when they came near Harry's. They turned a corner and saw him in front of them, waiting at the head of the street. He looked big in the twilight and broad. Beyond him was the house, with Grace in the doorway, a pale shape. They were lined up in the dusk like Judgement.

Sandy had to walk towards him.

'Where have you been? Do you know the time? What have you been doing?' He almost couldn't speak, he wanted to hit her, she remembered him holding her and shoving her downstairs. He was as violent as Nick underneath.

'I'm sorry, I lost track . . .' Her excuse petered out. She thought, he's my child, why should I explain? She slunk down the road like a culprit while Harry walked ahead.

He opened the gate.

'Go in, David.'

Sandy watched him go up the path. Grace was on top of him, 'Oh David!' she repeated as she snatched him inside.

Harry trembled beside Sandy, full of menace. She avoided looking at him, she didn't want him to speak.

She crept down the street. When she looked back he was still there, like a dog on a boundary, watching her go.

TWENTY-SEVEN

The streamlined car crept beside Davey, Nick's head was on the same level as his. The engine made non-stop revving noises.

'Nick, Nick, can I get in? Please.'

'What do you think, Eric?'

Lloyd puckered his face, his long nose looped bigger. He looked in pain.

'Go on, then,' he said quickly.

Frowning he lifted Davey, and lowered him gradually into the cockpit. Somehow they squeezed him in the tight space, and strapped him in with Nick.

'Let's go. Go, Nick.'

'OK, man. Hold your horses.'

In splitting revs the car inched forward. Nick turned, until they had ahead of them the wide concrete strip which ran to the horizon. All round them, empty, stretched the disused airfield. Lloyd, in brown overalls, had his hands on his hips. Far away there were round-topped hangars.

'Are you ready, Captain Space? Fire engines!'

Slowly they started, bumping on the pitted runway.

'Oh faster, Nick, faster.'

'Cool it, captain.'

He thought, I'll give him a burst. He pushed his foot down, the car moved forward and faster. Davey was pressed into Nick. The whole airport shivered, the hangars on the horizon grew fast to big boxes. They disappeared.

The car shook to pieces going faster than speed, a jet-plane at grass-level. The hedge on the horizon swelled towards them.

The engine-noise dropped, they hung forward on straps. Still they were too fast, they'd go through the hedge and leave a car-shaped hole.

The hedge and trees stood still, a distance away.

'How you keeping, soldier?'

Davey looked up. His face was chalky and his eyes shone brilliant, streaming with tears from the wind.

'Great!' he said shakily, he had no voice.

Seeing him, Nick felt his own colour drain. What did I do that for? Slowly he drew the car round, bouncing on the grass. They faced back down the runway. He stopped.

'Return trip, mate. I won't take it so fast.'

'Can I drive?'

'What did you say? You?'

'Oh please, Nick. Please let me.'

'What! Babes on the track!'

'Let me, Nick.' He gripped the wheel, clinging forward.

'Are you sure you're OK, Davey? You look bloody pale.'

'Yes, Nick. I'm ace.'

'OK, Stirling. Take it away.'

Nick worked the pedals, the engine spat, the car crept forward.

'Here, a bit left, Davey.'

'Don't tell me, Nick. Let me.'

Davey moved the wheel, the car swung the other way.

'Straighten her up.'

'Don't tell me.'

They made a snake's path down the runway. Gradually Davey got the hang.

'Arms!'

'What's that?'

Nick's arms hovered above Davey's small arms. He moved them back a little.

'More.'

'No way, mate. That's enough. It's my turn now.'

'It isn't your turn. It's my turn. It's Davey's car.' He hugged the wheel.

Nick let the car slow till it stopped.

'Oh make it go, Nick. Make it go!' He bounced up and down, his legs kicking hacked into Nick's legs.

'Shut it, mate. I mean it.'

Davey sat back, Nick drove them down the runway. Davey's fingers touched the wheel as he shared the driving. They drove like one person, Nick surrounding Davey gently.

Lloyd stood waiting, deep trenches down his cheeks.

'I drove it, Mr Lloyd. Did you see?'

'Course I saw, Nick couldn't drive like that. I hope you taught him a thing or two. He needs putting right.'

Davey smiled, he looked tired and strained. Nick lifted him out and passed him to Lloyd, then climbed out himself, and stretched his limbs.

Davey came and clasped his leg. He clung as if the leg were a person he loved.

Lloyd bent down, adjusting the engine. Nick and Davey joined him.

'Do you know what this is, Davey? This is the fuel injector.'

'Fuel injector.'

They stood up. Nick went a few steps off with Lloyd, while Davey walked slowly round the car. He trotted to the runway making revving noises, then looked round him imagining cars and planes. The empty airfield stretched flat all ways. The sky was wide with big clouds, very white, slowly boiling up in shapes. One cloud was like an armchair.

He could tell Nick and Lloyd were talking about him. He stole closer.

'No, he's a good lad.'

'You didn't say you were bringing him.'

'Yeah, but I had to.'

Their voices got quieter, he heard Nick say, 'They're afraid that some time she'll be off with him.' Nick's face was red, the other man looked serious. He knew they meant Sandy: because of Sandy everyone was serious. The two men were whispering like Harry and Grace.

Lloyd shrugged, Nick turned on his heels.

They all looked round, something was happening on the runway. It was the strangest old car, big and square, very upright. Because the wind blew the other way it made no sound. It drove towards them like a ghost car. It moved in a funny way, wobbling as much as when Davey drove.

Lloyd said, 'Jeepers creepers, that's just what we want.'

'What is it? Who is it?'

'Learner bloody drivers,' Nick muttered.

Lloyd explained, 'That's old Mr Jackson, he won't give up. That's his son in there trying to teach him.' His long nose laughed slyly. 'Yes, it's the sons teaching the dads today.'

Davey laughed, Nick smiled. The old-fashioned car came nearer, then seemed to see them. Jerkily it turned round. There was a crash of gears, a bang from the exhaust, a little ball of black smoke rose in the air. It started back down the runway, the one upright shape on the flat world.

Lloyd shook his head. 'Hope they've had enough, it's getting late.'

Slowly the car left them. In the distance it stopped with an explosion, then retreated.

'Off you go, Nick. This'll be the last run.'

'I'm coming too.'

210

'Not now, mate.' Nick was sharp, Davey's face crumpled.

Lloyd stooped down beside him. 'Let him go, Davey. The man's got to learn. You'll put him straight another time.'

Davey watched seriously as Nick worked himself into the machine. The car stirred then jumped away like a missile. It was funny seeing Nick disappear like that. Lloyd held his hand.

Nick, in top, pressed the pedal flat home. The car leapt from itself like a rocket leaving stages. Its metal, his bones, the airfield shook. The ground nearby was nothing but a blur. He felt he had left his blood behind. He was at the sharp edge, edge of life, edge of death.

Davey remembered the hedge running towards him.

There was no noise, no car. Lloyd looked down just as Davey's face folded.

'It's all right, Davey. Nick's all right.'

He stooped down and hugged him. Funny child, he thought, he's not his age, he's like a babe. Davey's eyes hung on Lloyd as if he were a mum.

The car reappeared. It hovered in the distance like a buzzing fly then grew at them quickly.

The car stopped beside them, Nick's head smiled from the cockpit. 'Great engine. No misfires.'

Lloyd was smiling. Davey looked at them, then took a flying jump that carried him head first, arms out, half into the cockpit.

'Steady, mate, you'll throttle me.'

'That's it. Pack up. Let's go,' Lloyd said.

They pushed the car up ramps on to the trailer. They all got in Lloyd's car.

Davey bobbed on the back seat. 'Where are we going now?'

'We're heading home, mate. Eric'll drop us off.'

Davey nodded then said, 'I've got three homes I can go to.'

'What do you mean, Davey?'

'There's Sandy's home, and there's my home, and there's Nick's home.'

'It's your home we're going to.'

Davey sat up. 'Yes, we mustn't be late.' He looked at Nick uncertainly. 'When I go out with Sandy, she always keeps me late.'

Nick looked half round and caught Lloyd's eye.

'Oh yes,' said Davey, 'Harry and Grace get very worried. Sandy shouldn't do that, should she? She's nice really.'

Nick sat like a low hill. 'What things does she get you?'

'Oh very nice things, Nick. She got me an ice-cream milk shake.'

'Christ!' Nick muttered to Lloyd. 'Great mother love! Ditches the kid all this time, then turns up and buys him ice-cream milk shakes. Bloody Christ!'

Lloyd tilted his head. They were all quiet.

TWENTY-EIGHT

'Davey, do you want your fortune told?'

It was cheap night at the fair, with a crush of crowd. Davey looked at the picture of Gypsy Lee.

'She doesn't really know!'

'Of course she does! She's only got to look at your hand.'

'Mum!' he said, she held his hand tighter. 'I'm not a baby. You haven't got your fortune written in your hand.'

'Yes you have. Let's go and see.'

He scoffed. 'My fortune in my hand!' He led the way, excited, into the caravan. A sallow woman with a scarf round her head smoked wearily.

'Go on, Davey, give her your hand.'

He gave a shy smile and kept his hands at his side.

'Which hand is it written on?'

'Are you right-handed or left-handed?'

'I'm both-handed.'

'Let me see them both, then.'

He put out both hands quickly and looked shyly, with thrill, at Sandy. Gypsy Lee's heavy-lidded eyes peered steadily.

'What do you see?'

She looked up. 'There's something good in your hands.'

Davey turned open-mouthed to Sandy.

'Something good in my hands? What can it be? I can't guess.'

Sandy smiled. On an impulse she said, 'Can you look at my hand?' The gypsy smoked, and studied it.

'Will the person I want be with me always?'

She caught Davey's eye: they both waited for news. She thought, this woman can't know.

Gypsy Lee pushed back some grey hairs that wandered from her scarf, and looked heavily at Sandy.

'Yes.'

'Oh! Thank you.' From nowhere happiness flowed. She wanted to sit. Somehow the word made everything right.

'Thank you,' she said again to the woman. 'Davey, isn't that good?'

He was impatient.

'All right, Davey. Let's see the fair.'

He hurried ahead, pulling her. She followed laughing, enjoying the feelings of a put-upon mum. She began to spend pounds.

'Oh look, Sandy, there's the ghost train. It does look frightening, doesn't it. Can we go? But you must come with me.'

They had a ride on the ghost train. In the dark he clung tight to her.

'I'm glad we're out of that. I was frightened when that thing came in my face. But I wasn't really. Oh look, there's the two-headed man. I have to see him, he must be very funny. Can you imagine having two heads?'

He couldn't leave the booth, with its bright-coloured picture of a savage man with two heads growing from one neck.

'That's not real, Davey. You don't want to waste your money on that.'

'Oh no, I have to see it. I have to see the two-headed man.'

He kept craning round the canvas, trying to see past the entrance. She paid and they filed inside. All they saw was a long box like a big coffin, covered in glass, with an emaciated figure in it that must be seven foot tall, brown,

dry, shrivelled to the bone. At the top there were two
heads. It was all so dark and rough and damaged, they
couldn't make out if the heads were artificial. Sandy shook
her shoulders, the lifeless figure disturbed her stupidly.
Davey looked up at her with brilliant eyes.

'Do you think it's from space? I think it must be. I'll
draw it when I get home.'

She was glad to be outside again. She bought Davey
candyfloss, which came in a polythene bag.

'Are you having a good time, Davey?'

'Mum! I am!'

A bloodshot man, his big belly bursting his vest, sold
china. He lifted a platter with plates and cups and saucers
on it, and swung it in the air so the china separated and
landed again with a tinkle and clatter. He held a cup to
the light-bulb so the white glare came through.

'Here's a tea-set I'll throw in and the platter too. Now
I won't take twenty pounds and I won't take fifteen pounds
and I won't take twelve pounds, no I'll sell this for under
ten pounds, and not only that but I'll tell you what I'll
do.'

'Come on, Mum, this is boring.'

'Oh no, Davey, I want to see this. Isn't the china lovely?'

She took a bowl from the pile and cupped her hands
round it. It had a pattern of flowers, it held homes and
families, dresser cupboards, cheerful grandmas. She
wanted to bid for it, but Davey wouldn't wait.

'Oh please, there's the guns, I have to shoot the guns, I
can shoot everything. And the dodgem cars. I have to go
on the dodgem cars.'

They watched the dodgem cars bang and bounce, while
blue light flashed from the metal tongues overhead.

The turn ended, people staggered out, new people
shoved for the cars. Sandy was good at that. 'Here! Watch
it! Do you mind!' A gormless man who looked like a

215

doctor was hesitating with his kid beside a car. Quick as a spark Sandy was in, pulling Davey after her.

The man began to get red in the face. The power came on, their car jerked forward.

'I can drive. I can drive a racing car.'

'All right, Davey, you drive.'

Still he took time getting used to the controls. The car jerked and turned on the spot, other cars jolted into it.

They were away. Davey crouched at the wheel, going full speed. He drove crash into the nearest car, the couple in it looked round startled. He smashed into car after car. When other cars hit them he shrieked with laughter.

'Davey, stop! I'm being shaken to bits!'

He couldn't stop, he was a devil in Heaven. The rubber tyre bumper bounced car after car, he chuckled, spinning the wheel.

'Look, Sandy!'

'What's that?'

'It's Nick!'

She hadn't noticed, she must have been out of it, letting herself be chauffeured by Davey. But there were Nick and Barney, in a car at the other end of the floor. She'd faint, she felt completely weak.

'Stop, Davey. I don't want him to see.' They must get away quick, drive out of the fair in the dodgem car.

Davey wouldn't stop: she was carried at Nick. She saw only him, there was no one else. He was thinner but he still had his grin. He was demon-driving like Davey, while Barney, who'd got fatter, overflowed the car.

'No, Davey! Stop!'

They hit Nick and Barney hard amidships. Their heads bobbed, they looked round amazed.

'Hello Nick!' Davey chimed with laughter.

'Wotcher mate!' Nick's sharp wide smile came at once, then disappeared. As she watched, his face went white.

216

'Hello, Sandy.'

'Hello, Nick.'

They stared at each other. She didn't know what she felt, it was the dead stop of everything. The cars behind impacted on them, there was a pile-up.

Nick and Davey spun their wheels and veered clear. All the cars swept on again, battering, in a whirlpool. Nick looked round lost. He set to driving, furious, funny. Davey raced after him, chortling and trying to crash him. It was a play-race, cars bashed like murder, each crash was laughter, no one was hurt. Sandy was dizzy, then she started laughing. They were all caught up in it. Barney was falling half out of his car, combing his quiff. Now Barney worked the pedal and Nick sat on the back, steering with his feet. He got up to standing, holding on to the pole. He hung out to one side then to the other, a swinging gorilla. Davey crashed them again. Sandy shrieked, Nick gasped, for a second he was in the air, then he was on their car, he'd caught their pole and clung to it, standing over them.

'Come back, Nick, I can't drive.' Barney was going round in circles. Nick had climbed up their pole like a monkey. Davey screamed laughing, Sandy was screaming, Barney was shouting, 'Nick, you're up the pole! Come down, man, there's nothing up there.'

The flashing ceased, the cars all stopped. Nick climbed down. They left the floor panting, other people shoved in.

Barney teased Davey. Nick and Sandy didn't speak: they tagged after, apart, like confused kids. Sandy glanced shyly, Nick's face was unhappy.

They came to the hammer, where Barney took off his big jacket, with a shouting check pattern, and folded it solemnly and gave it to Nick. He spat on his hands, worked his shoulders, then took the mallet, wagged his bottom, and with a great swing whirled it high in the air.

217

With a samurai shriek he swung it hard on the knob: and the indicator rose a few feet only. He was shattered. With a grieving face he took his jacket, and slowly put it on.

Then Nick came: the driver. Davey took Sandy's hand.

Nick swung the mallet. On the second go he hit the bell.

'Well done, Nick,' Sandy said without thinking.

Nick came up to them like any pleased father of a family.

'That was good, Nick,' Davey said. 'That was a very good hit.'

'Thank you, squire.'

He took Davey's other hand, so they made a threesome. Davey took charge, pulling them forward. Then he ran on ahead, so they followed as a couple. Nick looked at her tensely. She wanted to touch him, but there was an electric fence between them.

Davey led them to the rotor and for a time they were plastered to the wall, tipped and spinning round fast in the sky.

'And the helter skelter!'

Afterwards he was tired, he had to lean on someone. His head seemed ready to roll off his shoulders.

'Davey!' Sandy said. 'Isn't it time you were home? Oh dear, I've done it again. Come on, Davey, we must run.'

'I'm not going home.' Davey's eyes closed as he mumbled. Barney propped him up.

'I'll take him,' he said.

'Oh no I must.'

Barney insisted. Sandy looked at Nick: she saw that they both wanted Barney to take Davey.

'All right, mate, ta,' Nick said.

'Come along young Dave.' Fat Barney was now like a comic uncle. Davey yawned his goodbyes. He was dropping, happily. Barney walked him off, supporting him.

218

She looked at Nick. He was keen, thin, all straight lines, a tall shrewd handsome man: she felt that over the many months she had forgotten what he looked like. She remembered his eyes as sharp and slitty, cunning eyes, bad eyes: but tonight they were like anyone's eyes, human and pleased to see her.

He asked gently, 'How are you, mate?'

'I'm tired too.' Sandy started yawning. The yawn once started opened wide, till she felt she could swallow herself. It was a sweet tiredness. She couldn't find her rage with Nick, she was too tired to search for it.

'You're looking good. That's London, I suppose.'

'You too. You've lost weight, it suits you.'

As they walked they leaned together. When the row of booths ended they walked on into the black.

'Come round mine, lover.'

She looked back at the bright-lit, swarming crowd.

'I've got to work tomorrow.'

'It's OK, I'll take you down the station first thing.'

It was strange hearing him close to her, he was like Nick, and like a different person.

'All right.' She stood closer into him.

TWENTY-NINE

'You know, we may get together again.'

'What? Have you seen Nick?'

'I took Davey to the fair, and Nick was there.'

'Yeah? Oh. You went to bed with him.'

'Yeah. Why not?'

Pearl was silent.

'What's wrong with it, Pearl? You screw when you want.'

'Sorry, Sandy. No, that's nice.' But still Pearl looked as though she'd cry in her tea.

'I don't know if we could get together again.'

'You used to say he was death.'

'I hated him, Pearl.'

Pearl looked at her. Sandy was thoughtful. She could feel her mouth wanting to smile.

'You know, Sandy, I don't think you should have.'

'Well, that's my business, isn't it?'

'Yeah, but you gave him what he wanted.'

'Yes, well, it was what I wanted.'

'Please yourself.'

For days Nick was close to her. If she closed her eyes she saw him. When she lay down she felt he was all round her, warm, with his smell of man, taller than her in the bed. At will she could feel his breath on her nipples.

At the office she thought of him, she remembered him in his sports car when he first came beside her, as she walked the pavement hurriedly, late for work. He was as low down as if he sat in the gutter; encased in shining unpainted metal, revving his engine so it made deep throbs that shook the air.

'Can I give you a ride?' His glint of eyes, his sharp grin of teeth.

'No thank you very much.'

She walked on oblivious; but the low machine hovered, quietly thundering, behind her. He would not go without more from her.

She wondered, would he ring today? How would they get in touch?

He didn't ring. The night with him receded, like a holiday or something not real.

'Has he rung?'

'No.'

'I'm afraid he won't.'

'Don't say that, Pearl. That's not very nice.'

'But it's true, Sandy. What can I say? You let him use you.'

'Shut your sodding hole.'

She left Pearl's room but Pearl's words stuck. Her anger with Nick began to come back.

'You know, Pearl, maybe I'll ring him.'

'I can see that. You're off your chump.'

Sandy left it a day then she rang Nick's lodgings. She rang several times but he was always out.

He didn't ring, she couldn't trace him. Her old rage was back, she remembered his face the moment before he hit her. His mouth went down at the corners, his eyes had white all round the blue.

Each time the phone rang she shook like a leaf.

'Are you all right, Nick?' Her eyes didn't blink.

'Yeah, never better. What are you getting at?'

'Well, you haven't said a thing, you just sit there eating.'

221

'Yeah. I'm whacked. Sorry.'

It sounded lame, his skin was hot. He felt her nose and small chin point at him, like a gun-turret swung at a black bit of jungle. He would be made to tell her about Sandy.

She resumed eating. He drank.

They made love but she said afterwards, 'Where were you, Nick?'

'What do you mean, where was I?'

'Well, you weren't with me.'

'I'm with you, baby.' He made his voice and his arms hold her nicely, but sleep didn't come.

The next evening he said casually, 'I saw Sandy the other day.'

'Oh, where?'

'She was at the fair.'

He made it sound as though Barney and Davey were with them all the time.

They watched the telly. From the corner of his eye he saw her sitting stiffly.

She stayed silent, he could see she had worked everything out. He wanted to say, 'Why not, she's my wife!' but Teresa wouldn't speak.

He went out to have a drink. In the pub he was depressed and came back early. Teresa had gone to bed. He took another beer and sat in front of the telly. Finally he went to bed. Teresa was pretending to be asleep. When he touched her, she stiffened; he lay awake.

He wanted to have things out, but she wouldn't let him. He thought, you're bloody, Teresa! He thought, all this, just for one night with Sandy.

Whenever he was round Teresa's he seemed to see her side-on, at the sink or at the cooker, or with a basket of washing, her hair at the back tied tight, her mouth tight. The only time she spoke was to ask him to do something she couldn't do.

222

They were eating.

'Why don't you go back to your wife, Nick?'

'Perhaps I will.'

She pushed her plate away. 'Go then, I'm not stopping you.'

He got up. 'Christ! Bloody fuck! All this just for one night!'

'It was a night, was it?'

'Of course it bloody was. What do you expect, she's my wife, isn't she? My Christ!'

'That's it, Nick, shout at me, swear at me. It's a good reason for doing it, isn't it?'

'Yes Teresa, and you know it. You know how to make people mad.'

So: they were having the row. She was clever and mean, he felt clumsy roaring back. Still he was relieved, it was time they quarrelled.

She got more harsh: he came at her, his arm up. She flinched and looked murder. Later she collapsed weeping, all he could see was her white neck and the tight red bun with stray hairs waving.

She sat up. Her face was blotched red, her eyes were red, her nose was red. Still crying she slanged him. He sagged with shame. Later they made love. Afterwards she said nothing about Sandy.

Things went back to how they had been. His night with Sandy was somehow spoiled, a net had pulled across it. He thought, that night was a chance, I shouldn't let it go.

He had to drive north. Stopped in a lay-by he shut his eyes. Here the night with Sandy was clear. He could hear her bubbling laugh he liked. He could count her big freckles. She slightly shrank her shoulders when he came on top of her. He couldn't drive on. Hands in pockets, hunched himself, he sat in the cab with eyes shut thinking of Sandy. He remembered being in the cottage without her. He remembered being with her, painting the walls, with paint on both of them like confetti.

When I get down south, I'll ring her. I'll go round Sandy's before I go to Teresa. I can say I was delayed.

When he got back to the depot he was tired from driving. He went home to Teresa's. He had bad nights, he was tired but lay awake. He remembered his sweet-peas in the cottage garden: Sandy stood them in a jug in the bedroom. In the mornings they smelt them as they lay in bed loving.

Other times he thought: Sandy, ditching me, ditching Davey. His anger was still there, just under his skin.

Teresa talked of visiting her parents. Nick thought, I'll ring Sandy then. In the meantime he spent more time out at Lloyd's. The car needed more work and he must get himself in shape too.

Nick visited his mother.

'Ooh!' she said, looking up from the kitchen table. 'You did give me a fright!' She pulled a bottle of stout from her lap. 'I thought it was the vicar.'

'What vicar?'

'The Reverend Baker. He's on my track, Nicholas.'

She poured stout into a big mug with hearts on it, and passed it to Nick. With a graceful movement she lifted her own. 'Your very good health, Nicholas.'

'Down the hatch, mate.'

'Are you in good work now?'

'Sure. HGV.'

'HGV. And your grandfather had a newsagent's!'

'Yeah I know. If he'd left it to me, I'd be a tycoon, but as it is I'm on the lorries. Still, better than the buses, eh?'

'Better than being a farm labourer. I died of shame, Nicholas.'

'That's a pity, then, because they were the happiest

224

days of my life, I reckon. Still there's one good thing.'

'What's that?'

'The car goes all right.'

'What car? You sold your car.'

'Got a racer now, mate. You'll see me at Brands before you know it. That'll be all right.'

She didn't understand or didn't want to understand.

'It's not all right.'

'What's not all right?'

'Your life, Nicholas.'

'What's wrong with my life? I enjoy it.'

'Don't be so bloody ridiculous. You don't enjoy it.'

'Excuse me, I didn't know.'

He turned sideways to the table and stretched his legs out long.

'You know what I mean. At your age you should be settled. You should have a good job and be married with a kiddy.'

'Well, I was, wasn't I?'

'Anyway it's time you got back on the rails. You've got this girlfriend, I think?'

'Yeah, Teresa.'

'Do you live with her or what?'

'I'm round there some of the time.'

He looked in his stout. His mother waited. He looked up with a serious face.

'I saw Sandy the other night.'

'I know you did.'

'How do you know?'

'Harry said.'

'Harry!'

His mother watched him.

'Do you think you'll get together again?'

He met her eye. He heaved himself to sitting upright. He gazed through the oilcloth on the kitchen table.

225

'I don't know. I don't know that I see it.'

His mother said hesitantly, 'It would be good for David if you got back together.'

'It would.'

'Is she changed, do you think?'

'Maybe she is.'

She slowly turned her mug of stout. Her lips closed and opened with a smacking sound.

'I wonder what she wants.'

'What do you mean?'

'I mean, what is the woman after? Does she want to get back with you? Does she want Davey for herself? When she wanted to be shot of him, she left and she didn't give a tinker's cuss.'

'So?'

'All I'm saying is, go easy, Nicholas. Be careful she's not just using you, to make you sweet so she gets Davey. I have to say it, she's a selfish woman. You won't be soft with her, will you?'

'I don't know that I'll be anything with her.'

They were silent. The room had got small and hot like an oven.

'How does she live now?'

'She's got a job. She talked about taking some course – Business Studies, I don't know, it was beyond me.'

'Did she ask for anything from you?'

'No.'

His mother sat at the end of the table with her arms folded and her shoulders square, the mug and plate and the bottle in front of her. Her face was solemn. Behind her, like a dusk, was the question of his life: with Sandy, and Davey too; without Sandy, and Davey elsewhere. He wanted light to see his way.

His mother said, 'Be careful, Nicholas.'

He nodded sadly. 'I'll be careful.'

226

THIRTY

Day passed day, still nothing came from Nick. The night after the fair had not gone away, it stayed beside her close like the Invisible Man. It brought back other times when they made love. They had their clothes off in the rape field, the rape was slightly scratchy, itchy, Nick was over her big like King Kong against the stars.

'Nick, wait a bit,' she said.

He did, he loved her nicely then. All round his black head the stars were bright as bike-lights.

She thought, he hasn't rung, he won't ring, he tricked me. She remembered him in the cottage, hulking awkward in a rage. She remembered him sulking like a babe; and being a weasel, sniggering with Davey. She remembered him making dinner and setting it nicely, he did try to pull his socks up. She thought of him driving; however fast he demon-drove, she always knew she was safe.

Her thoughts scattered all ways, all about Nick. She said to herself the words, husband, wife. I married Nick, we haven't divorced.

She'd stopped speaking to Pearl, Pearl didn't understand. On her own in London she was in a haze or smoke of marriage.

She saw Nick at the party, jigging his thighs at the cow. He was always screwing other women. That didn't hurt in the same way, now she'd had other men; nor could she love him, his cheating killed that. Better he didn't ring, better she stayed clear.

At night her dreams broke different ways. In the day she banged between different futures. She'd think of her and Nick together, just like the first days but in a bigger house. Quickly she felt cramped, I don't love him any more. If she thought of them divorced and nothing left between them, she'd remember their first year: the nice times tugged so painfully she wanted to cry.

Her next time with Davey came. In the train on the way to see him everything cleared. Davey was the answer. If she and Nick came together, it would be through Davey. Through Davey everything wrong could come right. She almost skipped through the town: it was possible for things to come good.

'Hello, Harry!'

He looked like a graveyard but her good mood couldn't falter.

'Come in, Sandy.'

The hall darkened as the front door closed. They entered the chilly front room.

'How are you, Harry? Got a stomach bug? I'm sorry, I'm in a silly state.'

'Do you realize what time David came back?'

'It was the fair, he was having a good time. So he was late. It's OK, Harry, really.'

'He was more than three hours late.'

'It wasn't three hours. But I am sorry. We were at the fair, he liked it.'

'You know what this does to Grace. We worry.'

'I know that, Harry. But you don't have to worry when Davey's with me. I am his mum.'

'His mother. Yes. Do you really think the way you behave is how a mother behaves?'

'Well, I'm more of a mother than you are, Harry, whatever you think.'

Harry said nothing. She thought, God, I've shut him up. Somehow his gloominess made her happier.

'Sandy, I have to say it. It wasn't his mother who brought David home to us.'

'So it was Barney. Barney's all right.'

'Evidently you don't know what Grace and I think of Barnabas.'

'Did you say Barnabas? He's wonderful, Barney. He's ever so funny.' Smiles bloomed, Harry's gloom was comic: it had no place in a happy world.

'He may be funny, Sandy. But we don't think he's a fit person to trust a child to at night. Do you know what noises he was making in the street?'

'No I don't, I wasn't in the street.'

'No, you were at the fair. That's what we can't get over, Sandy. You preferred to stick there, and let some other person see your child home. We don't see how a mother could do that. And the state he was in. He was exhausted. That child had been dragged around long after his bedtime. He was almost ill.'

'Was he ill?'

'No.'

'Well then.'

'That doesn't alter anything. You said you would bring him home, and you didn't.'

'Harry, I was with Nick!'

'I know what you were doing. You got someone else to bring David home, tired as he was, all so that you and Nick could –' He started speaking and stopped himself several times. 'Bang away.'

'Harry, what do you mean? We're married. It's our business what we do.'

'Married? Do you call that marriage? And is that what Grace and I are? The babysitters? Are we just minders, to look after David while you and Nick frig about?'

'But if Nick and I got together again –' She stopped. Harry's fingers moved, he was breathing in and getting taller. She saw she had said the wrong thing. They were terrified they would lose Davey. They hated her for coming back, they wanted her gone, dead, anything.

Harry was saying his words one by one. 'Sandy, I have to tell you we don't think it would be good for Nick if you and he got together again. He has someone else now.'

'What do you mean?'

'You know what I mean. He has another girl now. They get on very well. Grace and I think they're right for each other.'

'Another girl.'

She thought, Harry's saying this to annoy me, he's saying it to set me against Nick.

'Who is this good woman?'

'Teresa, of course.'

'Teresa? Who's Teresa?'

'Oh, don't you know?' He couldn't stop himself grinning. 'They've been together now a while.'

'You're a bastard, Harry.' His spite worked, his words grew like a thorn bush inside her. She knew it was true. Of course old Nick had another woman, what else would he be doing? At the fair he was cheating, he was cheating the other woman and he was cheating her: that was Nick, he cheated. She had been these days in a stupid dream. She must go where she could shout.

She took in breath as if she were about to dive.

'All right, Harry. Will you let me take Davey and go.'

Harry made no move. He stared directly at her.

'Would you get him please, Harry. This is one of my days.'

Harry moved his weight from one leg to the other.

'No.'

'I'm taking him, Harry.'

'No you're not. You don't look after him. And you haven't kept your word. You're hours late every time, then you send him back with someone else. In a terrible state. Nothing's changed, you're as selfish as you used to be. You neglected him then, you're just the same now.'

'I don't believe this, Harry. We've arranged —'

'Yes, we had an arrangement, and you've broken it every way you could.'

'Harry, I want to see Davey. He's my son. Get him. I mean it.'

'No way.'

Harry's face was so red it looked black.

'I'll go and see Nick. Nick will make you give him to me. He has to do that.'

'Go and see Nick.'

'I will.'

'Do that. Go round Teresa's and see him.'

'What?'

'He's round Teresa's. Go and see him. See what you find.'

'Oh!'

He shouted the address after her as she walked quickly out of the house.

THIRTY-ONE

Sandy knocked and waited.

The door opened. The woman had a high forehead like a Martian.

'Is Nick here?'

'No, he's out.'

'I want to see him.'

'Do you?'

The woman had padded shoulders, high and pointed. Her head looked as if it were on a stick.

'Are you Sandy?'

'Yes, of course. You're Teresa.'

'Yes.'

The woman's voice was a clear bell.

'You'd better come in.'

She walked down the hall, leaving it to Sandy to follow if she wanted.

In the kitchen Teresa scraped a chair round, its legs screeched on the tiles.

Sandy sat, Teresa went back to work. She was doing things with shoe-boxes. She worked in a quick jagged way that told Sandy not to look at her.

The kitchen was full of old things: a sugar-pot shaped like a cottage, a tea-cosy like a broody hen. There were posters on the wall of little maids in pinafores.

Teresa looked round with her staring blue eyes.

'Would you like a cup of tea?'

'Thank you.'

Sandy watched her make the tea. Does he kiss her

down there, does he lick her? There was a mirror on the window-sill, she saw herself looking back, hunched down, beady, mad and looking murder: Christ, I look like the criminally insane.

Teresa brought the tea. They drank without speaking.

They sat over the cups.

'What do you do with all these shoes?'

'I've got a stall. I sell afghan stuff.'

'Yes?'

'Yes, but I'm moving into espadrilles.'

'Maybe that's right.'

Poor Davey, if he ends up with this scrawn for a mum. She'll give him nothing.

No, Teresa won't want Davey. If Nick stays here, he'll leave Davey where he is.

Perhaps she smiled. Teresa got up quickly.

'I've got to do something, do you mind?'

Sandy heard her moving things in different parts of the house.

Teresa came back.

'I must say you've got a nerve, coming here like this.'

'He's my husband, isn't he? If this is the place he dosses then I have to come here to see him.'

'You don't have to see him in my house.'

'I don't care where I see him. But I'm not going now till he comes.'

Teresa had her sleeves rolled up, her hands on her hips. Sandy sat with her fists on the table, clenched.

Teresa went to the sink and started washing up plates and cups very quickly.

Nick came.

'Hi there!'

He walked down the dark hall like someone at home.

Teresa called in a cut-glass voice, 'Nick, there's someone to see you.'

233

'Sandy!' He was at a loss. He blushed. He looked young, a kid in a fix. 'What are you doing here?'

'I've got to talk.'

His face was open and unhappy. She thought, he looks like Davey.

Teresa, arms folded, watched them. She said, 'I'll be upstairs.'

She left with sharp steps, she went up the staircase like a pony on tin.

'Let's go in the front room.'

By the fire there was a brass coal-scuttle and a green china cat with blue boils. There was a standard lamp like an old fashioned lamp-post, and posters of Ronald Colman on the wall. Everything was old but somehow smart. It was all more solid than she had expected, a home.

'Why did you come here, Sandy?'

Nick stood near the fireplace, it was his home not hers.

'Where the hell can I find you, Nick? They said you were here.'

He waited. He looked unhappy and serious, he reminded her of Harry.

She said, 'I'm very unhappy. We have to talk.'

He thought, she wants us to get together. He looked at her hurt face. He remembered the fair.

'Sandy.'

He was confused and full of love.

'What is it, Sandy?'

'I'll tell you. I went round Harry's today, to get Davey. It's my turn to take him out. And Harry wouldn't let me.'

'You came about Davey?'

'Of course about Davey, I wouldn't come here otherwise. You know, Nick, you could have told me that you were fixed up. That wasn't very nice, what you did at the fair. You haven't changed. Still, that's not my business. Right now I need your help. I want to see Davey.'

234

She thought, what's up with him, he looks as if someone sat on his face.

Nick said, 'Harry'll let you see him.'

'He didn't. And I hate Harry. He's such a bloody stick. When I think my Davey's with him I can't bear it.'

He looked gloomy and in pain, and not sure what to say.

'Yeah, well, you did it.'

'What's that mean?'

'I mean you walked out and you didn't care who had him.'

'You can bring that up if you want to, Nick. I know I ran away. I left him. But for a long time now all I've wanted is to see Davey.'

He made a face, depressed, sarcastic.

'I want to see him more than you do, Nick. I come every time I can. I come bloody miles. You go sometimes, other times you don't go. It makes you feel good, to think I don't care. But you don't care like I do, now.'

He was thinking, why row? A row won't help. But what else to say? He hurt as if a wrestling match were occurring inside him, two fat giants were stamping on each other.

'The fact is, you left him.'

'You left him too. You dumped him with your mum. Then you dumped him with Harry. You're just as bad, so don't talk about me.'

With sadness, with relief, he let go, the words came. 'Oh I'll talk, Sandy. I've got things to say to you. Because I've tried with Davey. I've looked after him all I could. And my mum's tried, she had him a long time. But you didn't think of him for months and years. You ditched him and ran and didn't give a fuck if he was alive or dead. So don't come to me now playing the mum. "I want my baby." You're no mum. You shouldn't have had a kid, the sort of woman you are. There's something wrong with

235

you. All this about Davey, how you have to see him now. Why can't you leave him be? He's happy as he is. It messes him up when you come round. You walked out, so stay out. Let him alone. Don't tell me all how you care.'

He felt strong, he was telling her like God.

'Nick, please –'

He thought she'd say a lot. He waited.

She shook her head. He wondered if she'd go down.

'You walked out on him, Sandy. And you walked out on me, we don't talk about that. Don't come here asking for favours.'

He'd spoken, he felt complete.

She was making such eyes at him, almost frightening.

She said, 'Nick, I won't argue now. There's things I could say except I can't bloody bother, you're not worth it. There's one thing I care about and that's it. I want to see Davey.'

'Yeah, well you won't see him.'

'All right, Nick. You'll see what I'll do.'

'What'll you do?'

'You'll see.'

Things got less certain. He had the funny sense that Barney was in the room. 'You're taking the wrong turning, Nick.'

They looked at each other. They were both in trouble.

Teresa called, 'Nick, have you finished?'

Sandy said, going, 'He's finished.'

Nick said, 'That's right. That's it.'

In the street Sandy turned and gave him a look.

He gave back as good.

Teresa came downstairs.

'I told her.' He put the kettle on with decision.

He was in a bad mood, they bickered all evening.

236

THIRTY-TWO

Sandy tried once more to see Davey. She wrote to say she was coming, there was no reply.

It was a low-cloud day, the panes in the windows were black. Her mind filled with accidents.

No one came to the door, no curtain moved.

She looked through the letter-box, she could see a milk-bottle on the kitchen table.

There was no sound from the house.

She waited on the step while the daylight failed.

THIRTY-THREE

As soon as Nick saw the letter, he knew it came from Sandy's lawyer. It was very short, it frightened him.

He sat going whoo! and waving a hand to disturb the air. She can't come out of the past and take Davey. He held the letter up and shook the paper so it rattled. The cow, going to law. Where'd she get the money?

He looked in the mirror, his face was hot and working like a close-up on the telly. Let her go to court, let people see her, the woman who wasn't a mother.

But to go to law with Sandy – they were man and wife, whatever happened. The letter was a bluff, she couldn't want the courts.

He went to Harry and Grace. They had had a letter.

'What do you make of it?'

Harry's face was red like Davey crying. Dear old Harry, Nick thought and shrugged.

'It's wicked, wicked.'

Grace said, 'She's bad at heart.'

'She can't get him, though. Can she, Harry, after what she's done?'

Harry shook his head. Grace reached out her arm and held his wrist hard.

Nick watched them, worrying.

At home he read the letter again. It frightened him more. Courts, the law, lawyers, they were foreign, strong, heartless. It would all go on for months or years. Some-

238

thing had arrived which would not go away. It was something iron, treading steadily in his direction. He couldn't run, all he could do was watch it come.

He took advice from his boss and went to a solicitor.

He was kept in a waiting-room. A girl in a white shirt with a white bow-tie came and asked his name.

They went to an office and the girl sat behind the desk. He blinked: was she the solicitor? She had a pale face and pale eyes and pale fair hair. She seemed white everywhere, she was whiter than he liked.

He thought, 'Oh God, she won't scare anyone.' Still he smiled, she was young and cool.

She didn't smile back. She was like a white grasshopper. She asked questions quietly that were sometimes hard to answer. Now and then she made a note.

He got red and hot, remembering the party, and Sandy with Brian. She jotted her notes and didn't seem surprised.

He wondered, whose side are you on? What am I doing with a woman lawyer? She'll take Sandy's part.

He said how Sandy left and never asked about Davey. The solicitor's eyes moistened.

He said something, she laughed. Her face went slightly pink, her pale eyes brightened. He thought, it's a good thing to have a woman lawyer. It takes a woman to catch a woman.

They came to the nub.

'Where's Davey to live?'

'Well, he's with Harry and Grace.'

'Yes, you've said. But is it just for now, or are they foster parents or what?'

'Well I suppose you'd say they're foster parents. I suppose that's the word for it.'

She'd stopped making notes, she looked at her white hands which lay on the desk-top.

'You're not divorced?'

'Well, I don't know what you call it. She ran off and I never heard a word after.'

She put one of her hands on top of the other.

'Can she give Davey a home?'

'I don't see how.'

'Can you look after Davey? Can he live with you?'

'How can he? I work all day.'

'Do you plan to re-marry?'

'No chance. I'll never try that one again.'

'Do you live with someone?'

'In a manner of speaking, yeah.'

'Does she want to look after Davey?'

'I can't see it.'

She looked at him some moments seriously.

'We must say something better than this. Do you understand?'

He nodded.

'Right.' She put the papers together and started to explain.

'I'm not with you. Do you mean she'll get Davey?'

'I'm not saying that yet.' Her face got kinder.

His blood hurried.

Her little voice said, 'It may happen.'

'It isn't right.'

She tilted her head. 'You'll write down everything for me. All the details, everything.'

He scarcely heard.

'When will you let me have it?'

'Oh in a week or two. I'm up to my eyes.'

She gave a small smile. 'The sooner the better.'

At home he got a biro and a sheet of paper. He sat and looked at them. How could he write? It wasn't his thing.

He got up, then sat on a different chair. Sandy and me in court, that's stupid. What I should do is go and see her.

For a time it was clear: he'd visit Sandy in London. They'd talk until they worked it out.

He read again her lawyer's letter, and the idea of seeing her thinned like smoke. This was something harder, harsher.

He returned to his sheet of paper. Again he stared at it, helpless. He remembered something Sandy said, how she couldn't love Davey, and Davey didn't like her. He wrote it down.

Once he started, it was easy. Sandy had told him how she ran into the rape-field, leaving Davey who was crying, having a fit, he could have suffocated. Another time Davey split his head on the cooker, when she punched him flying.

As he wrote his anger grew, he hated her steadily more. Let it come to court, he knew what to say.

He read over what he'd written. 'Oh it's coming to you, Sandy,' he murmured, impatient.

THIRTY-FOUR

Nick saw his lawyer again. As she read his notes, her eyelids flickered.

He was leaving her office.

'We'll do what we can.' She looked solemn as a doctor.

'Do what we can.' He said the words over all evening. Did she mean Sandy might still get Davey? He shut his eyes and shook in his chair.

'It won't happen. Davey must live with me!'

They would live together, he and his son. He'd take him to school, sometimes they'd go in a lorry. In the weekends, when the car was ready, they'd go to the races together.

He must work all day, there was no way Davey could live with him.

He wondered, what if I marry Teresa? If she stayed home, she could look after Davey. But that wouldn't happen. And how could they marry, up and down as they were?

Still it was a thought, to marry Teresa. Holding the idea was like touching a live cable: it gave him big jolts, he couldn't let go of it. He went round to her house with Davey.

'Hello, Davey! I've got something for you.' Her voice was bright and direct.

He looked at the box, there was a crimson car on the side.

'Well, do you like it? I thought you liked cars.'

Davey turned the box over. He didn't put it down but he didn't open it.

Teresa went to get tea.

'Christ, Davey, what's the matter with you! That was really nice, what Teresa got.'

Davey stood with his hands in his dungaree pockets.

'Nick.'

'Yes, mate.'

'Is Teresa your girlfriend?'

'You know she is.'

'I have a girlfriend.'

'You never. Good for you, old mate. Who's that, then?'

'It's Sandy!' He ran across the room and buried his face in one of Teresa's giant cushions. He looked shyly out of the cushion at Nick.

Nick whistled. 'Good for you, mate.'

Teresa came back with the tea.

'Here you are, Davey.'

He was busy pulling crayons from a little satchel.

'Say thank you, Davey.'

He squatted on the floor drawing and wouldn't lift his head.

'Here's your tea, Nick.'

'Thanks, love.'

Davey drew busily. Teresa went and looked.

'Oh that's very nice.' Bright colours jagged.

She came back and sat. None of them spoke.

Davey took his other toys out. They were all cars and space-robots. Soon they were fighting while Davey made their noises. The robots shot the cars and each other, the cars ran over the robots.

'Zash! Gopp!'

There was a big collision, a robot shot across the room and hit the wall.

'Davey, you bloody behave!'

Davey went to the robot and crouched down nursing it. He caught Teresa's eye. He caught Nick's eye. He stared up at them green-eyed like a squatting monkey.

'I don't like this, Nick. What's he up to?'

As they watched, there was a new explosion. Metal objects flew all ways.

'My Christ!' Nick was up and over him.

'It's all right, Nick.' Teresa calmed him; her face looked a headache.

'You're coming with me, mate.'

He took Davey home and came back to Teresa's.

'Well, I tried, Nick, you can't say I didn't.'

'Yeah. Thanks, lover. It needs a bit of time, I guess.'

'It needs more time than I've got. He's a difficult child, Nick.'

'He's good at heart. He's been knocked around.'

She sat looking strained, all points. He sat on her sofa, sinking deeper in a silence like lead. Teresa, Davey – his different hopes were at odds and desperate.

He told his lawyer Teresa was no go.

'Oh, that's a pity.'

Looking down she shook her head.

She looked up. 'Still, never say die. There's your wife, after all. Can she give Davey a home? She doesn't sound your average good mother.'

For a few weeks anyway they were safe, Davey was with Harry and Grace and Nick could see him whenever he wanted. But slowly they were sliding towards the horizon, there Sandy waited with her lawyer.

THIRTY-FIVE

Barney rearranged his posture. His hams stuck back behind the stool, his chin dug deep in his folded arms, he pushed his lips forward as if he'd kiss the pint glass in front of him.

'Man, it looks murky.'

'Thanks, mate. God, that puts heart in me.'

Barney came up. 'I suppose you don't think you'll get together again? No, excuse me, squire, no chance, out of order, definitely not, phew, God, I am the arsehole, the original one, beware of imitations for I am it.' With his open hand he struck his forehead so he reeled back, lost balance, and flung his limbs for support and couldn't find it. He clutched at the bar and clung like a drowning man. 'God, I thought I was a goner there. Give us a drink, mate, I need it badly.' He grabbed his glass and drained it, sat upright a moment, then fell forward on the counter his arms spread-eagled like a fallen crucifixion. His head arrived on the wood with a sound like a big piece of cork on hardboard.

Nick waited till he settled.

'Sandy and me? That's a big joke now, mate. She's hard like you don't know. She's changed.'

'You can't judge her by her lawyer, man.'

'Oh no, that's Sandy, she knows what she wants.'

Barney rocked on his stool and slowly pivoted round, till he sat with his elbows on the counter behind him.

'Still, Nicholas, I'm wondering – don't say yes if you'd rather not – would you like me to talk to her?'

245

'You can spare your breath, mate. There's no point.'

'True man, true. Fair enough. Course, the way it's look-ing, she could get the kid. There's a chance, right?'

'She's not getting him. No way.'

'Right! Sure. Enough said. But like I was saying, if you wanted me to speak to her, I would.'

'What would you say?'

'No idea! Inspiration of the moment, man. See if there's an opening.'

Nick was silent.

He said in a low voice, 'Yeah all right, mate. I'd be grateful.'

Sandy was surprised to see Barney, in an enormous sooty fur-collared coat. He had a kind of fur fez on his head.

'Barney!'

'Hello Sandy.'

This was a grave Barney, deep-voiced as a funeral. His large white chops were clean-shaven and shining, his blue eyes were honest and kind.

'What do you want, Barney?'

He doffed his hat, which was like a fluffy flowerpot. 'And good afternoon to you, madam. Can I interest you in a micro mini vacuum computer? Pardon me while I get my foot in the door.'

'Come in, Barney.'

He took off his coat of black hair and black fur, that made him look like a Russian. He was wearing a suit, light grey with grey pinstripes. It was a wide airy suit but still strained in places like a stretched balloon. She thought, he's a great big man, that Barney.

'I haven't seen you in a suit, Barney.'

He smoothed his skirts, the suit was smart.

'No you wouldn't have. I'm a man of the world now, you know.'

They chatted till she asked, 'Did Nick send you?'

'No, mum.'

He continued in his jokey way. A good past mood came back.

He said, 'It's a pity, isn't it?'

'What's a pity?'

'You and Nick.'

'What do you mean?'

'You know, man.'

'Say it, Barney.'

'I mean, look what you're doing to Davey.'

She didn't speak.

'There's no other way, right?'

She looked at her knees. He hadn't seen her for a long time. Her face was serious and thin, her red-brown hair looked good. Perhaps it was make-up, her freckles didn't show so much. She looked older. He thought, she's elegant.

'You may get together again.'

'Get together? We'll get divorced.'

'Big D, eh?'

'What else?'

'Search me, man.'

'It's nice that you came, Barney. I don't mind if Nick sent you. It's really good to see you. But Nick and me — that's over. You should see what they say about me, him and his lawyer.'

'You got on once.'

'That was a hundred years ago.'

'You with someone else?'

'That's my business, isn't it?'

'Sure. Sure. Sorry.'

'But I'm not with anyone else. I don't reckon to, either. There's only one person I want to live with, that's Davey.'

'You'll live on your own?'

'I'll live with Davey, Barney, like I said. That's all I want. That's all I can think of.'

'How will you manage?'

'I'll manage. I can give Davey a home. I'm switching to part-time, I'm down for a flat. I've changed all my plans from what they used to be.'

'You'll never make it. I'm sorry, Sandy. I mean, it'll be bloody difficult.'

'It'll be difficult. With benefits I can do it.'

'And you don't want a man around, not even as a pet or for decoration?'

'No way. I don't want a man. I don't want a husband. I want Davey, that's all. It's funny, Barney, isn't it? It seems that's how I am. But if I get Davey – oh God, that'll be my dream come true.'

Barney had made his cheeks droop long. He nodded up and down slowly and sent his brows into his hair. He heaved a big sigh then blew out so his lips blubbered.

'And there isn't a place for old Nick in the picture?'

'It's dead, Barney.'

'Yeah, but . . .'

'It's been dead a long time.'

Barney nodded ponderously a ten-ton head. 'It's bloody sad, isn't it?'

'I suppose.'

'Yeah.' He stood up. 'Yep.'

'Are you going?' She looked up at him big-eyed. He stood over her towering, an enormous man with a round kind face.

She got up.

He put on his big coat. His fleshy face was serious and handsome. She thought, old Barney's a better man than Nick.

He said, 'I'm sorry it's ended like this.'

A wave of strong sympathy came from him over her: a

big sorrow and kindliness. Everything went sad. She gave a sob, she was surprised, but the tears, once started, streamed. She moved within his arms, crying. His hands soothed her.

'There, love, there.'

Presently she raised her face.

'What happened, mate? Tell us, then.'

Barney didn't seem pleased, his face had a mottled look.

'What she say?'

'I'm an arsehole, Nick.'

'Yeah, well, OK, mate. What's new?'

'No, I mean, you know I said I'd see if there was hope, like you and her could get together and that.'

'Yeah, I remember.'

'I reckon I was wrong. I reckon it's not on.'

'Well, thanks a million. I could have told you that.'

'Yeah, I reckon it's over.'

'Christ, Barney, I heard the first time!'

Barney stared deeper into his drink.

'There's something else, Nick.'

'What's that, then?'

Barney's mouth fumbled.

'Come on, mate. Make my day.'

'We snogged.'

'What?'

'She fell into my arms. She was unhappy, Nick.'

Nick was talking to the bar.

'That's all it was. But I'll tell you something, Nick.'

His knee would go into Barney's stomach. As his big head dropped, he'd get the glass in it, a triangle of glass would be flapping in his cheek.

'Nick.'

Nick turned.

'That's OK, Barney. Good one. Thanks a bunch.'

249

THIRTY-SIX

Sandy stretched straight. Brown street-light came in. She couldn't sleep, they'd be in court tomorrow. She lay answering questions her lawyer had given her. What would her income be on part-time? Could she collect Davey every day? How would she describe their early married life? She was scared of Nick's lawyer, Nick always played dirty.

She tired of questions. She lay in the dark urging, let Davey come to me. If she didn't get him, her life would stop. How had she left him? How could she do it?

She thought of her mother, her real mum who left her. Where was she? Who was she? She could have tried to find her mother, but she decided not to.

She had avoided thinking about her mother. Now she tried to see her. She saw different women's clothes and a face a bit like her own that kept changing. 'Why did you leave me? How could you do that?' She wanted to catch hold of her mother and hurt her but the woman wasn't there. There was just a smoky dark-brown space within the changing clothes.

She grew quiet again. She lay on the bed like floating in water. Slowly she felt her mother, hovering underneath her like a shadow.

She prayed to God. Would things come right? Her wishes turned. She knew if she got Davey, she would find her mother too and her mother would get better. The bits of the circle would join up inside her. She would be complete, he was her baby.

Oh let Davey come to me. If he doesn't I'll die.

THIRTY-SEVEN

Under a stone sky and beside the wide road there was a building with pointed windows.

Feet echoed, and the odd loud voice, in the low-ceilinged passages. Knots of men and women talked to men and women in black.

The big room was divided in pews like a church. Nick sat with his solicitor. He wore the dark suit he wore to get married in.

Sandy came in with her solicitor. She saw Nick and turned away. She looked pale and frightened.

She sat down across the room from him, and she and her solicitor leant their heads together. While they talked, the solicitor's eyes located Nick. There was something mocking in her face.

Harry and Grace came with their solicitor, a middle-aged man who talked in a loud voice from outside the room. They sat down near the back, while their solicitor came and talked to Nick's. He looked gloomy but he clacked his loud voice, and stretched his arms freely as if the room were his theatre.

Nick looked at Sandy. He could tell she felt his eyes, but she wouldn't look back. She had her head up as though everyone looked at her, her watery eye gazed ahead.

He turned to Grace and Harry but they were looking down. Harry began whispering solemnly to Grace. She looked at him sweetly, she looked as if she'd cry. He took her hand and squeezed it.

Nick looked at the high desk at the end of the room, the chair backs were carved in a fancy way. He looked at the men who stood round near the doors. They were at home, they opened doors and shut them and told people where to go.

Time passed, the little groups waited quietly. Apart from them the room was empty.

Nick sat back. He shut his eyes tight and tighter. He stayed moments wishing. This was the judgement day, he needed help. God, let me get Davey.

They opened doors and shouted, everyone stood up.

Three serious people entered in a leisurely confident way. They made space for each other as they got to their chairs behind the high desk. They seated themselves comfortably and looked out on the court.

THIRTY-EIGHT

Harry closed the front door. Without taking their coats off they went into the living-room and sat in separate armchairs.

Harry said, 'We couldn't have kept him. They'd never have let us. If Sandy hadn't got him, Nick would have taken him sooner or later.'

Grace said with difficulty, 'She is an evil woman.'

'Evil?'

'She's not a mother, the way she behaves. She shouldn't be a mother.'

Harry went and sat on the side of Grace's chair. He put his arm round her while she grew smaller, her face shrank together.

As Grace lifted her head, she wailed: a growing cry that didn't stop. He held her.

Harry was sitting again in his chair. They saw they still had their coats on, sitting in the cold room.

Harry said, 'I'll put the heating on.'

They stayed in the two armchairs.

THIRTY-NINE

'I'll have Davey tonight. It is the last night.'

'It's our last night too,' Harry said.

'Please. He is my boy.'

With pain they consented. Nick drove Davey home and made a nice tea. After his bath Davey put on Nick's dressing-gown. They sat holding mugs of cocoa and watching the telly. Davey was white-faced and hardly spoke, he was being grown up.

He looked at his father through the steam of the cup.

'It's for the best, isn't it, Nick?'

'Do you reckon?'

'Oh, I think so.'

'Well, that's all right then.'

But Davey still looked at him, like a little old person who was very alert.

'Yeah, it's for the best, mate.'

'I'm glad.'

They watched the screen. There was a programme on about the start of the universe, how it all came from nothing in a moment: in a huge crash and all the forces were there. Nick nodded, he liked the scheme. Davey was staring as if he saw the big bomb.

Nick switched off the set.

'We'd better turn in in good time.'

'That sounds a good idea, Nick.'

When Davey stood up he said, drowned in dressing-gown, 'I'm all packed up, you know.'

'You've got everything, have you?'

'Oh yes, I thought it best to have the lot.'

'You'll make out.'

'I'll cope, Nick.' Like an old fat rich man in a film, he toddled off to bed.

Nick had bought him a Superhero comic, and sat beside him reading out the speech-balloons. Davey made the sound-effects. 'Wharg! Zoing! Goof!'

When they said good night Nick held him close. Davey clung tight. Afterwards Nick heard his firm voice reaching through the half-open door.

'Good night, then, Nick.'

'Good night, Davey. Sleep tight.'

'Oh I will, Nick, I'll make sure I do.'

Nick, on the sofa, hardly slept. He rolled in fever repeating, she won't get him, I know my way all over Europe.

Davey rubbed his eyes.

'What is it, Nick?'

'Get dressed, soldier. We're going.'

'I think it's very early, Nick.'

'Yeah that's right, an early start. Come on, mate.'

Davey was bewildered but he got up and dressed. They had cornflakes, then stepped out in the grey dawn light. The air was sharp, the street was empty.

'But Nick, will she be awake?'

'Who's that?'

'Sandy of course. Aren't we going to Sandy?'

'Sure we are. But I thought we'd go for a trip.'

Davey gazed at him, his mouth a bit open.

They loaded the car and got in.

'No Nick, let me.' He insisted on strapping the seat-belt himself.

Nick drove fast through the empty streets. There was a lost white face beside him, but when they started on

256

the motorway Davey soon fell asleep. Nick had the world of roads to himself. The sun was in his face.

The roads were clear through to Dover. On the quay Davey woke and they got out. They walked on the concrete while Nick explained about hovercraft.

'I don't think air could hold them up, Nick.'

'That's how they work, mate. They sit on an air-cushion.'

Davey was doubtful. But when a cloud of spray and steam appeared out at sea with a hovercraft inside it like a travelling castle, and entered the harbour with a swoosh of wind, slid smoothly from the water up the concrete ramp, and hung gigantic roaring in front of them and then like a big creature sighing breathed out and sank down on its blubbery sides: then Davey clung to Nick's hand in ecstasy, Nick had never seen him excited like this.

'Are we going on one of those? Oh, I have to go on one of those, Nick, I have to.'

'That's where we're going.'

'Oh Nick.'

'We'd better get tickets. Are you coming?'

They went and got tickets, then came out and sat in the car. There were rows of other cars already waiting.

'Let's go and look, Nick.'

'OK, mate.'

They went up close to the hovercraft, and inspected the thick rubber skirt and stared up at the giant engines. They walked back to the car.

'I know which one we're going on. It's that one.'

Nick shrugged.

Another hovercraft arrived beside the first, which loaded and departed in a sounding cloud.

'When are we going, Nick? Is Sandy coming with us? Will she meet us here?'

'Just wait, Davey.'

'No, it won't be long,' Davey said firmly. The other cars had left, they were by themselves.

Nick didn't answer. He walked back and forth. Davey squatted on the bumper, and buried his sight in the Superhero comic. He couldn't read the speech-balloons and made up his own words. He made shooting noises, hitting noises, flying noises.

The hovercraft left, another appeared. Its top had a big square snout and eyes as it approached in spray through the sea. It slid out of the spray as it mounted the shore.

'Is it this one, Nick? Is it? Is it?'

But Nick was looking back with a very funny face.

'Get in the car, Davey.'

'Oh but Nick.'

'Just get in.'

Crestfallen, bewildered, Davey got in. Nick revved the engine.

Davey said quietly, 'Nicks don't cry.'

Nick turned to him with a flowing face, then started. He drove fast out of the harbour and up the hill and back the way they had come. His mouth was open, his man's voice made loud sobs.

FORTY

They were in the park. He stood in the swing-seat and thrust his legs down so the swing hurled faster.

'Davey! Stop, love! Do slow down!'

He kicked again, the swing flew high. He would fall out and break his head. He came back so fast that if he hit her he'd kill her.

'Oh Davey love, stop please!'

He looked at her, laughing, as again he drove forward. He'd crash to the ground, he'd be shot through the sky.

The chains of the swing gave, they were stretching out longer. The rubber-tyre seat was flying clear away and Davey was hurtling like a stone from a sling. She wanted to scream but her voice stuck. She tried to run and catch him but her body froze. How would she find him? He was small in the sky.

Davey, Davey. She sat up in bed. He would be killed. Oh Davey. She was confused, not sure where in her life she was. Had she got Davey, had she not got Davey, everything was broken.

She lay getting breath, making herself calm. Her heart made a noise. She scanned the room. On the mantelpiece she saw a picture. In great big letters it said Captain Space, it was one of his Superheroes pounding the Supervillains. She looked at it smiling, the colours were like fireworks. He drew nothing else. She was happy looking at the shooting lines.

There were noises in the flat, clumpings, she heard him

talking to himself. Her door opened bang, she saw his head above the bed-frame. He'd brought her a tray with cakes and sweets.

'Breakfast time!'

'Davey, have you brought me breakfast in bed? Oh what a treat! Isn't that lovely!'

He put the tray on the bedside table. She looked up at him, he was very big over her.

'I'll feed you, Sandy.'

Before she knew it he had put a big piece of fruit-cake to her mouth. She took a small bite, crumbs scattered on her and the bed. Eating, she laughed, they both laughed. She lay back still and he fed her as though she were a child. She looked up at his big head, pleased with looking after her.

'Was it a nice breakfast?'

'It was lovely, Davey!'

He coiled shyly. He took the drawing and looked at it making fighting noises.

'Davey, that's ever so good. You are clever. What's he saying?'

'He's saying Weeooowww and he's saying Zonk!'

'Davey, it is exciting. When you're bigger you'll make comics like that.'

'Mum!' he said. He laughed.

There must be some funny look in her eyes. He reached a plump hand and moved her hair back.

She reached out and held him. She sat up in bed and hugged him close, shutting her eyes and clasping him to her.

'Davey Davey Davey,' she said. 'I've got you.'

He was big now to hold, she buried her face in his front. The two figures locked in one rocked back and forth on the bed.

'My darling.'

She glanced up. His face was different, he looked troubled or frightened as if he met something too big. He was dead in her arms. She thought of how she used to be, how she was frightened, and had to run. How could she feel those things? She could make them up to him by loving him.

She calmed, holding him. She was still. He eased and warmed, his small hand patted her back.

'There, there, Sandy,' he said gently.

She didn't answer, she only sat, resting while his hand moved on her shoulder. She was getting smaller, softly falling back until she was tiny. She was a baby and smaller than a babe. Her eyes were shut, she was at home. She was nothing, an atom hidden in a safe place inside his warm body. They were one person that had hurt itself, together in one.

FORTY-ONE

The day of the first race arrived. Lloyd came round, with the car on a trailer.

'Are you ready, Nick?'

'I guess so, mate. This is Teresa.'

'Pleased to meet you, love.'

'Is that the racing-car? I like the colours!'

Lloyd smiled, they got in and started.

Lloyd asked, 'Feeling nervous?'

'I suppose. Didn't sleep too good last night.'

'You'll wake up. Got your medical?'

'Sure.'

'Your licence? Your membership?'

'Yeah mate, yeah.' Nick had everything but he felt in pieces.

Teresa watched the countryside pass.

'Look at that house for sale! Isn't it great, Nick?'

She sat very upright, almost springing from her seat, her head up on her tall neck.

Lloyd watched the weather. 'There's a sky full of promise.'

The sun had gone, the grey clouds thickened till the sky was black. A shower began, then the downpour pelted ruthless. Rain drummed on the roof of the car, they could hardly talk.

Teresa shouted, 'What happens if it does this during the race?'

'You change tyres quick!'

'Change tyres!' She had a funny picture of racing-cars stopped all round the track, with drivers frantically jacking up axles.

The rain pattered and stopped, the clouds broke up in tree-top shapes, white as icebergs.

'Oh look, Nick, a rainbow! That's good luck.'

The sun was brilliant, hedges glittered.

Traffic thickened, they met other cars on trailers. Nick studied the competition. They crested a hill overlooking the track.

Teresa said, 'Oh, that's a good view!'

Below them, for acres, the wet grass sparkled. So far there were only a few parked cars, like bright-coloured insects on the green. The grandstand with its lettering was brilliant blue and white, the shining track wound away between trees. Beyond were hills, clumped with copses. Overhead the shower-clouds made a separate country, dazzling, arctic, with long glaciers. There were mountains in the air like crouching polar bears.

'Be an interesting surface, Nick.'

Nick nodded drily.

They entered the track and drove to the paddock. Within the enclosure it was like an open-air garage. Mechanics in bright tunics dipped in and out of motors, there were sudden revs of sound like yelping dogs. Lloyd called out a name, a man waved to him from deep in an engine.

'Nick, I love this place. I don't know how I gave it up.'

In the next bay a man in red carried a helmet. Lloyd said his name and Nick stared at him, nervous. The man was short but confident, he had a grin without humour, he was a driver. Further off were other drivers, Nick knew them at once, they were more visible than ordinary people. He watched them hungrily.

'Hello there!' A car-sized motor-bike pulled up beside them, a man all in leathers got off. He had a white fleshy face and thin hair cropped close. He let his engine throb before switching off, then stood in his leathers, looking like a driver.

Lloyd hailed him, 'Hello Geoff!'

'Morning, Eric. Morning, Nick.'

'Hello Mr Dixon.' Nick introduced Teresa to the sponsor.

'How's she sound?'

'Satisfactory.' Lloyd tilted his head.

They went to the car. Lloyd reached into it and pressed a cable, so the engine-noise shot up harsh.

The sponsor knit his brow. 'What you got in it? Paint stripper?' He knelt down and poked in the works. Lloyd answered his questions smiling deeply, like a doctor completing a long delivery.

Nick watched them chatting about the car. They were knowledgeable together: and he was the driver but he felt like a spectator. He reflected, if things had gone differently I'd be here with Sandy and Davey.

Teresa came and clasped his arm, together they walked to the edge of the track. They sniffed the air and gauged the weather. The world was dry and sunlit again, a breeze blew out the flags on the grandstand. Overhead there was one giant cloud, a mountain, shaped like the shoulder of a person. It was an Everest. The sun caught its edge but its inside was deep violet-black.

'I hope you've got your waterproofs, Nick.'

He put an arm round her and drew her close.

'I like it here, Nick.'

'Do you, lover?' Her words made him feel more sad than happy.

He looked at her and his feeling for her dropped through a trap-door. All feeling left him, he hung in a void.

Lloyd called him and from then on he was busy. They checked the car then the scrutineers vetted it. Nick did

264

his practice and attended to Lloyd's post-mortem. He went to the drivers' briefing. Finally he put on mask and helmet and worked himself into the car.

'Let's hit it.'

The sponsor gave a thumbs-up with both his thumbs. Teresa came and kissed him through his coverings. With wide eyes, wide smile, she urged him ahead. Bright sharp face: he smiled to her.

From the car Nick looked at them: Teresa, Lloyd, the sponsor still in his leathers, standing in a row with the bustle of the pits all round them. This was his new family, wishing him well. He raised his hand in salute.

He rumbled forward in spits of engine. Lloyd walked beside him, touching the fairing as if he held the car's hand.

Nick drove on to the track. When he had manoeuvred into the grid, Lloyd came and shouted last instructions.

'And keep your weather eye open!'

He nodded at the sky which was ugly again, torn in smokes and streaming fast. Brown clouds bubbled like a cauldron of trouble.

The loudspeakers crackled, Lloyd withdrew. The cars hovered on the spot, in splitting engine-revs.

He thought: here I am, seconds to go. It was really happening, but everything felt different from how it should feel. He was lost.

The lights changed, engine noise deafened. The first cars zipped out of sight. Nick pumped the accelerator, jumping through the gears. The track was blocked with jostling cars.

The cars thinned. He swerved to get through but the cars in front were pulling away, soon they were strung out loose.

The back of a car appeared right in front of him, his front end would hit the exhaust. Already it was shrinking as it left him behind.

265

He was neck and neck with a car inches off. The road took an S bend, they stayed side by side. They came to a corner and the other with no difficulty drew ahead and lost him.

Other cars passed him. He had moments of panic then he thought, I'm a new boy, I'll learn.

There was a car ahead that he was catching. As a curve approached he got behind it, slipstreaming. When it slowed for the curve he moved out and passed it, cutting in close.

There was another car ahead, slowly he drew nearer.

Steadily he gained ground, passing cars. Was he still in the tail of the race? The same trees passed, the pits and the grandstand one more time. Should I make a pit-stop? He didn't want to stop, or go back anywhere. His home was speed, he'd race for ever. He was following his line, changing gears and missing them as he and Lloyd had planned. There was a red car ahead he had set his sights on.

A car pulled past him effortlessly. It was enormous, black, a powerful dark machine like a higher formula car descended in his race. It swung away and left him standing, it was like a god-car shooting through. What was this car? How had it been behind him till now? Was it one of the leaders lapping him at last?

He set off in pursuit, no way would he lose it though he could not catch it.

It approached the red car, he followed after. It overtook the red and disappeared. Nick took the red and saw the black in front again.

Alternately he caught the black and lost it, as it overtook other cars and he tried to do the same. There was a green car ahead and the black went beside it. Was there another car in front of the green? He couldn't see clear.

The rain came back, a cataract, his windscreen turned

to stripes of water. His foot played on the accelerator, he could tell he'd lost grip, he was sliding or flying as if the road were half ice.

His wiper raced but his windscreen was a river. The cars in front disappeared in spray. There was a corner coming, how would they make it?

Two cars slewed round, the black had touched the green. They grew bigger quickly, he'd slice them.

This was the crash, in seconds he would be dead. Someone inside him flung up his arms, soaring. He was happy as trumpets, he saw clear what he wanted. He thrust down the accelerator, racing to the crash.

The green car was rolling to the side of the track and the black car lifted, it was rising in the air and turning over so presently he saw the whole car upside-down and very close, he saw the eye of the upside-down driver through his goggles, for an instant there was a car like his own facing back the way they'd come wheeling round in the air only inches above him, a fraction lower it would have struck off his head, he passed underneath it as if under a low bridge.

The road was clear. He was alive, he was cheated, something was lost. The rain had gone again, the sun shone jewelling.

Was he in the lead or were there more cars in front? He must go faster, he had been crawling. The car was at its limit, juddering and vibrating as if it would explode. He cranked the gears, pressed the pedals, accelerating further, falling forward into the wide track ahead that was clear all ways he could see.

FORTY-TWO

THE ADVENTURES OF CAPTAIN SPACE!

Collectors' Album
Written by: Davey Grant
Drawn by: David Grant
Inked by: Dave Grant
Lettered by: Davo 'Art' Grant
Published by Davicom
Copyright © David Grant 1980

Hi, folks! Meet Captain Space! But first, for new readers, we proudly present . . .

The Legend of Captain Space!

How did Captain Space get his superpowers??? This is the story! The legend begins . . .

Captain Space was flying along one day in his space-ship when . . .

'What's that?'

It was a Black Hole! The gravity was terrible! He couldn't get away! Then something very strange happened! The gravity of the Black Hole pulled him out long till he was 200 miles long! It hurt terribly! He was like a spaghetti man!

He kept on falling and it got blacker and blacker!

He got to the centre of the Black Hole! He was going so fast, he went through the middle! He came out in a Parallel Universe! But something very funny had happened! Because only half of him was there! The other half was in the Black Hole! But it was all right in the Parallel Universe because people there could live like that!

But he did look funny because he had his head but he only had one arm and one leg and he hopped along! Here comes Captain Space! Bomp! Bomp! Bomp! If you went round the other side of Captain Space you could see all his insides wobbling about! He could only eat sticky toffee! Anything else fell out!

But there were people in the Parallel Universe and they were all scientists! Some of them were androids! They made Captain Space another arm and leg, of Supermetal! Then he could walk properly and he was bionic! His bionic arm could smash a person in half! If he punched your face with his bionic fist, your face went splat! If he kicked your bottom with his bionic foot, your bottom went inside out! These are the enemies of Captain Space, before and after! This is before! They look like people or monsters! This is how they looked after they tangled with Captain Space!

'Yeeurugggh!'

'Oh that's horrible!'

He had a rocket in his bionic foot so he could fly!

But Captain Space was unhappy! He was lonely because no one was like him there! So Captain Space flew back to the Black Hole! He got through all right this time! But something terrible had happened! Time is different in the Parallel Universe! When he got back, millions of years had passed! Everyone he knew was dead!

'My old friend Jack! That's his grave!'

He was very sad!

Everything was different! There was dust on everything! There was only one person still there! It was the Queen of Space! She was very old now but she was a magic person! Her hair was made of fire! She lived in Universe

City! Sometimes Captain Space went to stay with her! They talked about old times because she was very old!

'Do you remember when there were people?'

'I just can, I think.'

She was married to someone called the King of Space! He went off in a rocket when Captain Space came! No one knows if he will ever come back!

She is always kind to Captain Space! In return he saves her life! He does it lots of times! Because there are terrible dangers now! Because the universe is ruled by a terrible monster!

What the monster is made of is a chunk of the Black Hole! All wriggling and shaking! It fell out of the Black Hole when Captain Space went through! It has tentacles and claws and arms and tendrils! It will sit down on a planet and suffocate it with its giant bottom! It will pick up a planet and suck it out, so there is nothing left but the skin which it throws away! Sometimes it appears as an Evil Witch! There are lots of mutants that are slaves of the Witch! They are horrible to look at, dripping green! Captain Space has lots of fights with the mutants!

This is Captain Space, he is fighting twenty mutants at once!

Whoom! Thwupp! Krakk!

'Aaaargh!'

'There's a mutant behind me!'

Clunk! Wopp!

'Errrr!'

'OK, mutant, let us battle hand to hand!'

'You don't scare me, Captain Space!'

'Oh no?? We'll see!'

Donk! Klanng! Kroosh! Wowl!'

'Eeeeurgh! I die!'

Look at what Captain Space has done to the mutants! This one is chopped in twenty bits! The face of this one is flat as a wall! This one was fat, now he's thin as a pin! This one is cut in half like Captain Space used to be! Look at his insides spilling all over!

'Well done, Captain Space!'

'Captain Space has saved us!'

'Take Captain Space to our City!'

'I didn't expect to be a hero!'

'You have saved our planet, Captain Space!'

And that is how Captain Space got his superpowers! He has bionic bits in his brain! He is cleverer than a million computers! His body is bionic! And he can fly! He can fly faster than light! He is the fastest man in the universe!

Does Captain Space have a weakness??? He has a weakness!!

'Having superpowers makes you alone!'

He has a bit of the Black Hole stuck inside him! He can control it! He can make it grow and swallow things up! It is all dark inside and frightening!

This is a picture of Captain Space! He is flying through space! You can see he is sad because he is alone! You can see he is clever and strong! He is the cleverest and strongest person in the universe! He is in Outer Space! There is nothing there at all! The nearest planet is light years away! But he is shooting at Superspeed! You can see how his rockets are blasting! He is heading for Universe City! He has had a message from the Queen of Space!

'Come quickly, Captain Space! There is a terrible new danger!'

If he hurries he will be there for tea!